JUSTICE

BOOK 4 ~ TIN STAR K9 SERIES

JODI BURNETT

Created with Vellum

To all who fight for justice, both human and K9.

I pledge allegiance to the flag of the United States of America and to the republic for which it stands, one nation, under God, indivisible, with liberty and JUSTICE for all.
~ The Pledge of Allegiance to the Flag (1892)

JUSTICE

PROLOGUE

Wind groans at my windowpane. The hollow sound slithers up my neck. I pull my blanket over my head and try to go back to sleep. Bleak weather carries warnings, so I'm not surprised when my phone rings in the dark hours of the morning.

"Hello?" The covers muffle my wary voice.

"Paytah is dead."

Instantly, I sit up and grip the phone to my ear, ignoring the cold. "What?"

"They found him. Someone beat him to death." The sentence ends in a bleak wail.

"Who?" I ask, though I already know.

"Paytah." His name is sung on a moan of grief.

I say nothing. My mind tries on images of the teenage boy broken and suffering. I quickly discard them. "What happened? When?" I reach for my blanket robe at the end of my bed.

"All I know is that he's dead. His body is a bloody mess. Hikers found him down by the hot springs in

Mammoth." A sob echoes through the phone and into my soul. "They didn't think it was a human. One of his arms is broken and many of his ribs. His skull… they smashed in his skull."

I try to breathe and wait for the crying on the phone to soften. "Are you with him now?"

"At the morgue. I had to..."

I squeezed my eyes shut, not wanting to imagine what it would be like to identify the body of someone you love. "Who would do such a thing?"

"The police have brought in three senior boys from Paytah's high school for questioning."

"Is it the same kids who've been picking on him for the past year?"

"Ever since he moved in with his grandfather."

"The principal should have done something. He turned a blind eye." A hot, sticky sense of injustice ignites in my belly. "This is a hate crime."

"There is no doubt about that."

"This has to stop." My retort is sharp.

"It won't."

"It will."

"It's in the hands of the court now."

"We'll see how well the court handles this. I don't have a lot of faith. If Paytah isn't given justice. We'll *take* it."

One month later…

"All rise," the court bailiff's voice bounces off the plaster walls, and goosebumps race across the surface of my skin. "The Honorable Judge William Hughes presiding."

Everyone in the courtroom stands and waits for the man. Judge Hughes, though a minor federal judge, is a major personality. He sweeps in through the door that leads to the courtroom from his chambers. His black robe flares out as he rounds the corner to mount two steps to his bench.

When he drops himself onto it, the leather desk chair releases a sigh, and the spectators sit along with him. "Bailiff, bring in the jury." My hands are cold as I lace my fingers together and stare at the entrance. The bailiff nods at the judge and opens the door at the side of the room. A mix of seven men and five women files in, taking their seats in the jury box. Hughes smiles at them benevolently. "Good morning, ladies and gentlemen of the jury. Thank you for being here again today to hear the closing arguments in this case." His gaze pans to the bailiff.

"Court will come to order in the matter of the State of Wyoming versus Mason Clark, James Martin, and Andrew Wright on charges of first-degree murder." After the proclamation, the bailiff moves to his position beside the juror's door. I've been waiting for this day for so long, I had begun to think it would never happen. My heart pounds like a gavel.

Judge Hughes peers down from the bench. "Mr. Getts, is the government prepared to give closing arguments?"

"Yes, Your Honor." Donald Getts, the federal prosecutor, spreads his hands over a manilla file folder but rises to his feet without it. He moves around his wooden table, nodding to the judge on his way. "Thank you, Your Honor." He stands before the jurors, looking each one in the eye. Getts is a handsome man. Distinguished, but with a boyish charm that will hopefully sway some of the female jurors, even if the facts of his case don't.

Before he addresses the twelve, the prosecuting attorney looks down at his polished wingtips. He releases a breath, raises his face to the panel and in a warm, unwavering baritone, he begins. "Thank you, ladies and gentlemen of the jury, once again, for your presence here and your careful attention in this trial. In the beginning, Judge Hughes instructed you on the law. He clarified that any comments or arguments made by either counsel are not part of the actual evidence. Evidence is what you have heard from the witnesses, along with various documents and exhibits that were presented. You are not to consider my statements," Getts sweeps his hand in a wide gesture that includes the defense attorney, "or any of what Mr. Ward has told you, but rather purely what the witnesses have said in their testimony and what the evidence shows you. Then, using your good judgement and common sense, you are to interpret the testimony and determine the truth therein. The path to justice is entirely for you to determine.

"The judge also discussed the difference between direct and circumstantial evidence. When someone sees something happen, that is direct evidence. If a man sees another man fire a gun and kill someone, that is direct evidence. Circumstantial evidence is inferred from a set of known facts. For example, if a man hears a gunshot and runs into the room to see a corpse lying on the floor and another man standing over the body holding a smoking gun in his hand, it would be reasonable to infer that the man with the gun shot the dead man on the floor. If you add to that knowledge that the day before the man with the gun had threatened to kill the dead man, you now have more evidence to convince you of his guilt."

I notice the eyes of two of the jurors stray to the defense table where the three sixteen-year-old boys who murdered Paytah sit with their attorney. My soul stretches out to theirs, willing the jurors to recognize the boys' smug wickedness.

Getts offers his listeners an understanding grin. "We've all seen courtroom dramas on TV, and it is common to believe that criminals cannot be convicted on circumstantial evidence, but that is a falsehood. Most criminal convictions are based on circumstantial evidence as long as there is enough of it to meet the burden of proof, which I believe I have presented to you over the duration of this trial." The soft clicking of the stenotype machine whirs to keep pace with the prosecutor's speech, and I concentrate on the sound—silently imploring the jury to agree with the prosecutor.

"Let me point out the type of inferences you could make during this trial." Getts holds up his finger. "We have heard testimony that students frequently saw these three white defendants bullying the deceased, Paytah Kanoska, a young man of Native American Crow descent, at their school: pushing him and taunting him with racial slurs. And the end result of this bigoted behavior was murder. Murder in the form of a racially motivated hate crime." Getts clenches his jaw and shakes his head. "An eyewitness saw these same three boys forcing Paytah into the trunk of Mason Clark's car, the same car in which a red bead, that likely came off a beaded scabbard belonging to Paytah, and a packet of methamphetamines were found by forensic investigators."

"Objection." Alan Ward, attorney for the defense, interrupted. "The boy in the trunk was never positively identified as Paytah Kanoska, and the methamphetamines have no bearing on this case."

"Sustained."

Getts nodded and continued. "That same night, Paytah's grandfather, with whom the boy lived, reported his grandson missing. One week later, Paytah's brutalized body was found by hikers near Mammoth Hot Springs. And finally, another student witnessed these same boys," Getts points to the defendants—their parents crowding the long bench behind them, "showing off the beaded scabbard that Paytah was known to carry with him, a symbol of his proud native heritage."

The prosecutor pauses, and the silence in the room presses down on my shoulders. His arguments are clear, and I'm certain they'll lead to conviction. They must.

"The defense will claim that all of this evidence is coincidental; that there is no proof of murder. But I say that the only reasonable inference you can make from these facts is that these three young men, James Martin, Mason Clark, and Andrew Wright, with premeditated thought and malicious intent to kill, abducted the victim, Paytah Kanoska, a Native American boy, viciously beat him to death, and left his body to rot in the wilderness of Wyoming."

I squeeze my eyes tight against the mental image Getts paints, and my stomach roils. He grips the railing of the jury box with both hands and leans forward. "I appeal to your sense of righteousness. You *must* find all three of these boys guilty of first-degree murder in an obvious racial-hate motivated crime. This disgusting and violent bigotry must be punished." The attorney pulls in a long breath and studies each juror's face. "I am confident you will do the right thing and bring justice to young Paytah Kanoska." He turns to the judge. "Thank you, Your Honor."

Hughes nods and waits for the prosecutor to return to his seat before addressing the defense. "Mr. Ward, are you ready with the final argument for the defense?"

The barrel-chested defense attorney, Alan Ward, glances back at the boys' fathers sitting on the other side of the bar and smiles confidently. Both the curious and the indignant fill the courtroom benches. The dead boy's grandfather sits alone in the last row of the gallery near the door, as stoic as the chiefs of old.

"Yes, Your Honor, if it pleases the court." Ward places a beefy hand on the shoulder of the young defendant sitting closest to him and gives the boy a pat. The three teens all have fresh haircuts and are wearing suits with ties, each doing his best to look innocent. None of them fool me.

Ward ambles toward the jury with a good-ole-boy saunter. He looks certain that the jury will side with his defendants, whom he has craftily portrayed as hard-working local ranch boys. One of their own. "Good morning, folks. I'd like to echo Mr. Getts' appreciation for the kind generosity of time and attention you've given to hear the discussion of this trial." He smiles at the jurors and ten out of the twelve smile back. My stomach twists tighter.

"You have all heard Judge Hughes speak about the spectacular form of justice system we are fortunate to have in this blessed country. One unlike any other in the whole world. One where every accused person is presumed innocent unless proven otherwise beyond any and all reasonable doubt. *Proven,* ladies and gentlemen. That is a strong word and one you must hold fast to in your assessment of this case.

"We've heard quite a few stories over the past several days, but no hard facts that could possibly lead any thinking person to conclude that the poor dead boy found here in Wyoming met his fate at the hands of these three fine young men from Montana. Now, the prosecution—since they have no solid case—would like you to believe that if you string together all his snippets of circumstantial incidents, that you should come to the weak supposition that these boys were somehow involved. But let's go through those glimpses one more time, together.

"We've heard about a few afternoons when these boys were seen teasing Paytah at school. Now, none of us like the idea of this kind of schoolyard banter, but as the saying goes, boys will be boys." Ward's full lips purse in humor. "A 911 caller claimed he saw the boys helping another dark-haired boy into the trunk of a car, but when questioned, the caller couldn't swear that the boy he saw was absolutely Paytah Kanoska. The witness watched the incident from almost a full city block away and couldn't possibly have had a clear view of the teenage shenanigans." The attorney turned and smiled indulgently at the defendants. "It was pure coincidence that Paytah Kanoska didn't return to his grandfather's home that same night.

"Now, there is the question of the red bead discovered in the trunk of Mason Clark's car. The bead could have come from any one of a hundred or more places and when the FBI searched the boys' homes and school lockers, no Native American knife nor beaded scabbard were located. They found no other loose beads either, for that matter.

"Next, a young girl believes she saw the boys at the movie theatre looking at something that resembled a scabbard several days after Paytah went missing, and yet this item has not been recovered or entered into evidence, nor was anything like it found by federal investigators.

"Ladies and gentlemen, we all feel horrible about what happened to that young man. But wouldn't you rather find the true killer than blame his death on these three innocent boys and effectively allow the actual murderer to go free?" Dropping his chin, Ward shakes his head as though the thought greatly disturbs him. He lets out a deep sigh and continues. "The prosecution has the burden of proving his case to you *beyond a reasonable doubt*. He has not done so. All Mr. Getts and his team have been able to do is parade a handful of witnesses before you with unconnected, unprovable tales of boys who admittedly treated another student unkindly. For that behavior, they should be reprimanded. Even disciplined. But there is no conceivable way that you can, in any good conscience, find them guilty of first-degree murder. I have every confidence that you agree with me on that point. I ask you, therefore, to do the just thing and find these boys *not* guilty."

A trickle of sweat skitters down my spine. The

certainty in his voice and his wide grin as he turns back to the defense table causes my blood to simmer. How dare he reduce what Paytah went through on a daily basis to childish hijinks! I glance at the jury to see if I can guess their thoughts before the judge sends them out to deliberate, but I can't read anyone's intent as they all turn their eyes to Hughes and await his direction.

My ears are hot and ringing. I barely hear the judge give his charge to the jury for their deliberation of the case. He reminds them of the standard of proof beyond a reasonable doubt.

"You are required to adhere to the written law in making your decision, regardless of what you believe the law is or ought to be." The judge sits back in his chair and says, "You are excused to deliberate this case."

Hughes calls a recess while we wait to hear from the jury, and as soon as I can, without drawing undo attention to myself, I rush outside to the lawn at the front of the courthouse and suck in a huge breath of fresh air. The fury in my chest threatens to explode as images of Paytah's beaten body flash through my mind. Surely, no matter what the jury comes back with, Judge Hughes will make certain justice is served. He can over-rule the jury. Right now, that's the only thought that keeps me inside my skin.

I'm not hungry, but needing something to do with my agitated energy, I walk to a nearby deli and buy a packet of potato chips. The springtime sun warms my shoulders, and I find a spot to sit and nibble on the salty snack while I wait for the call to return to the courtroom. I get no call.

On the third day, we're called back to the courtroom.

It seems to take forever for the people in the gallery to find their seats and settle down. The members of the defense team look relaxed. Alan Ward leans back in his chair and chuckles at something one of his clients says. Donald Getts, on the other hand, has a grayish-green pallor and stares down at the single notepad he placed on his table.

"All rise," the bailiff calls, and the courtroom fills with the ruffling sound of people standing. The judge enters and I hold my breath.

Everyone returns to their seats. Judge Hughes swivels his chair to face the jury. "Madam foreperson, has the jury reached a verdict?"

A tall, weather-worn woman rises to her feet. "No, Your Honor. We cannot come to a consensus."

Judge Hughes sighs, and my heart slams against the walls of my chest. "Ladies and gentlemen of the jury, must I impress upon you the importance of your role? You are here for the sole purpose of assessing the evidence presented to you during this trial and determining if there is enough actual evidence to prove, beyond a reasonable doubt, that the defendants are guilty of first-degree murder. That is to say, an intentional murder that is willful and premeditated with malice aforethought. Now, I ask that you return to deliberation and do not come back to this court without a decision."

I grapple with the fact the jury didn't automatically come back with a guilty verdict. One look at the haughty faces of the three teens and it's obvious they are guilty. Surely, I'm not the only one who can see that. I want to scream it out loud. Instead, I pin my mouth closed with my teeth and stare straight ahead.

We vacate the courtroom once again and are not called back again until the next day. The bailiff goes through his script of announcing the judge and we wait for the jurors to file in. The foreperson rises to her feet. "Your Honor, I am sorry to say we are still unable to come to a decision." She hands a slip of paper to the bailiff, who walks the message to the judge.

The hefty defense attorney jumps to his feet. "Your Honor, sidebar?"

Getts's knuckles are white as he grips his notepad.

"Very well, Counsel, please approach the bench." The judge waves the attorneys forward and they speak quietly. "Your Honor, the prosecution has brought forth no substantial evidence or argument to warrant any conviction here. And these poor boys have been through enough! They should not be forced to spend another minute incarcerated for a crime they did not commit."

"Mr. Getts, do you plan to re-try these boys in the future?" Judge Hughes raises his bushy brows.

The prosecuting attorney frowns. "I'll have to get back to the court with a final decision, Your Honor, but I'm not inclined to retry this case unless new evidence is discovered."

"Very well. Please return to your seats."

The judge unfolds and skims over the note the bailiff handed him and clears his throat. "Though the nature of this crime is wholly disturbing. I'm inclined to rule in favor of a mistrial. The prosecution has failed to bring forth enough substantial evidence or argument to warrant a conviction here. And the jury is unable to come to a consensus. Therefore, Mr. Getts, unless you come up with any new and substantive evidence—schoolyard bullying aside—that would suggest we push forward, I must declare a mistrial and dismiss this case without prejudice."

My skin goes cold and damp, but a searing blaze flares in my belly. I can't breathe past the heat of the internal flame that scorches my throat. My hands tremble as I stare at them. *A mistrial?*

Once they sit, the judge addresses the defendants and the gallery. "This case is a mistrial, and I am dismissing it without prejudice." Judge Hughes slams his gavel down and I feel the vibration of his ruling in my bones. He turns to the defendants. "That means the jury has not found you young men guilty. However, because there is a hung jury, the prosecution has the right to re-try you for this crime in the future if new evidence comes to light and he may or may not choose to do so." He glowers at the teens until they fidget in their chairs. "We have heard many witnesses testify that you boys have participated in unsavory schoolyard bullying. This court will not stand for that behavior, whether or not you have been convicted of a crime. Therefore, I am assigning each of you to 20 hours of community service. Is that understood?"

In unison, the defendants say, "Yes, sir," and my ligaments stiffen over my bones.

"Very well, Mr. Ward. Your clients are free to go."

Unsavory schoolyard bullying? Community service in exchange for a life? They committed a hate crime. A murder! How dare Judge Hughes come out with such a pitiful punishment? My skin is on fire, and pure, liquid-hate boils in the pit of my stomach. Not only for the murderers, but also for the inept judge who set them free.

Another native boy's death goes un-avenged...

But not for long.

1

Gunfire echoed against the firing bay walls. The sound of the blasts was muted through Caitlyn Reed's range hearing-protection earmuffs, but the reverberation of every shot she fired from her Glock .40 ricocheted through her forearm and slammed against the healing break in her radius. It had only been a little over two months ago when she'd broken her arm falling from her horse while chasing fugitives in the high country. Caitlyn clamped her teeth together to keep from crying out in pain, and she inhaled deep breaths of the gunpowder-scented air; its bitterness stinging the back of her throat.

"Ready to retrieve the targets?" Dirk Sterling, her mentor and sometimes partner as a US Deputy Marshal, flipped a switch, and the dark human-shaped forms printed on the paper targets flew toward them on their pulleys. Dirk's shots had all landed within two six-inch circles—one at the center of the head and one at center mass in the chest. Caitlyn's shots resembled buckshot.

Most were at least inside the black shape, but none were grouped in the ideal target spots.

Dirk raised a dark brow. "How's the arm feeling?" he asked as he unclipped the targets.

"Fine."

"Yeah, right. It doesn't do you any good to downplay your pain. I know how well you shoot when you're healthy." He held up her target and chuckled. "And it looks like you have more rehab to attend to."

Caitlyn shook her wrist to loosen the ache. "It's so frustrating. I've never shot this poorly in my life."

"You've never broken your arm before, either. Be patient with yourself. What does the doctor say?"

"Another month of PT." Caitlyn scoffed. She cleared her Glock .40 and placed the weapon in its hard plastic travel case. She removed her safety glasses and headset.

"Sounds about right. How's the counseling going?" Dirk asked without looking directly at her, which she was thankful for.

Caitlyn was dealing with the aftereffects of her first fatal shooting, and though she was feeling better since she'd been seeing a therapist, she still didn't like to talk about it. "I'm cleared to return to work."

"That's great. Good for you." Dirk latched his gun and gear in his case and folded the paper targets. "Any word from Chief Spencer?"

"I expect to hear from him this week."

"And until then, you're just lounging around getting lazy?" He winked at her, and they headed toward the door. "How's Renegade's rehab going?"

"He's doing great," Caitlyn chuffed. "But then he's a lot

younger than me. We've been running together, and he's pretty much back to a hundred percent already."

"And Colt?"

Caitlyn's boyfriend, Sheriff Colt Branson, was healing from a gunshot wound and subsequent surgery. A gift from the same group of outlaws. The memory of the incident that left them all injured fueled Caitlyn's desire to hunt down the two remaining fugitives and throw them in jail. "He's back in the office, but only on light duty. Deputy Cooper has taken the brunt of the load."

"I noticed you're wearing a ring on a certain finger." Dirk pushed open the door and held it for Caitlyn to walk through.

She smiled and brandished her left hand. "Yeah. It's official."

"So, when's the big day?"

Caitlyn signed them out of the range and waved at the attendant. "We haven't set a date. But if my mom has anything to do with it, it's likely to be a huge black-tie affair at Reed Ranch in July." She and Dirk had parked side-by-side, and they stopped in front of their cars. "What's the news with Sam? How's his leg doing?"

Dirk's partner, Sam Dillinger, had received a bullet to his thigh during the mountain shoot-out. "He's milking it for all it's worth. I don't know how his wife puts up with him." He grinned and slid mirrored sunglasses over his eyes.

"Laurie is a saint, and their little Caleb is the cutest thing ever. Any word on when Sam will be back on the job?"

Dirk pressed his fob and unlocked the doors of his

SUV. "No, but I imagine he'll need light duty for a while, too."

"Any trace of Ray Burroughs or Elaine Woodrow? I'm itching to track them down and make them pay." Of the four, two dirtbags were in the wind. One of the murdering jewel thieves was in jail, and the other was the primary topic of Caitlyn's PTSD therapy sessions.

"I figure they headed north. I've been searching through Elaine's past. Seems she was a middle-school teacher before she married her husband and had a family. I still have no idea how she and Burroughs hooked up, though." Dirk tossed his keys up and caught them. "I'd better get going. Give me a call as soon as you and Renegade are ready to help me hunt them down."

"Count on it." Caitlyn waved and climbed into her truck. She and Dirk met weekly at a gun range halfway between Billings and Moose Creek for practice. She had almost two hours of driving before she'd be home, but if she stepped on it, she could shave off some of the time. Renegade still needed to get a run in before Caitlyn got ready for her dinner with Colt.

Her phone rang, and she pressed the button on her steering wheel to answer. "This is Caitlyn Reed."

"Hello, Deputy Marshal Reed. This is Chief Spencer. I'm glad I got a hold of you."

"Hi, Chief. What's up?"

"I received your therapist's recommendation for your return to work."

"That's great news."

"Yes, but your doctor reports you still need some rehab before you're fully healed."

Caitlyn rolled her eyes and bit down on her lip to keep from blurting out an angry retort. Blake was far too protective for her taste. Too bad he was the only doctor in town. "I feel fine."

"Good to hear. Either way, I have the perfect job for you while you wait. I need you to go up to Mammoth in Yellowstone, near the hot springs. A US Magistrate Judge assigned to a small federal court up there has received a couple of vaguely threatening letters and some phone call hang-ups following a recent hate crime trial. The letters did not mention the trial specifically, and they might not be related. In fact, I'm sure none of this will amount to anything, but I thought it would be the ideal situation for you and Renegade while you're both on the mend. Your mission would be to search the courtroom and Judge Hughes's chambers each day and to protect him while he's out of court, as well."

"As a bodyguard?"

"No. He is resistant to that idea. I think if you watch from a distance, that'll be more than enough. He claims his home security is top-notch, so if you escort him home from work and run a check in the evenings, he should be fine until morning. You can follow him from his house to the courthouse in the a.m. and stay with him there during the day. I'm certain the threats will fade away, but it's better to be safe."

"Of course." Though the job didn't sound exciting, it thrilled Caitlyn to be allowed back at work. "When do I report for duty?"

"Tomorrow morning."

"I'll be there. Thank you, sir." As soon as she ended the

call with her boss, Caitlyn called Colt. "Hey, I have great news."

"You've picked a date for our wedding?" His warm laugh vibrated through the speaker.

Caitlyn smirked at his not-so-subtle prodding. "No, not yet. You're not in a huge rush, are you? So much is going on right now."

"I get it. What's your news?" Colt's voice was even—lacking inflection—so she knew he had been hoping for a decision on their special day. With that in mind, she figured her good news wouldn't seem so great to Colt.

"I just got off the phone with my chief. He's letting me come back to work."

"But your arm hasn't fully healed yet. How did target practice go?"

Caitlyn sighed. "Not great. My arm hurts less, but I still have a lot of strength to build back before I regain my aim. In a weird way, that's part of the good news. I got the go ahead from my therapist. She agrees that I'm dealing with killing Reggie Burroughs in a healthy way, and the officer-involved shooting investigation is complete. I've been cleared of any wrongdoing."

"That was obvious to anyone who was there."

"I know, but it still feels good to get the clearance. With all that, Chief Spencer called and wants me to come back to work."

"Will you have to go to Casper?"

"No. Spencer's easing me back in. He assigned Renegade and me to guard a US Magistrate Judge up in Mammoth."

"In Yellowstone?"

Caitlyn chuckled. "Yeah. There's a small federal court up there, believe it or not. The presiding judge recently ruled for the defendants in a hate crime murder trial."

Colt's brow furrowed. "He let them off?"

"Yes. Since then, he's received a couple of threatening letters. So, they want a deputy marshal up there to guard the courtroom, the judge, and his chambers. I get to go because I have a K9 partner who can sniff out any trouble."

"I don't want to be there when you tell your mom you aren't going wedding shopping with her next week."

Caitlyn had forgotten about her mom's plans. "Oh, man. I don't want to have to tell her either. She's in hog heaven with all her planning."

"You are her only daughter."

"Don't remind me." Caitlyn needed some breathing room. Now that she and Colt had officially agreed to spend their lives together, she wanted some time to focus on her new career as a US Deputy Marshal. The pressure from her mom was too much, all at once. If it were entirely up to Caitlyn, she and Colt would enjoy a long engagement. "Colt, you don't mind if we wait a while to get married, do you? You understand I need to concentrate on my new job, right?"

"I do, but I am looking forward to being married. The sooner the better, as far as I'm concerned."

"I want to be married right now, too. What I don't want is to get bogged down in my mother's princess wedding dreams."

Colt laughed. "So, you're saying I should let the Westminster Abbey reservations go?"

"You think you're kidding, but you know my mother. I wish we could just get married outside with family and a few friends."

"Now you're the one who's dreaming."

"I know. I don't want to disappoint my mom, but she is going to have to wait at least until I'm back from this job babysitting the judge."

"How long do you think you'll have to be up there?"

"I'm not sure. I guess until the powers that be decide there's no longer a credible threat."

"I'll miss you. It's been so nice having time off together during our recuperation."

"It has, but don't go getting shot just so we can spend time together."

"I'll do whatever I have to." A smile warmed Colt's voice. Spending most of their time together over the past few weeks had been the silver lining to their injuries. She, Colt, and Renegade took full advantage of their mandated rest. "I could drive up and visit you on my days off."

"You'd better." The reality of being separated from Colt again dulled the shine of her excitement.

"Count on it. For now, though, I need to go. My deputy just took a report about some missing cattle from Harbor's ranch north of town."

"Stolen?"

"That's the report, but before we jump in that boat, we going to drive out and check for a busted fence. You know how cows are."

"Well, tell that deputy of yours to watch your six. You aren't planning on riding the fences, are you? I doubt your chest is up for that kind of bouncing activity."

"If I do, I'll take an ATV."

"Be careful."

"You do the same and say hello to your mom." Colt teased as he disconnected the call. Caitlyn stuck her tongue out at his verbal poke as if he could see her, then pulled in a deep breath and dialed her mother.

2

As soon as Caitlyn got home, she changed and took Renegade for a run. They were almost back up to their five-mile per day norm. Doctor Moore, Renegade's vet, assured her that her Belgian Malinois K9 partner was ready to push into the full run, but Caitlyn didn't want to rush him. Her dog always had her back, and she was determined to take the best care of him in return. He proved his stamina had returned, however, when they jogged through the trees at the end of their stint. Colt was there, leaning against his Jeep waiting for them as they rounded the bend. As soon as Renegade saw him, he bolted forward, his body stretched out in full stride.

"Hey, buddy!" Colt greeted her dog who in return acted like a hound who'd found his long-lost boy.

Caitlyn jogged up. "Hi." Panting, she gave him a quick peck before placing her hands on top of her head. She walked in a small circle until she caught her breath. "Are we late? I thought I had time for a run before our date."

"No. But I have to postpone. Wes and I still haven't made it out to Harbor's yet. I stopped by because I didn't want you to leave town without kissing me goodbye." Colt reached for her and pulled her close.

"Ugh, Colt, I'm all sweaty."

His lips met hers, and he chuckled. "That's how I like you."

She swatted his good shoulder and tried to push away, but he held her tight, kissing her until she relaxed into him and returned his farewell. "This is the kind of thing that makes a girl have second thoughts about going to work, you know." She murmured against his lips.

Colt held her face between his hands and gazed into her eyes. "Tell me about it. Drive safe and call me when you get settled."

"I will. And Colt—I love you."

He kissed her again and Renegade, jealous for their attention, whined and barked at them until they drew apart. "I love you back. I'll call you tonight." Colt reached down and scratched Renegade's head. "Take care of our girl."

Caitlyn watched Colt's taillights until they disappeared in the trees before she ran inside to shower and pack.

ONCE SHE AND Ren were on the highway the next morning, Caitlyn called her mom. "Good news, mom. I'm going back to work!"

The slight pause on the line spoke loudly. "When?"

"Ren and I are on the road right now. We're headed up

to Mammoth to guard a judge and his courtroom. It's an easy job, but I'm thankful they're letting me come back a little early."

"How long will you be up there? We had plans to go shopping this week." Caitlyn felt her mother's disappointment in the pit of her belly.

"I know, Mom. I'm sorry. I don't know how long this job will be, but we could do some online shopping. That might be better anyway, you know? We could get a good idea of what to look for when we are together."

Again, the pause. Her mother could use silence like a battle club. "I suppose." Caitlyn bit her lip and waited. "Have you and Colt picked a date yet? That really needs to come first. I bought a wedding planner notebook and I've started filling it out, but without a date, it's almost impossible to move forward."

Caitlyn shook her head. "Shouldn't I be the one with the planner?"

"Ha! If I waited for you to get a planner and actually start filling it out, you'd be eighty before you got married." The brittle laughter did little to disguise her mom's true feelings.

"Well, good then. That will give you something to do while I'm away." With his nose firmly planted on his paws, Renegade peered up at her with his tiger-eyes. Caitlyn held her finger to her mouth as if to shush him. Even her dog was ganging up on her.

"We just need a date, Caitlyn. Will you please settle that one thing? July would be perfect—just pick a weekend."

"I don't know what I'll be doing with work in July, Mom. It's not like fugitives take weekends off."

"Caitlyn Rose, if you wait until all crime stops before you take a weekend off, you'll never get married. Now, I mean it. Pick a date."

"Fine." She released a long-suffering sigh. Her mother hadn't used her middle name since she was in elementary school. "I'll call you after I talk about it with Colt. Changing the subject, how is Dad?"

"He's doing well. Ever since the weather has been warming up, he's been getting outside more and helping your brother with chores around the barn."

"Tell Dylan not to let him overdo it."

"Dylan has been keeping a close eye on him, but I think they're both glad that Dad's able to start back. His spirits have been high, and he has good color back in his cheeks. I'm so thankful."

"I know, Mom. Me too." Caitlyn's dad's health scare over the past year had shaken them all. Her dad ended up in the hospital before he agreed to let Blake do a full examination. That's when Blake diagnosed him with diabetes and put him on insulin and a strict diet and exercise regimen. Her dad's strength had returned in spades. "Tell the guys I said hello. I'll call you in a few days."

"With a date."

Caitlyn rolled her eyes. "I'll try. Bye, Mom. Love you."

It wasn't that Caitlyn was reluctant to get married. She longed to. More than anything—even more than going back to work. It was that she dreaded whatever her mom was conjuring up in her mind for the ceremony. On the other hand, she didn't want to disappoint her mother, either.

Caitlyn was relieved when she pulled around the bend into the small town of Mammoth. It wasn't hard to find the city buildings on the main street, and she glided into a parking space in front of the courthouse. She clipped on Renegade's leash, and they went inside the building. She took note that the only security inside was a bored looking Court Security Officer leaning in a chair against the wall.

The CSO stood when she entered, and she showed him her badge. "I heard we were getting a Deputy Marshal up here. I see you brought your K9 too. Impressive." He held his hand out for Ren to sniff.

"This is K9 Renegade. He's unlikely to bite you, but FYI, you should never reach out to pet a working K9 without checking in with their handler. Not all dogs are stranger friendly. A bite-and-hold dog would have mauled your hand."

The guard snatched back his hand and tucked it under his arm. "Oh. Right."

"I'm Caitlyn Reed. Renegade and I are here to give you some backup, since the judge has received some threats."

"I'm glad to have you." He pointed the way to the elevator. "The courtroom and the judge's chambers are on the second floor."

Caitlyn nodded and opted for the stairs. She and Renegade made their way to the courtroom. It was empty, so they walked down the hallway to the back of the building and found a closed door with Judge William A. Hughes printed on a plaque. She knocked.

A shuffling sound came from the other side of the door before a man's voice called out. "Come in."

Caitlyn opened the door to a stout man sitting in a leather desk chair, straightening his tie. With his thinning hair and jowls, she guessed him to be in his early fifties. Her gaze panned to his left where a middle-aged woman with long, straight, dark hair tugged on the hem of her blouse.

"Excuse me," the angular woman said and without meeting Caitlyn's eye rushed past her into the hallway, closing the door as she left.

"Not hard to guess who you are. Few dogs come into the courthouse. US Deputy Marshal Reed, I presume?" The judge's eyes appraised her, and he smiled appreciatively before lowering his gaze to take in her furry partner.

"Yes, sir, and this is my K9, Renegade."

"Thank you for coming. I'm sure there is no real cause for concern, but we all have to follow our orders."

"Of course. We're happy to be here."

"Good. Well, at least you're much nicer to look at than the CPO assigned to guard the courthouse downstairs."

Caitlyn bit down on the inside of her cheek to stop herself from saying what she thought of his inappropriate comment. "We're here to keep you safe, Your Honor. Have you received any more threats or unusual communications since you reported the letters?"

"No. Not a peep."

"That's a good thing." Caitlyn glanced at her watch. "What time do you leave the office at the end of the day, sir?"

"I usually head home around five. Are you guarding me at home, too?" His grin broadened.

"I'll follow you to your house, make sure it's clear, and check out your security system there. You do have an alarm, correct?"

"Of course." The judge winked. "When I remember to turn it on."

"I suggest you remember that every time. I also recommend that you vary your schedule. Leave for work in the morning and return home at different times each day."

"That sounds very ah… safe. However, I am a slave to my docket." He rose to his feet and slid into his suit coat. "What did you say your first name is?"

"I didn't."

Judge Hughes chuckled. "Well, it's a good thing I looked at your paperwork. Caitlyn, isn't it? We're casual and friendly here. You can call me Bill. The woman you saw leaving my office is the court recorder. Her name is Una Murphy, and the fact that she was in my office is to remain our little secret. Is that clear?"

"It's none of my business, Your Honor. I'm here for the sole purpose of keeping you safe. Are you ready to drive home?"

The judge studied her face for a long moment before he opened the door. "Yes, follow me."

Caitlyn and Renegade walked behind the judge to the elevator. Inside the compartment, he leaned against the wall and studied her. Caitlyn kept her eyes glued to the lighted floor numbers. When the doors opened on the first floor, she and Renegade followed him out the back door to a gated parking lot behind the courthouse. He pointed to a silver Chrysler 300. "That's me right there."

"Please wait here while we check your car, sir." Caitlyn walked her dog to the Chrysler. "Renegade, *such*." She gave him the command to search for explosives. Renegade sniffed the wheel wells, the trunk, doors, and hood. Not surprisingly, he found nothing. "It's all clear. My truck is out front. I'll pull in behind you when you leave and follow you to your house."

"You do know all this is unnecessary, don't you?"

"I certainly hope so, sir. But it's my job, nonetheless."

"Very well. I'll see you at my place." Judge Hughes pressed his fob and his car doors unlocked. His arm rubbed across Caitlyn's chest as he passed her. She stepped back to give him more room while she fantasized about giving him a sideways kick and dropping him to the pavement. A low rumble sounded from Renegade's throat as the judge slid into his car. "My thoughts exactly, Ren. Let's go."

Caitlyn drove behind the silver luxury car the four miles to the judge's house. The town was even smaller than Moose Creek and it wouldn't take long to get her bearings. Not many people lived in Mammoth, Wyoming. The township was inside Yellowstone National Park, and the Mammoth Hot Springs lay just outside of town. They passed a couple of hotels on their drive, which Caitlyn imagined must burst with tourists in the summer. At the edge of town, the judge turned into an established neighborhood with plenty of old shade trees protecting the houses. He pulled into the driveway of a white, two-story colonial home with glossy black shutters that was much nicer than most of the other homes on his block. Caitlyn parked on the street, and she and Renegade met the man at his front door.

"Come on in," Hughes said as he unlocked his door and pushed it open. "After you, my dear."

"Your alarm isn't set." It wasn't a question.

"No. Like I said, there is no cause for such heavy concern. It's not like we're in New York City or DC."

"Crime happens everywhere, sir. It's better to be safe."

"Well, come in and check around. I like the idea of you keeping an eye on me." The judge placed his hand on her lower back as she passed him.

She turned away, out of his reach. *I wonder if he'll get the hint the next time he touches me and draws back a bloody stump.* Caitlyn maneuvered so that Renegade stood between them. "My partner and I will check your residence before we leave. Then you'll set your alarm."

"Oh, I figured I'd invite you to stay for dinner. It's your first night in town and all. I want to be hospitable." The man's grin spread across his fleshy face.

"No, thank you, sir. This is not a social job. I'm here purely to keep you safe. Tonight, I'll familiarize myself with the town, and I'll meet you here in the morning. What time are you planning to leave for work?"

"Too bad. We're simply not all that formal up here in nowhere's-ville. But if you insist on regulation, I'll be ready around nine."

"Sounds good. You need to lock your door and set the alarm as soon as we leave. Don't turn it off again until I get here in the morning. Is that understood?"

"You're very commanding, Deputy Marshal. I love it."

The judge chuckled as he made his way to the kitchen and poured himself a glass of wine. He held it up in question toward Caitlyn.

She shook her head, and she and Renegade cleared the main level, easy because of its open concept design. The living room and dining room stood across from each other at the front of the house, on either side of the entranceway. The kitchen and a family room were at the back. After checking the main floor, the pair jogged up the stairs to clear the upper level. They searched each of the four bedrooms, two bathrooms, and a linen closet. Back downstairs, Caitlyn was ready to leave within minutes. "See you in the morning, Judge."

He followed her to the door and closed it behind her. She waited to hear the beeping tones as he set the alarm system. Caitlyn had been excited to get back to work, but if the judge didn't stop his lecherous behavior, this assignment was bound to drag.

Caitlyn and Renegade drove around the town. It took them all of fifteen minutes. She went to an off-brand hamburger drive-through joint for dinner and then found the hotel that would be Ren's and her home for the next several weeks. Once inside, she kicked off her boots and ate two bites of the tasteless burger before she dozed off watching TV. Caitlyn woke with a crick in her neck to the sound of her phone buzzing.

She reached for the device and saw US Deputy Marshal Sam Dillinger's cheesy grin lighting up the screen. "Hey, Sam. How's the rehab going?" Sam had been shot during their previous manhunt, and it was that specific gunfight which resulted in Caitlyn killing the shooter. She'd had weeks of therapy and time to learn to deal with taking the man's life, though sometimes the memory was still sharp and filled her with a gritty sense of guilt.

"Not as slow as I'd like. I was hoping for a couple of months off to spend with my wife and kid."

"How are Laurie and Caleb? I imagine they're ready to send you back to work."

"Ha, ha. Well, that's happening whether they're ready or not. Looks like I'm coming up to Mammoth with you. I think it must be the place for Marshals' Convalescent Duty. The kind where you're away from your family and bored out of your mind. You either recuperate or go crazy."

Caitlyn laughed. "It's true. There's not much to recommend this town as a duty station. The judge is a handful."

"In what way?"

"He seems to think that since he's a judge, he can come on to anyone with two X chromosomes."

"I hate those kinds of guys. Have you had to hurt him yet?"

Laughing, Caitlyn answered, "Not yet, and it won't be me. Renegade doesn't like him either."

"What kind of idiot messes with a Deputy Marshal and her dog?"

"An egomaniacal one. Anyway, I'm glad you'll be up here. You can be a buffer between me and the judge, and the time will pass much faster with your company. You ought to bring Laurie and Caleb up with you. The hot springs are nearby, and there's some incredible hiking up there. You could hang out with them in your off hours."

"That was my plan—at least for a couple of days. We'll be there tomorrow."

"That's great! I'll see you guys then." Caitlyn signed off and took Renegade out for his bedtime constitutional. Back inside, she heated water in a mug for some Sleepy Time tea and shrugged out of her clothes. She slid on a cast-off t-shirt of Colt's for sleeping in. Renegade rested his chin on the edge of the bed while she sipped her hot drink and channel surfed.

"No, Ren. You know you're not allowed on the furniture." She should have set up his kennel. He watched her with sad eyes and flagged his tail slowly through the air. "Sorry, bud."

With a resigned groan, he curled up on the carpet by the door. After Caitlyn drained her cup, she snuggled into the covers to watch a medical drama but drifted off.

She sat straight up in bed at eleven-thirty in response to an alert on her phone indicating the judge's house alarm was going off.

"Ren, *kemne*!" Caitlyn sprang to her feet, threw on her clothes, grabbed her gun belt, and yanked open the door. She and Renegade sprinted down the stairs to her truck. As she flung open the truck door, her phone alerted once again, this time a text message flashed on her screen. It was from the judge.

Oops! False alarm. I opened the door to let the cat in and set off my alarm. I'm safe and sound. See you in the morning. Sweet dreams.

3

Colt climbed out of his Jeep and entered the Moose Creek Café. He and his deputy, Wes Cooper, had had a long afternoon helping Greg Harbor check his fence-line to see if the man's cows broke through and were merely lost, or were in fact stolen. As promised, he rode on an ATV all day, but the soreness in his wounded shoulder caused by bouncing around on the uneven terrain made him wonder if horseback would have been a better choice. He stretched his arm backward and rotated it in small circles to loosen the joint while he rubbed his aching trapezius and neck with his other hand.

His phone buzzed, and he retrieved it from his pocket. *Blake Kennedy.* "What's up, Doc?" Colt snickered at his own joke.

"Sorry to say, this is an official call. I have two young men here in the ER. They are both high as Mount Everest on something still yet to be determined. But I thought you'd want to speak to them when they come back down."

"Thanks. Wes is officially on duty, but I'll swing by

after supper and talk to them tonight. Looks like I'll be performing a random locker search at the school tomorrow, too. Unfortunately, Caitlyn and Renegade are out of town. Renegade's nose would make the job a whole lot faster."

"You'd think country kids wouldn't have to deal with this kind of thing as much as city kids."

"That'd be wishful thinking, Doc. When should I come by the clinic?"

"Hard to say. I'd give it a couple of hours at least."

"See you later, then." That gave Colt plenty of time for dinner, and he had his appetite set on chicken-fried steak with mashed potatoes and gravy. When he entered the restaurant, he waved at McKenzie Torrington, who was working the serving shift, then he claimed his favorite booth, the one in the back corner. He sat on the side that offered him a full view of the front door. McKenzie sat down opposite him to take his order.

The waitress was Caitlyn's best friend and had been Renegade's professional trainer and caretaker a lot over the past year. But now that Caitlyn was home from the US Marshal Academy, McKenzie had to choose between moving back to Florida and her old job of training police K9s or staying in Moose Creek. Since she was in love with Caitlyn's brother Dylan, McKenzie had decided to stay. She rented a small apartment in town and worked at the café for the time being.

"Hey, Colt. How's the shoulder?"

"Sore today, but nothing that a cold IPA and today's special won't cure."

"Comin' right up." She slipped out of the booth and

clipped his order to the round stainless-steel wheel in the kitchen window. She brought him his beer in a frosted mug. "How's Caitlyn doing?"

"I haven't heard from her since she texted me when she got to Mammoth safe and sound. I know she's glad to be back at work."

The front door opened, and three people entered the café. Colt recognized Mr. and Mrs. Snow, but he almost dropped his mug when their daughter, Allison, followed them in. There she was, in living color, the girl—woman now—who was at the center of the greatest mistake of his life. She was still beautiful—and still knew it. Allison swept her long blonde hair behind her shoulder and panned her gaze around the restaurant.

"This place hasn't changed at all." She smiled as her eyes paused at several pieces of familiar decor. "Even this mangy old moose head." She stared up at a mount that had been hanging there since before their generation was born.

Colt attempted to disappear behind his beer, wishing he was invisible. The last thing he wanted to do was share 'old home week' with Allison Snow. But, since he was the only other person in the diner, he clenched his jaw and waited for the inevitable.

"Colt? Colt Branson, is that you?" *Damn.* Alison rushed over and threw her arms around his neck, engulfing him in a too-sweet fragrance and gripping his sore shoulder, making him wince. With her hand still resting on his scar, she drew back and chirped, "It is you! Well, this day just can't get any better, now."

Colt ground his teeth against the sting in his shoulder,

and his face filled with heat. He slid away from her grip and ground out her name. "Allison."

"How long has it been?" Allison turned to her mother and mouthed, *Be there in a minute.* Then she slid, uninvited, into the other side of the booth and let her leg rest against his.

McKenzie approached with his dinner, and her eyebrows shot up when she saw Allison. *Great. The last thing I need is for McKenzie to meet Allison and end up mentioning to Caitlyn that Allison's back in town.*

"Here's your steak, Colt." McKenzie set his dish in front of him. "Extra gravy."

"Thanks." Colt kept his eyes on the plate.

McKenzie stared at him for an uncomfortable minute, but he pretended not to notice and stuffed a bite of meat into his mouth.

She shrugged and held out her hand. "Hi. I'm McKenzie Torrington. I don't think we've met."

"Allison Snow." The woman slid her perfectly manicured hand into McKenzie's. "I grew up here. Colt and I went to school together."

"Oh, then you must know my good friend, Caitlyn Reed?"

Allison's eyes darted to Colt and back up to McKenzie before she pasted on a plastic smile. "Yes. I remember Caitlyn." Then she laughed with a bright, trilly sound. "But I remember her brothers better. I used to have a huge crush on both Logan and Dylan."

"Is that so?" McKenzie made a show of searching in her apron for her order pad.

Allison reached across the table and touched Colt's

wrist. "Yes, but my true feelings were saved for this handsome guy." Her eyes sparkled and she pursed her grin. Colt reflexively pulled away covering his discomfort by wiping his mouth with a napkin.

McKenzie cleared her throat. "Can I get you something to eat, Allison?"

The woman hesitated, but when Colt didn't invite her to stay, she ordered a drink anyway. "I'm here for dinner with my parents, so I'll just have a glass of Chardonnay with Colt before I join them." She returned her gaze to Colt. "I see you're wearing a sheriff's badge. Good for you. Did you ever leave here, or have you lived in Moose Creek this whole time?"

"I stayed here." Maybe short answers would give her a clue. *Why won't she leave?* Colt had come here for a nice, relaxing dinner, but now the knots in his muscles twisted tighter. And he could only imagine what McKenzie was thinking.

Alison leaned back in the booth and drew imaginary circles on the tabletop with her long red fingernail. "You really should travel. There is so much more in the world to see than this dusty old mountain town."

Colt nodded and filled his mouth with another big chunk of steak. He felt no need to tell her that just because he never moved away, it didn't mean he hadn't traveled. In fact, he didn't want to encourage any conversation at all.

The café door swung open again and a family of five shuffled in, followed by Dylan. *Can this night get any more awkward?*

Dylan looked for McKenzie, and when he saw her, a

wide grin spread across his face. She swept by him with her hands full of plates and brushed a kiss across his bearded cheek. McKenzie said something Colt couldn't hear, but Dylan's gaze swung back to him. He nodded when their eyes met. Dylan removed his black-felt cowboy hat and hung it on a rack by the door before he sauntered across the room toward Colt's table.

When Dylan got there, he noticed Allison for the first time. He said nothing to her, but he shifted hard, dark eyes to Colt. After a tense few seconds, Colt swallowed his mouthful and said, "Dylan, you remember Allison Snow? She's in town visiting her parents." He pointed to the other side of the room. "They're right over there."

"How funny." Allison's silky voice purred as she reached out and touched Dylan's arm. "I spoke your name, and you appeared. It's nice to see you, Dylan."

Dylan glanced at the woman, but his sharp gaze snapped back to Colt. "You're kidding me, right?" His tone was cold and hard as steel.

Colt wanted to defend himself, or dissolve into the atmosphere, because anything he said would make the situation worse. "I was as surprised as you."

"Mm-hm."

McKenzie sidled up to Dylan and slipped her hand around his elbow. "I've put all the orders in, so I've got about ten minutes to sit with you. Want a beer?"

DYLAN TURNED McKenzie away from Colt's table and propelled her toward a vacant one across the room. "How long has this been going on?" His grip tightened when he spoke.

"What's wrong?" She stared up at him while her mind searched for clues to what he was talking about. "You seem angry. Did I do something?"

Dylan jerked out a chair for her to sit in. McKenzie's face heated as she sank into it. What could she possibly have done? "Talk to me, Dylan. Why are you so angry?"

"It's not you. You didn't do anything wrong." Dylan flashed a glare in Colt's direction.

"Colt? Who *is* that woman he's with?"

"She's the one who Colt… It was because of her that Caitlyn's heart was crushed for so long."

"The girl in high school? The one Colt slept with at the graduation party?"

"The very same." Anger seemed to seep from Dylan's pores. "When did they get here?"

McKenzie reached for his hand. "They didn't come together. She came in with her parents and when she saw Colt, she sat at his table."

"I don't see him asking her to leave."

"I'm sure she'll join her family when she's done with her wine." Dylan's glare didn't waver, so McKenzie pressed on. "I don't think Colt knew she was in town, and he didn't seem pleased to see her. He looked to me like a trapped rabbit."

"Or a rabbit that got caught." Dylan's obsidian remained pinned to Colt's booth. "It's a little too convenient that she shows up the day Caitlyn leaves for a couple of weeks, don't you think?"

"It could just be a coincidence." Hoping she was right,

McKenzie squeezed Dylan's hand to get him to focus on her. "Speaking of coincidences, you know how I said I've been thinking about breeding Belgian Malinois to train up and sell to police departments for their K9 units?"

Dylan shook his head slightly and returned his gaze to her. "Yeah. Did you decide?"

"Yes, and I'm really excited! As soon as I made the decision, I found a woman online who is a breeder in Sheridan. I'm driving over there on my day off to see the dam. The lady is going to try to have the sire on site too, so I'll get a chance to observe both of their demeanors. The pups are due in about a month, so that gives me time to get everything ready for my first puppy."

"How does your landlord feel about dogs? Are you allowed to have one in your apartment?" He fiddled with the saltshaker on their table and his gaze darted back to Colt,

"He said I can since I'll be training the pup as a police dog. But, of course, I have to pay a pet deposit."

"What did he say when you told him you wanted to breed dogs?"

McKenzie waited to answer until he glanced at her and she gave him a sly smile. "I didn't ask him because your mom said I could build a pen in her backyard when I'm ready to breed. But that won't be for over a year. I'm going to choose a female puppy and when she's old enough, I'm hoping to convince your sister to let me breed my girl with Renegade. Brilliant, right?"

His deep gruff chuckle warmed her insides. "Right." He lifted her hand to his lips and kissed her knuckles, but his gaze slid back to Colt's table again and the warmth in his eyes evaporated. "Do I tell Caitlyn that Allison is back in town?"

"I think you should give Colt the chance to tell her. Besides, they're just talking, and maybe she's only visiting for a few days."

Dylan scoffed. "It only took one conversation with the serpent to destroy the entire Garden of Eden."

COLT SHOVELED his food into his mouth, both to prevent having to talk, and to speed up his departure. Before he finished chewing his last bite of the chicken-fried steak that now tasted more like straw and paste, he wiped his mouth with his napkin and set it on top of his plate. As he stood, he gulped one last sip of beer to wash down his mouth full. "Got to go back to work, Allison. Say hello to your folks."

Allison gaped at his rudeness, but Colt didn't care. All he wanted was to put distance between him and the woman who could burn his world to the ground. He'd worked hard to regain Caitlyn's trust, and he wasn't about to let anything threaten that.

He passed McKenzie and Dylan on his way out. "Have a good night, you guys," he said as he settled his dove-colored cowboy hat on his head.

"You, too." McKenzie smiled up at him. "Headed home?"

"Nope. I'm meeting Blake over at the clinic."

Dylan didn't look up. Colt knew Dylan was only being protective of his sister, but hopefully he'd let Allison's appearance in town float away like water under a bridge and not feel the need to bring it to Caitlyn's attention. No reason to cause a problem where none existed.

Colt drove to the hospital and when he got there, he found Blake in the cafeteria with Kayla. Their relationship made Colt a happy man on two counts. First, Blake was no longer trying to move in on Caitlyn, and second, Kayla had met someone of her own. She'd thought Colt might be the one for her, but his heart had belonged to Caitlyn for as long as he could remember.

"Hey, you two," Colt greeted before focusing on Blake. "Sorry to interrupt your dinner, but are those kids ready for me to talk to yet?"

Blake shook his head. "No. They're out of it, but I can tell you that the lab report came back. Both boys are sailing on a wave of methamphetamine."

Colt's blood chilled, and he shuddered. Moose Creek had Raymond Burroughs to thank for introducing that horrible drug to their town in the little *rockeT* designer packets. His whole plan had been to get a bunch of kids hooked on meth and start up an empire. Colt's belly still burned at the thought of Burroughs escaping from their grasp last spring, and the knowledge that he and Elaine Woodrow had planned her husband's death twisted the dagger. Colt wouldn't rest until he found out if they were at the bottom of this.

"I'll go to the school as soon as I get a chance and see what I can find out. Hopefully, we can put a stop to this mess before more kids end up here in the ER."

4

Even though the judge claimed all was well, Caitlyn was still obligated to check on him. In less than ten minutes, she and Renegade pulled onto Hughes's street. The house lights were on and as she passed by, she peered in the living room window. The judge was slow dancing with a woman who looked a great deal like the court reporter Caitlyn had met earlier. *The cat, I presume.*

Irritation spurred by his cavalier attitude flicked up the back of her neck, and Caitlyn pulled a U-turn. She parked behind a blue Honda Civic at the curb in front of Judge Hughes's house, and she and Renegade strode up to the front entrance. Caitlyn pounded on the black painted wood. The judge peered out the window seconds before he swung open the door.

The Honorable Judge William Hughes stood before her in shirttails and black dress socks swaying to *Smooth* by Santana. A crystal tumbler, half full of golden liquid and ice, tipped precariously in his hand. Behind him stood the woman he had introduced earlier that afternoon, Una Murphy, the court reporter. "Change your mind, my dear? Come in. Come in." Hughes attempted an awkward courtly bow. "The more the merrier! Do you know how to cha-cha?" He performed a few steps.

This man was ridiculous. "Sir, I'm not here to party with you two. When your alarm triggered, I came right away to ensure your safety."

While holding his glass in one hand, he covered his mouth with the back of the other. "I forgot I'm not allowed to open my door without permission. I only opened it for a second to let Una in." His laugh was raspy reminding Caitlyn of Snidely Whiplash in the Rocky and Bullwinkle cartoon. "After all, it takes two to tango." Hughes swept an arm around Caitlyn's shoulders, puffing a cloud of scotch-scented breath into her face before he pressed his cheek against hers. He stepped forward in what Caitlyn presumed was his attempt at the tango.

Renegade curled his lips and barked at the overbearing man, and Caitlyn pushed the judge away. She swung her gaze to the woman behind him. Una wore the judge's abandoned tie around her neck over a tight-fitting Rolling Stones T-shirt. "Ms. Murphy, is it your habit to visit the judge this late at night at his home?"

Dark, almost black eyes narrowed slightly over a forced smile. "I don't think what we do in our private time is any of your business."

"What you do in private doesn't even pique my interest, Ms. Murphy. My job, however, is to keep Judge

Hughes safe. So, from now on, if either of you needs to turn the alarm system off between six pm and nine in the morning, I would appreciate a phone call ahead of time, and then another one when the alarm is re-engaged. Is that agreeable?"

"Of course, of course. Don't be angry, sweetheart. Come on in. You should probably check all around the house just in case. Then stay for a drink." He raised his tumbler to Caitlyn and quirked his brows in question.

"No, thank you, Your Honor."

"Bill—please. Especially when I'm at home. I prefer to be casual."

"Good night, Judge." Caitlyn watched as the judge set his alarm on the panel by the door, before she turned toward her truck. "Come on, Ren. We may as well go get me some coffee. I should probably stand watch on the street until the lovely Ms. Murphy goes home. If she does."

They climbed into the truck and drove to the Sinclair Station for coffee. Renegade swiped the side of Caitlyn's face with his long, wet tongue. "Eww." Caitlyn laughed and hung her arm over Ren's auburn shoulders. "You understand, don't you, boy? I hope we can get back to the real job soon. This guy is a total schmuck!"

Caitlyn and Renegade remained outside the judge's house for the rest of the night, and Una Murphy never left. *Big surprise.* Caitlyn glanced at her watch and decided to dash through the McDonald's drive-through for some breakfast and much needed caffeine before their day started. When they returned, she passed by Una's car on the street and parked her truck behind the judge's Chrysler in his driveway and waited. An hour ticked by. At that rate, Hughes was going to be late for work, but he was the judge, and she supposed he set his own schedule. Caitlyn poured a second bottle of water out into a portable dog bowl for Renegade and then sipped her coffee. Its extreme bitterness made her wonder if it was the same brew from last night's pot. She drank it, anyway, needing the boost.

As she bit into her egg and cheese biscuit, her phone rang. When she answered, Sam sounded tired. "Good morning. I thought I'd let you know we'll be pulling into Mammoth in about two hours."

"You guys made great time."

"We left early so we could spend the day at the hot springs together."

"That'll be nice."

"We're driving through McDonalds. I'd better go. See you in a while."

"Sounds good. I've got to go, too. Looks like the judge is emerging from his lair." Caitlyn ended the call and opened her door. The drapes in the window of the house next to the judge's shifted, and she made a mental note of the nosey neighbor. She and Renegade stepped onto the porch at the same time the front door opened. "Good morning, Judge Hughes."

The judge, shuffling out of the entrance, startled at her voice. He looked abashed and more than a little hung-over. He glanced back inside his house.

Una's words echoed from inside. "It's got to be one or

the other of your nasty exes, Bill. Did you tell the sheriff to investigate them?"

Caitlyn raised her brows at the judge. "Ex-wives? You didn't mention you had ex-wives."

Judge Hughes's fleshy cheeks turned red, and he rubbed the back of his neck. "Una is just leaving. You aren't supposed to be here for another ten minutes."

"Look, Your Honor, I don't care what you do on your own time. I'm not here to judge you, but I do need to be informed so that I can do my job." Behind Hughes, the woman who had been dancing with him last night studied her reflection in the hallway mirror. She tidied her hair before following him out the front door.

Caitlyn rested her hands on her hip. "Good morning, Ms. Murphy. Are you two driving together to the courthouse?"

The woman's jaw dropped, but she recovered quickly. "No. I have my own car."

"In that case, why don't you lead the way, ma'am? Then I'll follow you both."

Una walked past the judge and muttered, "You didn't tell me the marshal was watching us all night."

"I didn't know she was, but Deputy Marshal Reed will keep our... uh... friendship confidential, won't you, Deputy Marshal?"

Caitlyn stepped back to give Una room to pass by. "Like I said, my only concern is your safety, sir." Maybe now that she knew he was having a workplace affair, the judge would behave himself around her. Una strode out to the blue Civic, got in, and started her engine while Hughes locked his front door. "I'd like Renegade to check your vehicle before you get into it. If everything is clear, we can head to the courthouse."

The judge nodded and waited while Caitlyn followed Renegade around his silver car. "Renegade, *such.*" Ren performed the vehicle search and gave no alert or sign that there was any dangerous scent, so the pair returned to the judge, and Renegade sat politely beside Caitlyn.

"Ms. Murphy mentioned you have two ex-wives?"

"Yes."

"How likely is it that one of them is the author of the letters?"

"Not at all."

"Have you given their contact information to the FBI?"

"I didn't see a need to."

"Ms. Murphy indicated there is some tension between you and one or both of them."

The judge set his jaw and pushed by Caitlyn on his way to open his car door. "Surely the FBI already knows I have two ex-wives," he snapped. "If not, they're not very good at their jobs."

"I'm sure they do, sir. But if you think one of the women might be threatening you, you should inform them." *Never mind showing any gratitude for the two federal agencies working to keep you safe.* Caitlyn schooled her expression to remain neutral though she wanted to tell this pompous jerk exactly what she thought of him.

"Will you please get your truck out of my way?" Judge Hughes plopped into his seat and slammed the door. Caitlyn and Renegade jogged to her truck and hurried to follow him. When they reached the courthouse, the judge met Una on the walkway behind the building, but they didn't wait for their protective guard. Judge Hughes took the court reporter by the elbow and rushed her inside through his private entrance. The automatic door lock clicked in place behind them. Clearly, he felt that a security detail cramped his style. Caitlyn sighed and she and Renegade walked around to the front of the courthouse and entered through the lobby.

She nodded at the court security officer, and they made their way upstairs to the courtroom. According to the docket the day's first hearing was at ten. That gave Caitlyn and Renegade about an hour to search and clear the small courthouse. Caitlyn kept Renegade on a short leash as he sniffed up and down the courtroom gallery aisles, the attorney's tables, the jury box, and the judge's bench. Una entered the room and busily set up her stenotype machine.

"Old school, huh?" Caitlyn smiled as she approached the woman.

"We digitally record the trials as well."

"Makes sense." Caitlyn paused by the woman's setup, and Renegade sniffed her equipment. She drew her arm back away from his nose. Caitlyn wasn't sure if she feared the dog or just didn't like him. "Ms. Murphy, I heard you talking to the judge this morning about his ex-wives."

"Call me Una." She sighed and peered up at Caitlyn as impatience pushed her brows upward. "What of it?"

Running on no sleep, Caitlyn was short on grace herself. Didn't these two understand she was there to help? "Do you believe either of them poses a threat to the judge?"

"Yes, frankly, I do." She leaned back in her chair. "Well,

his first wife has a house in Boston, so probably not her. But the second one lives in Nebraska. She's always demanding more money from him, and he's started refusing her, so she could be the one threatening him."

Caitlyn chewed on her lower lip. "Have you met either of his ex-wives?"

"No. No one knows that Bill and I are… except you. And you promised to keep quiet."

This was a tiny town and Caitlyn guessed many people already knew about the judge and Una, but she kept her thoughts to herself. "So, there's no reason for either of them to feel jealous of you, or anything like that?"

"No," Una snipped.

"Is there anyone in your life that might not like the idea of you and the judge together? An ex-husband, boyfriend, anyone like that?"

Una crossed her arms and narrowed her eyes at Caitlyn. "I told you, this has nothing to do with me."

"Keeping the judge safe does concern you, however. You must let me know if you see or hear anything unusual."

"I will."

Caitlyn nodded, and she and Renegade walked down the center aisle and out the double oak doors. Together, they spent the day checking all the corridors, meeting rooms, and restrooms on both floors. By the end of the afternoon, Renegade had found nothing, but the pair continued to search the back hallways, storage closets, the jury room and, of course, the judge's chambers where Judge Hughes did his best to ignore them.

Renegade sniffed along the outer walls of the judge's

office before he turned his attention to each piece of furniture. Caitlyn walked past Hughes's desk, but Renegade tugged her back when he stopped. Her dog sniffed the outside and then the inside of a small trash bin under the desk. Renegade sat down and whined beside the basket, and an icy chill rippled across Caitlyn's skin.

5

McKenzie was still asleep when her phone rang. She surfaced unwillingly from the depth of her dream world, swiped the answer button, and mumbled. "Yeah?"

"Good morning, Ms. Torrington. I never figured you for a late sleeper." The man's voice was familiar, but McKenzie's brain was too groggy to place it.

She glanced at the phone screen. It was only 5:00 am. "It's still dark out. Is this Tony?"

"The one and only. Hey—sorry, I forgot about the time difference."

"Great. What do you want?"

"I'd forgotten you're a grouch in the morning." Tony Cross ran the Escambia County K9 Unit down in Florida where McKenzie had lived before she came to work for Caitlyn. Before she fell in love with Caitlyn's brother. "I'm just checking in with you. I'm still hoping you're coming home sometime soon."

McKenzie had worked for Tony, training all the new

dogs for his unit and working with his and other police K9 teams to keep them sharp. He wanted her back, and he'd made it clear that it was not for purely professional reasons. McKenzie had kept her options open, not knowing how things would turn out with Dylan. But now she was in love with the Wyoming cowboy and didn't want to go anywhere. Besides, she had grown to love the whole Reed family and felt at home in Moose Creek. She hadn't been sure before, but in that moment, she knew exactly what her future held.

"I hate to tell you this, Tony, but I'm putting down roots here in Wyoming. In fact, I'm going to apply for a business license today. I'm starting a Belgian Malinois breeding business."

"Did you win the lottery or something?" His voice rose and he rushed on. "Don't you need a chunk of property? Not to mention, those dogs aren't cheap."

McKenzie chuckled, giddy from admitting out loud to Tony that she was staying in Moose Creek no matter what. "I'm starting small, with just one pup."

"Doesn't it take at least two?" Tony's joke sounded strained.

"I'm getting a female and when she is old enough, I want to breed her with the dog I've been training up here."

Silence hung on the line. "So, you're not coming home?"

McKenzie softened her voice. "Moose Creek is my new home, Tony."

"Okay... Can I come up to see you?"

She knew Tony had feelings for her, and maybe if

she'd have never come to Moose Creek, never met Dylan, maybe she could have returned his feelings one day. But that was a different life. "I plan to sell you dogs for your unit when you need them, so I hope you'll fly up here when I have some K9s ready for work."

"You know I will." Tony's voice dropped. "McKenzie, have you met someone? Is that what this is about?"

"Yes. But it's not just that."

"And he's worth changing your whole life for?"

"He is. But even if that wasn't the case, I'd still want to stay here. I've built a life here in Moose Creek. I'm part of the community now in ways I never felt in Florida." McKenzie wanted to stay in Wyoming to be with Dylan, but as she talked with Tony, she realized there really was more to it than that. She had made some good friends and had come to feel like she was part of the Reed family. The clarity she felt as she told Tony about her future had her eager to plan her business and get started right away.

"So, what's this guy's name?"

"Dylan Reed. I'd love for you to meet him."

"Be sure and tell him he better take good care of you, or he'll have a whole K9 unit to deal with."

"I will." McKenzie laughed, relieved that Tony wasn't overly upset at her news. He may have wanted to start something with her, but he wasn't the kind of guy who wanted anything serious. She ended the call and reached for her laptop as the tangerine-pink dawn pooled across her white comforter. She researched how to apply for a business license in the state of Wyoming. Within the hour, she established Torrington K9s, LLC. She couldn't wait to tell Dylan, but at a quarter past six in the morning, she'd be lucky if she caught him before he rode out to work on his ranch.

After being sent directly to voice mail on Dylan's phone, McKenzie tried the landline at the ranch house. His mother answered the call.

"Hi Stella, it's McKenzie. I've missed Dylan already, haven't I?"

"Yes, but I'm pleased to say that John rode out with him this morning. He's been feeling himself again and getting stronger every day."

"That's fantastic. So, he's figured out how to keep his insulin balanced?"

"He hates having to do it, but not as much as being sick. He told me he'd only work a half-day, and Dylan promised to make him come in. I don't want him to overdo."

"That's smart."

"What are you up to today? If you're not busy, I'd love your opinion on some wedding details. I bought a half-dozen bridal magazines and I've been cutting out ideas."

McKenzie smiled to herself. Stella was far more excited about planning Caitlyn's wedding than her daughter was. She'd have to teach Stella about Pinterest. "I might have a little time later, but I have some exciting news of my own. This morning, I started my own K9 training business. I'm calling it, Torrington K9s, LLC."

Stella's smile threaded through her words. "How wonderful! We need to celebrate. First, that you are now a business owner, and second, that this must mean you've decided to stay in Wyoming for good."

McKenzie laughed. "Yep."

"Any other reasons that I should know about?" Stella would have loved to hear that Dylan had proposed, but he hadn't, and that thought pricked McKenzie's heart. She hoped he would too, and a couple of times she was sure he was going to, but he didn't. Was it wishful thinking on her part? Maybe Dylan was only looking for someone to do things with now that Colt was either busy at work or with Caitlyn. Was Dylan just out for a good time?

Swallowing a dejected sigh, McKenzie answered, "No other reason that I'm aware of. But a new business is enough to keep me busy for a while. I'm off today, so I'm going to drive up to see the dam and sire of the Belgian Malinois litter I've reserved a puppy from. I have about two months to get everything ready before I bring her home."

"I'd love to ride along with you if you want company. We could have lunch and maybe do a little wedding shopping."

"That sounds great. But we should probably wait for Caitlyn before we buy anything."

"If we wait for Caitlyn to make plans, the wedding will be a last-minute hill-billy hoedown!" Stella sounded dejected, but a laugh burst from McKenzie's chest. The thing was, knowing Caitlyn, she'd much rather have a casual celebration than whatever white taffeta and lace confection Stella was dreaming of.

6

Colt rested his dusty boot on the dashboard in his Sheriff's Jeep as Wes drove them back out to Harbor's ranch. Greg had called that morning to tell Colt he'd found a section of fence that had been cut and subsequently fixed. "At first glance, I thought it was an old repair I'd made, but when the sun hit the fresh silver end of the spliced wire, I realized all three lines had been snipped and then repaired." A distant Texan twang flattened the backend of Greg's words when he spoke. Rumor had it that he'd moved up north from Texas in the early 70s, but he'd been ranching this land for as long as Colt could remember.

Harbor's fertile green acreage stretched out along the flatbed of the valley and bordered the creek. It was prime grazing land, and in his heyday, Harbor kept over four hundred head of cattle on his thousand-acre spread. Back then, Mr. Harbor had a full mane of thick, red hair and a temper to match. Fortunately, he'd married a sweet woman with a cast-iron backbone for whom he kept his ire in check. Most of the time. Greg was a good man, the kind who would drop everything to help a friend. He was a smart and experienced rancher too, so when Colt got his call about stolen cattle, he and Wes had driven out to investigate right away.

On this second trip, they had stopped by the neighboring ranches to see if Harbor's lost cows had turned up in someone else's herd. Colt was certain the phrase "the grass is always greener on the other side of the fence" came from the fact that cows always wanted to push through their fence to graze there. However, when they checked the neighbors, it was easy to tell Harbor's cattle hadn't joined their herds because most ranchers in the area raised Black Angus. Greg's red Herefords would easily stand out among them. The missing cows were nowhere to be found.

Wes pulled up to Harbor's barn and the man, wearing a well-worn set of denim overalls over his round belly, approached the Jeep. "Didn't find 'em, did ya?" His now thin, all-white hair blew straight up in the morning breeze, and he patted it back down.

"No, sir," Colt stepped out of the car and inhaled a deep breath of air. The mixed aroma of cut hay, manure, and stock animals grounded him. "I have to admit, it's looking more like theft. Why don't you take us out to where you found the broken place in your fence?"

"Gol-dern cattle rustlers. There was a time, in a not-too-distant past, when stealing a man's cattle was a hanging offense." Harbor plodded to an open-sided shelter covering several parked farm vehicles. He climbed up onto a black ATV and tossed his chin toward another. "You two ride that one."

Wes drove and Colt sat backward behind him, holding on to the frame with his good arm. His shoulder, still sore from yesterday's jostling, screamed in complaint. Colt gritted his teeth against the pain. After a mile or so, Greg pulled up to the fence and pointed out the fresh, shiny cuts in the barbed wire. Colt nodded and took a photo with his phone. He held two barbed strands apart and climbed through the fence, then crouched down in the new spring grass on the other side. "Looks like double tire marks over here, too. The kind you'd find on a stock trailer." He peered up and down a rough two-track pathway. "Doesn't look like this road gets much use."

"Not since back when I kept a full herd. I use it maybe twice a year, now."

"Someone likely backed a trailer up to your fence, cut the wires, and took what they wanted. Then they mended the wire, hoping you wouldn't notice." Colt pulled on a long strand of grass until it slid from its sheath. He chewed on the tender white end, savoring the clean, sweet flavor.

"How will we ever find them? None of the neighbors saw anything." Wes studied the mend in the fence.

Colt climbed back through the barbed wire. "Exactly how long ago did you realize your cattle were missing, Mr. Harbor?"

"Three days ago. I looked for them before I called you, then as you know, we searched together yesterday."

"Do you know how many you're missing?"

"Twenty head. Ten cow-calf pairs."

"And they all carried your brand?"

"Yes, sir." Harbor rocked back on his heels and looped his thumbs under his overall straps. "The Rocking A."

Colt chewed on his grass shoot and nodded. "The next step will be to call the local auction barns and see if they've had any cows come in with your brand. Or something similar."

Wes cocked his head. "You think somebody fooled with the brand?"

"I don't know, but that's what I'd do. They wouldn't get away with selling them under Harbor's brand. It's registered to this ranch. Of course, the thieves would still need a brand inspection to sell the cows. Wes, when we get back to the office, I want you to call all the local brand inspectors and see if anyone has applied for transport papers for Herefords in the last week."

"Sounds good."

"I'll call Dylan Reed and see if he has any thoughts on how to hunt down these cattle." The men rode back to the barn and Colt shook Greg's hand. "I'll let you know what I find out."

"Thank you, Sheriff. I sure do appreciate it."

It was lunchtime when Colt and Wes returned to their office in Moose Creek. Hopefully, Dylan would be somewhere within cell range during the lunch hour. If not, John could probably advise him. Colt dialed his friend.

Dylan answered on the first ring. "Colt. Calling to tell me what the hell you were doing at the café with Allison Snow last night?" Dylan snapped through the speaker.

"What? No. I wasn't there *with* her. She just showed up."

"You think Caitlyn's gonna buy that?"

"Come on, Dylan. Allison is ancient history. Caitlyn and I are getting married, remember?"

Caitlyn's ridiculously protective brother remained silent.

"Listen, I need to ask you about cattle brands. Greg Harbor has twenty cows missing from his herd, and it's looking like somebody stole them. If so, how would the rustlers get away with selling them?"

"Their best bet would be to slaughter them and sell the meat."

"I hadn't thought of that. But, if that were the case, they'd need enough freezer space to hang twenty carcasses of beef. And besides, ten of the cattle are weanlings."

"They might have taken them out of state, but if they get caught hauling cows without a brand inspection, they'll be in a mess of trouble."

"I thought the same thing. Do you think they'd try to sell the cattle somewhere in Wyoming, then?"

"Unless it's to a private party, they're gonna run into trouble without an inspection, no matter what."

Colt scratched his chin in thought. "I have Wes calling local brand inspectors now. I'm going to call the auction barns, but I don't see any way that stolen cattle could get into an auction."

"It'd be better to go to the auction barns and look for yourself. I'm done here for the day—if you want me to go with you."

Colt hesitated. The last thing he wanted was to be stuck in a car with Dylan's unfounded suspicions all afternoon. "How many auction barns are we talking?"

"There are four you should check first. The closest one is Buffalo, then we could swing by the Big Horn Basin and Riverton auctions. If we find nothing, we could head south down to Chugwater. We could make a big loop."

"That'd take a full day. How about we head west today and if we don't find anything, we could go to Chugwater tomorrow?"

"I was planning to brand my calves tomorrow. But I could put the chore off a day, if you'll come out and give me a hand."

Colt smiled to himself. Apparently, Dylan was over being mad at him. "Done."

"It's gonna be almost impossible to find Harbor's cattle, you know. And you're talking a thirty to thirty-five-thousand-dollar loss. Is he insured?"

"I hope so."

"For old Harbor, that could mean the difference between keeping his ranch or losing it." Dylan's voice faltered.

Colt flexed his jaw. "Let's go find those cows then."

"I'll meet you at your office." Dylan clicked off.

Colt opened the mini-fridge they kept under the coffee counter and pulled out a rumpled brown bag. Sitting at his desk, he unwrapped a bulging ham and cheddar sandwich and took a huge bite. A greasy glob of mayonnaise rolled down his chin and as he wiped it off, his phone rang. He swallowed the too-big mouthful and rinsed the painful lump down with a swig of stale coffee from his morning cup. “Yeah? Branson here.” He coughed.

“Sheriff? This is Dan Nestor.”

It had been well over a decade since he’d been called by the high school principal. “Yes, sir? What can I do for you?”

“Unfortunately, I’m calling because I think we’re dealing with a surge of drug use over here at the school.”

Colt wiped his mouth. “What have you seen?” He thought of the boys he and Blake tried to talk to at the clinic last night.

“As you know, we generally have a case or two of kids smoking marijuana. But this is much worse.” Dan paused, and Colt waited for him to continue. “Three seniors have been ditching class regularly, and yesterday, they were reportedly seen sneaking off into the woods behind the school. At this point, I only have whispered rumors to go on, but I’d rather act now than wait until it’s too late.”

“Of course. Two of your students ended up in the ER last night. I wasn’t able to interview them, but Doctor Kennedy said the blood tests turned up methamphetamine.”

“You’re kidding, me.”

“I was going to call you about coordinating a random locker search this week. It will have to wait a couple of days, though. I’m currently dealing with another situation.”

“I was hoping Caitlyn Reed could bring her dog in. Renegade could find any hidden drugs, and we’d also gain the added benefit of scaring any kids who were considering trying something into changing their minds.”

Colt chuffed. "Unfortunately, she's out of town, but I'll see when she's planning on coming back. Until then, we'll have to do the best we can. Meth is no joke."

7

"What is it, Ren?" Caitlyn crouched down and peered into the small metal trash bin. Other than one crumpled up yellow sticky-note, the receptacle was empty. "Judge Hughes, when was this trash last emptied?"

The judge pushed his chair back from his desk and squinted under his desk to see what Caitlyn and her dog were looking at. "I don't know. Probably yesterday, when the cleaning crew came through."

"Where do they take the trash? Is there a main dumpster for the courthouse?" Caitlyn stood and looked out the window. The judge's office had a view out the front of the building, so all she saw was the neatly trimmed lawn and road. She turned back to Hughes.

The judge shrugged. "I'm sure there is," he muttered as he returned to reading something on his computer screen.

Caitlyn released a breath of exasperation before asking Renegade to continue searching the room. Her dog did not alert her to anymore scents, so she told him to heel, and they left the office. Side by side, they jogged down the stairs to ask the building security guard about the courthouse dumpster. Renegade had smelled some type of explosive material inside the judge's wastebasket and since it was empty, she wanted to check the trash that the cleaner had taken out.

"Yep. There's a cement wall around the dumpster on the east side of the parking lot out back." The security guard walked her to the rear exit door and pointed to it.

"Thanks. Do you know how often the trash truck comes?"

"They were here last Friday, and they come by every other week."

"Thanks." Caitlyn and Renegade dashed out the door. "Up for a little dumpster-diving, Ren?" She unlatched the heavy bear-proof lid of the big green container and flipped it up and over. Fortunately, most of the trash had been thrown away inside closed trash bags. That made Caitlyn's job slightly less disgusting, and Renegade could smell each bag individually. She took a deep breath of fresh air before she climbed into the dumpster to throw the bags out. Caitlyn landed on a cushion of trash which under her weight released a sickeningly sweet fog of rotten garbage so thick she could taste it.

There were only two- or three-days' worth of trash inside the container and Caitlyn tossed the bags out onto the pavement. She had four more bags to go when she heard Renegade whine and bark. She stood and looked over the edge of the bin. Her dog sat next to one of the white garbage bags and when he saw her face, he barked again.

"Coming." Caitlyn hoisted the remaining bags over the side. Then bracing her hands on the lip, she jumped up, swung her legs, and vaulted over the edge. She landed on her feet and hurried to Renegade's side. Her clothes and hair had quickly taken on the filthy smell of the rusting trash bin.

Gently, she untied the knotted plastic and opened the bag her dog had alerted to. She found only wadded up paper, envelopes, and two or three used tissues inside. With gloved hands, she held a few of the papers at a time up to Renegade's nose. He wagged his tail and whined again when she offered a handful of torn-open envelopes that were addressed to the judge. Some displayed his office address and others his home, but Caitlyn found nothing overtly dangerous in any of the trash.

She reached for her phone and called the judge's office. "Who brings in your mail?"

"I have a part-time secretary who brings it up. Why?"

"Do you have your personal mail forwarded to your office?"

"No, but sometimes I bring my mail in with me to go through during the day. Did you find something, Deputy Marshal?"

"My dog smells something on your discarded envelopes."

"That's all? Well, if you have nothing further, I've had a long day. I'm going home." The man clicked off the call.

Not sure what to make of Renegade's find, Caitlyn considered the possible scenarios as she bagged up the torn mail as potential evidence and planned to get it to the FBI as soon as she could. She tossed the remaining garbage bags back into the bin and waited for the judge to come out to his car.

The security bar on the backdoor of the building clattered and Judge Hughes emerged. He waited for Caitlyn and Renegade to meet him on the walkway, but when they did, he wrinkled his nose and a haughty gaze slid down its bridge. "I am certainly glad we didn't ride together. You are in great need of a shower and a change of clothing."

"No doubt. Do you have a meeting, or are you just taking off early?"

"I'm finished for the afternoon."

"Okay. I'll follow you home, check your house, and then head straight for my hotel for that shower." Caitlyn was grateful she wouldn't have to smell like garbage the remainder of the day. "Are you expecting any guests tonight?"

"No, but I promise to text you if that changes. I've learned my lesson." Hughes said in an exasperated tone as though he was doing her a favor. He reached into his pocket for his key fob.

"Good." *It's not like I'm begging to be your personal bodyguard*. "Hey, Judge, I know you don't think either of your ex-wives would try to hurt you, but have either of them tried to see you or contact you lately? Maybe one of them wrote to you?"

He stepped toward his car, leaving Caitlyn and Renegade to follow. "Other than the weekly plea for more money from my second wife, I did receive a letter from

Julia, wife number one." The judge made a sour face. "It was a list of expenses that she thinks I should pay for. She doesn't usually demand money. Still, as far as I'm concerned, she can try holding her breath."

"But nothing threatening or angry, that you know of? From either ex?"

"It's all angry, but nothing new."

"The threatening letters you received—were they via email or actual posted letters?"

"Paper letters. I received one at home and one at the office."

"Were the addresses typewritten or handwritten? Where were they postmarked?"

Judge Hughes wrinkled his forehead at her. "They were typed, and so were the letters. Both had a Cheyenne postmark. None of this is new, Deputy Marshal. The FBI has both letters and they're investigating." Hughes pointed and clicked his fob, and the Chrysler honked in response. "Besides, why would either of my ex-wives want to hurt me? If I were dead, I couldn't pay their bills."

Caitlyn followed Renegade around the perimeter of the car as he sniffed for explosive material. "Are either of them beneficiaries of your estate?"

"Absolutely not." The judge got into his car, started the engine, and pulled out before Caitlyn and Renegade had time to race to her truck.

She sped behind him but was still a full block behind when the judge parked in his driveway. Caitlyn pulled to the curb across the street in time to see him sauntering toward the road. He stopped on the sidewalk at a golf-cart-shaped mailbox mounted on a post which stood in the center of a tulip garden in the corner of his yard.

As the judge reached for the hinged opening, a terrifying thought bolted through Caitlyn's mind. Sweat broke out across her forehead. *There could be an explosive device inside his mailbox!* It would explain why Renegade alerted to the judge's personal envelopes. She pulled the handle to open her truck door, but it was locked. And not for the first time, she cursed the age of her vehicle and yanked the lock stem upward. She flung her door open and screamed, "Judge, wait!"

Caitlyn leapt from the cab and sprinted toward him with Renegade at her heels. As she stretched out her hands as though to stop the man, her boot slipped on loose gravel. She fell to her knees, shouting his name, and he glanced over his shoulder. At the same moment, he clasped the golf-ball shaped knob and opened the mailbox lid.

8

Dylan entered the front door of the Sheriff's Office followed by his Australian Shepherd, Lariat. "Ready to go?" He spoke to Colt but raised his chin at Wes in greeting. Wes bobbed his head in response and pointed to the phone he was speaking on.

Colt wadded up his lunch trash and tossed it like a basketball into the garbage can across the room. "Yep."

He stopped at Wes's desk and waited for the deputy to put his call on hold. "Contact the weigh stations on the interstates and ask them to be on the watch for the stolen cattle. Call me if anything comes up, otherwise, I'll see you tomorrow." Wes nodded in response and Colt followed Dylan out to the Jeep.

"I can drive, if you don't want Larry in your car." Dylan bent to scratch his dog's salt-and-pepper-colored coat.

"Not a problem. He can ride in the backseat." Colt opened the side door for the dog, who jumped in wagging his tail.

"Let's drive out to Riverton first. It's farther away, but if it were me, I'd take the cattle as far away as I could, hoping to buy myself some time to sell them. Plus, they're auctioning off weaned calves all weekend."

"The rustlers stole both calves and cows."

"More likely, they took the cows down south. If they're smart, they probably divided them up, and the barn down in Chugwater holds a mature cow sale every day. In fact, it's one of the largest sale barns in the state."

As Colt drove out to the highway and headed west, he called the State Patrol office and asked them to keep an eye out for the missing cattle too. After he hung up, he said, "Hopefully, the large number of cattle at the auction will slow the sale process down."

"Should."

By mid-afternoon, the men pulled into the stockyards of the Riverton Cattle Auction. After a quick sniff around the new area, Larry followed them into the auction office. Inside, two women worked behind a chipped gold-flecked Formica counter, sorting brand inspection forms and stapling them to their coordinating auction sales receipts. A table at the back of the office held a crockpot of chili, paper bowls, and a bag of Fritos. The food was obviously meant for the staff, but Colt's belly grumbled a plea for the spicy food, anyway.

"Good afternoon, ladies." Colt and Dylan both leaned against the counter. All three women stopped working and stared at them.

"The auction is over for today, boys. If you have cattle you're dropping off, just back your trailer up to the unloading gate." The oldest woman of the three picked up the stack of papers in front of her and set the bundle into a wire basket filled with more.

"No, ma'am," Colt replied. "I'm Sheriff Branson from over at Moose Creek. One of our local ranchers had some cattle stolen and we're trying to track them down."

"There's no way they're here, Sheriff. We've accounted for all the cattle that came through." The woman glared at him and crossed her arms defensively over her chest.

Colt realized she thought he and Dylan were questioning their work, so he softened his approach. "I'm sure they are, ma'am. What I'm wondering is, if I had twenty head of stolen Herefords, how could I sell them without getting caught? Do any of you ladies have any idea how thieves could possibly sneak stolen stock through the system?"

"They couldn't." The spokeswoman shifted her weight to her other hip.

"Well," one of the other women spoke up. She sent a worried glance at the self-designated leader before offering Colt a soft smile. "There are a few ways I can think of. We'd like to believe we're too savvy to let anything get by us, but to be honest, we've been so busy it could happen."

Dylan gave the woman an understanding nod. "It's that time of year, isn't it?"

"Don't you know it."

The older clerk pursed her lips and went back to work, choosing to ignore all of them, so Colt encouraged the friendlier woman to continue. "So, how do *you* think it could happen?"

"Every cow must be accounted for on an official brand

inspection form, but I suppose the forms could be forged. We get so much paperwork coming through here, it wouldn't be all that hard. Especially if the inspection was from out of state. Wyoming paperwork is familiar, but papers coming from somewhere else obviously look different." The woman pivoted, placed her completed stack of work in a box behind her, then turned back to face them. "Were the cattle you're looking for branded?"

"Yes, with a rocking A."

"Hm. It's harder to sneak by with branded cattle. Some smaller ranches send cows in that were born on their property but don't have a brand mark."

Dylan reached for a pad of paper advertising a local realtor and asked to borrow a pen. "Colt, can you draw a picture of the brand?" Colt took the pad, scrawled a capital A with a curved line underneath it that resembled a rocking chair rocker, and turned it to face the others. Dylan's eyebrows shot up. "It wouldn't be that hard to change that brand into a circle A."

"I'll check to see if we had either brand come through here in the last couple of days." The helpful woman took the pad and studied the drawing. Three cowboys entered the room behind Colt in time to hear her ask, "When did you say the cows were stolen?"

"Three days ago." Colt nodded to the newcomers.

One man stepped forward and after giving Larry a pat, he held out his hand to Colt and then Dylan. "I'm the auctioneer here. Did I hear you're looking for stolen cattle?"

Colt shook his hand. "Yes, sir."

"What type of cattle?"

"Herefords. Twenty of them."

"That's a mighty shame, but I can save you some time. I haven't seen anything, but Black Angus come through this barn in over a week."

The woman smiled. "Well, Hank, you just saved me an hour's worth of work."

"I appreciate it, too." Colt placed one of his business cards on the counter and handed another to the auctioneer. "Please call me if you see or hear anything that might help our investigation. Thanks."

Colt and Dylan left Riverton to drive back toward Buffalo. "How hard is it to change a brand? And wouldn't it be easy to tell?"

Dylan shrugged. "Not necessarily. That's why you want a brand that's hard to make into something else. That A could also be turned into a flying A by adding a wavy bar at the top."

"So, we're looking for fake brand-inspection papers and a re-crafted brand? This feels like the proverbial needle in the haystack. Harbor will be lucky if we find any of his cattle at this rate." Colt's neck muscles tightened, and his shoulder ached.

"What recourse do you have if we find fake paperwork for cows that have already been sold?"

Colt released a puff of pent-up air. "We contact the buyer, I suppose. We'd also have an address because the barns send the sellers checks for their sales the following week."

"You might just catch the rustlers then, if the cows aren't already headed to the slaughterhouse."

The friends rode in silence, both deep in thought, on

their way to the next auction barn in Buffalo. They had the same bad luck there, and Colt was glad to be headed back home to Moose Creek.

Wes called as Colt turned onto Main street. "Sheriff, Mr. Nestor called again from the high school. He said the baseball coach found some small plastic packets in the locker room that are printed with the word 'rocket', and one still has two small pills inside."

A spike of adrenaline ignited in Colt's brain. "Did he say if the rocket label ended with a capital T?"

"He did. Sounds like the drugs we found in that case a few months ago, doesn't it?"

Colt ran his hand over his face. "Sure does."

"The coach is waiting at the school. He's making the team stay in the locker room until we get there."

"Good. I'm just now dropping Dylan and his dog off at his truck. Are you at the office?"

"Yeah, but I'm headed over to the school."

"Meet me out front. We'll go together."

9

"What has you so excited, my dear?" Judge Hughes shoved his hand inside the mailbox and pulled out a few envelopes, along with an ad magazine.

Caitlyn climbed to her feet in the middle of the road—her chest heaving and her heart slamming against her ribs. She bent over and propped her skinned palms on her thighs above her stinging knees and struggled to catch her breath. The moment the judge had reached to open his mailbox, it occurred to Caitlyn that the envelopes at the courthouse could have explosive material on them from a device that was possibly left inside the judge's home mailbox. Her cheeks blazed with embarrassment but thank God she was wrong. Whoever handled those envelopes might have had explosive material on their hands.

"I thought," she panted, "there might be a bomb inside your mailbox."

"Why on earth would you think that?" Judge Hughes

shook his head and sorted through his mail. "Honestly, Deputy Marshal Reed, I think you are over-dramatizing this whole situation. I received two threatening letters, but nothing has happened since then. I'm sure it was just some disgruntled plaintiff blowing off steam."

"That could be, sir. But it's my job to keep you safe." She didn't mention the scent Renegade alerted to in his office trash. There was no point until the lab confirmed what he sniffed was explosive material on the papers. Self-doubt crowded in, causing Caitlyn to second guess Renegade's alert. Maybe what he smelled was some type of drug residue instead. He could tell the difference, to be sure, but she couldn't. And though she'd used the command to search for explosives, maybe he alerted anyway.

Renegade, who had followed her from the truck to the street, bumped her hand with his cold nose, bringing her back to the present situation. Caitlyn stroked his face and moved to the sidewalk to stand next to the judge.

"On my way home, I made dinner plans for tonight. I'll be leaving my house at six-forty-five and returning sometime later. So don't panic when I turn off the house alarm. "Okay?"

"I'll be here to escort you to the restaurant, Your Honor. Who are you having dinner with?"

His eyes displayed his irritation. "I hardly think that's necessary. I'm meeting Don Getts, the federal prosecuting attorney, and I'm quite certain he doesn't want to kill me."

"I'm sure he doesn't, but someone is threatening you, so I'll be going with you, anyway. For now, I need to clear your house before you go inside." Caitlyn led the way to the front door but stepped aside to let the judge punch in his security code. She and Renegade made quick work of checking the house. When they finished, she looked for Hughes and found him in the TV room in stocking feet, with his shirt untucked. He was watching the news and enjoying a whiskey.

"Let me guess. The house is empty?" His sarcasm was thick as he stared at the giant flatscreen.

"It is. I'll see you at 6:40 p.m." Caitlyn and Renegade let themselves out, and she drove to the hotel. After a quick shower and change of clothes, Caitlyn fed Renegade and listened to Jason Aldene and Carrie Underwood sing, *If I Didn't Love You*. The song made her think of Colt and how much she missed him. She tapped off the music icon on her phone so she could call him, but as the music silenced, Sam Dillinger's face lit up the screen.

"Hey, Sam."

"Hey, yourself. Just wanted to let you know we're here. Is there anything to do in this town?"

Caitlyn laughed. "Not a lot."

"When we got here, Laurie and I took Caleb out to the hot springs like you suggested. We're getting settled in our hotel room now. Have you had dinner?"

"Not yet. I'm headed back out in a few minutes to guard the judge while he goes to dinner, though."

"Has he had any more threats?"

"No. But on our courthouse search today, Renegade alerted at the judge's trash bin. So, lucky me, I got to go sort through all the garbage."

“Find anything?”

“Yeah, Renegade signaled he’d found an explosive scent on a handful of personal envelopes the judge brought with him from home into the office. There’s something on those envelopes, but I have no immediate way of knowing what it is. I gave them to the FBI, and now we have to wait for the lab.” She didn’t bother telling him about her blunder at the judge’s house.

“This job might end up being more exciting than I thought. Want me to join you on guard duty?”

Caitlyn tossed Renegade’s squeaky toy across the room and watched him race after it. “No. You take your family out and have a good night. I’ll see you at the courthouse in the morning.”

“Do you mind if I bring Caleb to your room real quick to see Renegade? He’s been asking all day when he gets to see him. He’s like a broken record.”

Caitlyn grinned. She’d love to see Caleb herself, and it was good for Ren to be around kids. “Sure. I’ll meet you on the square of grass by the hotel lobby.”

“Thanks.”

Caleb bounced on his chubby legs when he saw Renegade. “Doggy, doggy!” he squeaked.

Caitlyn asked Renegade to sit before she let Caleb approach. She taught him how to hold out his hand for Renegade to sniff before he was allowed to pet him.

With a serious expression, Caleb waited for Renegade to lick his fingers, but then he threw his arms around the dog’s shoulders. Renegade’s tail wagged like a propeller, and he licked the little boy’s face and hair, leaving one white-blond lock in a soggy curl across Caleb’s forehead.

Toddler giggles chased all the tension out of Caitlyn's shoulders. Caleb's chortle was the best sound in the world. After the two wrestled on the grass and Caleb threw Renegade's toy several times, Caitlyn checked her watch.

"I better get going. Say goodbye to Caleb, Ren." Caleb's lower lip plumped and turned down, and Caitlyn widened her eyes at Sam. "I don't know how you ever say no to that boy!"

Sam grinned with pride. "Come on bud. Let's go see if your mom's out of the shower. I'm hungry." Sam scooped his son up in one arm, and the little boy clung to his daddy's neck.

Laurie opened the door to their room and waved. "Thanks, Caitlyn!"

Caitlyn waved back and headed for her truck. If she left now, she'd be right on time to meet the judge.

They parked on the street until the judge came outside, then they followed him to the town's single steak house. Doing her best to give the judge some personal space, she waited until he met a man, she assumed was the prosecuting attorney, at the door. She waited for them to go inside before she and Renegade followed.

When Caitlyn and Renegade entered, she showed the hostess her badge and pointed to Ren's K9 vest, explaining that Ren was a US Marshal K9, and she needed him to stay with her. She then asked to be seated at a table where she had a direct line of sight to both the judge and the entrance. Renegade laid under the table at her feet. She sipped iced tea from a straw and nibbled on a basket of salty hand-cut fries while she scanned the dining room and watched the judge and his friend talking.

The men shared a bottle of wine and by the time Caitlyn was finished with her fries, their dinner arrived—two plate-sized steaks, along with a second bottle of wine.

With no warning, a loud *BANG* sounded igniting Caitlyn's internal alarm as the plate-glass window beside the judge's table burst inward, showering shards of glass across the room. People screamed and Caitlyn was halfway across the dining room before she had time to think about what had caused the glass to break. In a fluid movement, she gave Renegade a hand signal to stay so he wouldn't slice his paws on the broken glass.

"Everyone, get down!" Caitlyn shouted as she ran. When she reached Hughes, she yanked him from his booth to the glass covered floor. She up-ended his table to give them cover and drew her gun from her shoulder holster. She peered around the edge of the thick wood. Her heart thundered, but her mind was sharp and on high alert.

Seeing no one, she yelled to the hostess who was crouched behind her podium in tears, "Turn off the lights!" If the shooter was still out there, darkness would help her see and provide cover for the human targets.

Caitlyn searched the judge's cowering form. "Were you shot?" A few flecks of blood were scattered across his face from the spray of glass, but she didn't notice any major bleeding. "Are you injured anywhere?"

"I—I don't think so. Where's Don?"

Caitlyn pointed to the man huddled next to two other diners hiding behind an indoor fountain. The water flowed happily over the stones as though nothing had happened. "He's over there."

Restaurant patrons scrambled on hands and knees toward the kitchen in the back of the building. Caitlyn called to the hostess, "Call 911!" The young woman nodded and with a trembling hand, reached for the phone.

"I guess you were right to be paranoid, Marshal."

"I'm just glad you're safe, Your Honor. My partner got into town tonight, so we'll be able to give you twenty-four-hour security from here on out until we find the person who's doing this."

The judge visibly swallowed and nodded. "Thank you."

Catching her breath, Caitlyn dialed Sam. "I'm at the steakhouse with Judge Hughes. Someone just shot out the window next to his table. Only one shot was fired, and as far as I know, no one was hurt."

"On my way." Sam clicked off.

DAMN IT! I swallow a surge of rage. *I had a clear shot and I missed. It would have been so easy. I could have taken out the prosecuting attorney too, if that Marshal hadn't been there to cover them. She's making my mission so much harder than it needs to be. I should have killed Hughes before she got here.* I look for the casing in the fading light, but I can't find it and I have no time to waste. The Marshal and her K9 will be out here searching for me any minute. Panic threatens to suffocate me as I run my fingers over the dirt.

A SIREN BLARED, and a local cruiser screeched to a stop at the front door. The sheriff exited his car and darted for the cover of a stone wall along the walkway. He scanned the vacant land across from the steakhouse before making his way inside. Caitlyn waved him over and told him everything she had observed.

The sheriff studied the inside of the restaurant before he said, "I didn't see anyone in the field across the street."

"I'm sure they're long gone by now."

"If you've got things covered here, I'll go search the lot and see if I can find anything."

"Actually, it would be better for you to stay here with the judge. We need to get everyone to the back room, then you can start talking to the witnesses. My dog and I will try to locate the place the shot came from. Renegade could track the shooter if he ran away on foot."

The sheriff bobbed his head in agreement and gestured to Hughes that they were going to move to a more secure location. Together, Caitlyn and the sheriff corralled the guests and restaurant staff into the kitchen area.

Caitlyn gripped the sheriff's arm. "My partner will be here in a few minutes. Are you okay in here without me? I don't want to lose any time tracking this guy."

The sheriff assured her he had the situation under control, so Caitlyn and Renegade made their way outside. She itched to be in on the witness interviews but reminded herself she was now a US Deputy Marshal, and investigating was no longer her primary job. She and Renegade were in Mammoth to protect a federal judge and needed to focus on hunting down the person who tried to shoot him.

10

Dylan hopped out of Colt's Jeep and left the door open for Wes to take his seat. Colt waved to Dylan as he drove off toward the high school. "Do the coach or principal think they know who the drugs belong to?"

"Nestor didn't say."

The school was only five minutes away, but Colt turned on the Jeep's red and blue flashing lights and parked outside the gym door. Normally, he hated feeding the local gossip chain, but on certain occasions, it could be useful. In this case, he hoped his presence at the high school would scare the kids out of trying the new *drug-de-jour*.

He and Wes entered the building and walked down the hallway toward the sports office and boys' locker room. The smell of floor polish mixed with basketball-leather, adolescence, and soap, hadn't changed over the years. It didn't seem that long ago that Colt spent most of his time in this very hall, back when he had played varsity baseball with Logan and Dylan but seeing the fresh-faced students sitting on the floor against the wall now made him feel old.

"Wes, you stay here with these boys while I talk to the coach. I'll be right back." The kids' eyes followed Colt as he walked by and entered the head coach's office.

"Hey there, Branson. Sorry to call you in to the school this evening, but I wanted to deal with this right away, even though it's suppertime." The man who had coached him in baseball stood from behind his desk and shook his hand. He looked the same except for a little less hair. "Seems like yesterday you were running bases. And maybe I'm getting old, but I don't remember having to discipline any of you boys for using drugs."

"There were a couple of kids who smoked weed back in our day, but it wasn't the athletes. But times are changing, and the drugs are getting worse."

"Well, I have to tell you, I'm disappointed in these boys."

"It's not all of them, sir." Colt turned to look through the office window at the baseball team lining the hall. "And I'm glad you and Mr. Nestor called right away. Hopefully, we can find out who's bringing the drugs into the school and put a stop to it."

The coach lifted a file folder from his desk and underneath it sat two plastic packets with *rockeT* printed on them. Colt recognized the logo as the same one they'd come across when Ray Burroughs and his gang of drug-pushing thieves killed Paul Woodrow and his son Tom. The scar from where Ray's younger brother had blasted Colt in their shoot-out throbbed at the memory.

"I found these under a towel on a locker room bench after practice yesterday." The coach puffed a sigh through his bulbous nose.

With a gloved hand, Colt slipped the packets into a clear evidence bag. "I've seen baggies like this before. Do you know who brought these to school?"

The coach rested his hands on the waistband of his polyester athletic shorts. "I could offer a guess, but I don't know for sure."

"Okay, well, do you mind if I use your office? I'd like to talk to each boy individually."

"Not a problem. I'll send in the first one."

"Thanks, Coach." Colt perched on the edge of the desk so that he towered above the solitary chair he would ask the students to sit in.

Colt believed the first five students he interviewed genuinely knew nothing about the drugs. When the sixth boy entered the office, he raised his chin in way of greeting and slumped into the chair. "I don't know anything, Sheriff."

"You've never seen this before?" Colt held up the evidence bag with the logos on the packets.

The kid didn't look at the bag but stared Colt in the eye and wagged his head. "Nope."

"And you haven't heard any of your teammates talking about it?" The young man shook his head again, but when he did, his eyes shifted away. "Did you know Tom Woodrow?"

"Yeah." The boy's jaw bulged. "We played ball together since Little League."

"The man who killed him deals this exact drug." The

boy flinched, and Colt knew his words struck a pain point. "We need to find him and bring him to justice. If you know anything, you'd be helping us do just that. You want justice for Tom, don't you?"

The boy's face went ashen except for two red blotches that formed underneath his cheek bones. "I'm not a snitch, Sheriff."

"We're not interested in busting you kids. This is bigger than that, and you could be a part of putting the man who shot your friend away—for the rest of his life."

A weighted silence filled the small office, until finally, "When you find out who the drugs belong to, what will happen to him?"

"There's not too much here, so providing it's a first offense, I could probably convince the judge to issue a fine as the punishment. Of course, since the drugs were on school grounds, the student will most likely be suspended for a few days. But if he aided in the capture of the true pusher, I'd make sure everyone went fairly easy on him."

The boy thought it over. His shoulders drooped, and he shook his head. "I don't know anything."

Colt let the young man's words sit between them for a long minute before he leaned down to his level and stared him right in the eye. With his face inches from the boy's, he clamped a hand on the teen's shoulder and said, "If you *do* know something and someone else gets hurt or killed, you will be an accessory to the fact. Even if we couldn't prove it, you'd know that you could have done something… could have saved someone from harm or even death… but you chose not to."

The boy dropped his gaze to the floor and Colt watched the inner struggle play across the expressions on his face. Finally, keeping his head down, the kid murmured, "It's Zach's. He got it from his cousin in Montana." With that said, the boy stood up, yanked open the office door and stalked out.

McKenzie and Dylan stood at the bar in the Tipsy Cow waiting for their drink order, and she told him about her day up in Sheridan with his mom. "The whole way up and back, your mom leafed through a stack of bridal magazines. You know she's planning an event fit for a queen."

Dylan chuckled. "I'm sure Caitlyn is thrilled."

"I don't think she knows how far it's gone. Your mom has already talked to the florist and has set up a cake tasting appointment with a baker over in Rapid City."

"My poor mom. She wanted a daughter so badly, but she ended up with three sons."

"That's not true." McKenzie shoved his arm. "Caitlyn has a feminine side."

"Rarely." He gave McKenzie a skeptical look from the side of his eyes. "Anyway, how did it go with the dogs?"

McKenzie let out a long sigh. "Fine."

"Just fine? You were so excited to go up there. Is the dam not all you hoped for?"

"No, she's great. She's beautiful, perfect conformation, and has a sweet temperament."

"Then, is there something wrong with the sire?"

"He wasn't there. When we arrived, most of the

kennels were empty. I didn't think much about that until we met the lady who owns the place." The bartender handed Dylan a dark brown bottle before setting a napkin on the bar with McKenzie's vodka-soda. McKenzie smiled at the woman and guided the small straw to her mouth for a sip of the lime-flavored drink. "She invited us inside, and her house was a mess."

Dylan's brows dipped. "You're not hiring her to clean."

"I know. It wasn't that. The lady told us her husband had passed away a couple of weeks ago and that she found she couldn't keep the place up. She'd sold or given away most of her dogs and wants to get out of the breeding business altogether."

"That's sad."

"I know. The property was set up well for the business, but it was obvious that it hadn't been taken care of in a long while. The empty kennel yards still had dog poop all over, and weeds and grass were taking over."

"Was she taking good care of the pregnant dog you went to see?"

"It looked like it. She keeps her inside the house along with another pregnant dog—a gorgeous Rottweiler."

"What's the woman going to do when their litters arrive?"

McKenzie scrunched her brows together. "That's the thing. She doesn't want to keep either of the mammas that long. She wants to move in with her daughter in Kansas and has no intention of raising any more puppies."

"Oh, no." Dylan smirked. "Let me guess. You and my mother came up with a brilliant plan…"

A laugh burst from McKenzie's throat. "Sort of. I

mean, I was only planning on getting one dog and then *eventually* breeding. But if I don't take the Belgian, I'll lose my opportunity to keep one of her puppies."

"There are other Belgian Malinois puppies out there, you know."

A dull ache pressed in on McKenzie's heart. "I know, but..."

Dylan laughed aloud, and the warm sound wrapped comfortingly around her. "But... you want to care for this dog and her litter, don't you?"

"I do. I mean, I know it's all happening sooner than I planned, but maybe that's a sign."

"How does your landlord feel about a litter of puppies living in his apartment?" Dylan chuckled.

McKenzie rolled her eyes at him. "You know fully well that your mom offered to have the puppies out at the ranch."

"You're right. I figured as much. She's never been able to resist baby animals, either." He grinned and shook his head. "What about the Rottweiler?"

McKenzie clasped her hands under her chin and bit her lip. "The thing is... her puppies are spoken for already. Same with the Belgian. I'd have to keep them for six weeks, but then they'd be instant cash flow for my business. It seems like a small investment in time and money for an excellent return. Then I could roll the proceeds back into my breeding business."

"And you would have two Belgians and a Rottweiler to take care of after that, right?"

"Well, yes..." McKenzie didn't need Dylan's approval,

but she wanted it. She wished he'd catch the thrill of the new twist in her dream.

Dylan took a long swig from his bottle and side-eyed her with sparkling mahogany eyes. "I suppose my dad and I could build a nice shelter for them in the backyard."

Excitement burst into shimmery bubbles that tickled McKenzie's ribs. She threw her arms around Dylan, and he responded by lifting her up and spinning her in a circle. When he set her down, she stood on her toes and kissed him hard.

"Wow! If I knew this was the response I'd get, I'd have already brought home a couple of litters of puppies myself."

She slapped his chest playfully. "Thank you, Dylan. You won't regret it. I can't wait for you to meet these sweet dogs. And I just know their puppies are all going to be perfect." They lifted their drinks and tapped them together.

The bar door swung open, and the evening sunlight glared into the dark room behind Colt's unmistakable silhouette. Dylan raised his hand to the bartender. "Can I get another IPA?"

Colt walked straight toward them. "Hey."

"Howdy, Sheriff," McKenzie smirked. "I always wanted to say that."

Colt grinned and shook Dylan's outstretched hand. "What a day. I sure have been looking forward to an ice cold one."

"Dylan told me about the stolen cows. Do you think you'll find them?" McKenzie sipped her drink.

"I seriously doubt it. But we'll give it our best."

Dylan passed the fresh bottle of beer to Colt and tapped it with his own. "Cheers." He pointed to an empty booth, and the friends wove through a few free-standing tables to get there. Colt chose the side facing the door.

"Have you heard from Caitlyn?" McKenzie asked.

"Yeah." Colt took a swig from his bottle. "She's staying busy keeping an eye on the judge, though it sounds like he's not real cooperative."

"How long will she have to be up there?" Dylan slid his arm around McKenzie's shoulders, and she snuggled into him.

Colt gave them a wistful look and pulled another gulp from his bottle. "Don't know. Could be a while. Catie told me her partner, Sam—the one who got shot in the leg last spring—is joining her for the duration. She'll have a little more free time once he gets there."

McKenzie stirred the ice around in her drink to better mix in the vodka and tested it through her straw. "Are you going to go up to Mammoth to visit her?"

"I'd like to, but I've got a couple of situations going on right now myself—the stolen cattle for one, and now it looks like we've got a meth problem at the high school." The entrance door swung open again and Colt squinted at the beam of light shining behind two women. He raised his hand to shield his eyes against the glare of the setting sun.

Dylan grinned. "That's what you get for always having to face the door."

"It's a law enforcement thing. I like to see what's coming."

Ironically, no one saw what, or who, was coming until

she was standing at the edge of their table. "Hi Colt. I saw you waving." Allison Snow stood, dressed to the nines in a red micro dress that might have worked at a trendy club in Manhattan, but she was as out of place as a shark in a pool of minnows in Moose Creek. She beamed down at him, but before Colt could respond, she prattled on. "Hello again, Dylan. And it's McKenna, right?"

"It's McKenzie." Dylan corrected Allison while he glared daggers at Colt.

"Oh, right. Sorry." Allison made a little bow, and she pressed her hand over her heart. Then, swinging her scarlet-clad hips around the corner of the table, she lowered herself to the seat next to Colt. "Mind if we join you?"

Colt slid sideways fast, narrowly avoiding her ending up in his lap. As it was, the woman sat close enough in the booth next to him that her shoulder rubbed against his arm. Her heavy perfume filled the entire booth and McKenzie felt sorry for Colt who looked miserable as he scooted closer to the wall.

Allison pushed up against him again and patted the seat beside her. "Sit here, Cindy," she invited her companion. "You all remember Cindy Coleman, right?"

Colt stared at the mouth of his beer bottle, and McKenzie's heart swelled in sympathy for him. He looked like he'd swallowed a cactus. McKenzie glanced between Dylan and Colt. Neither introduced her, so she said, "We haven't met. I'm McKenzie Torrington."

Cindy had the grace to look uncomfortable as she said hello to McKenzie, then murmured, "Alli, I thought we were here to play pool?"

"We will." Allison waved her friend off. "After we catch up with old friends and—"

"If you ladies will excuse me," Colt choked. "I've got to get back to the office."

Cindy jumped off the end of the booth, but Allison took her time sliding out. "Really?" She frowned, plumping out a pouty bottom lip. "I was hoping we could have a couple of drinks together."

Dylan stood too. "I'll walk you to your car."

Colt nodded in answer and slammed the rest of his beer down his throat while he waited for Allison to move out of the way. McKenzie tapped his leg with her toe, and when he glanced up at her, she gave him an understanding smile. He smiled back, but it looked more like a grimace. The poor guy sat completely still until Allison had shimmied all the way out of the booth before he made his escape.

"Should you be drinking while you're on duty, Sheriff?" Allison ran her hand down the length of his arm and gave him a sly grin.

His neck turned red. "I'm not officially on duty. It's my deputy's shift, but I need to do some research." Colt's excuse was flimsy, but it worked. "See you later, Kenze." He said before making a beeline for the exit.

Dylan pressed his fist into the small of Colt's back and half pushed him through the door. McKenzie knew there was nothing going on between Colt and Allison, but Dylan could be unreasonable when it came to protecting his baby sister. A woman who, by the way, had no problem protecting herself. They were all like that—the

Reeds—another reason she hoped to belong to their fiercely loyal family one day.

"So, how did you and Dylan meet?" Allison slid back into the vacant bench seat.

"I'm a good friend of his sister, Caitlyn's."

"Right. You mentioned that." Allison scanned the room and waved at the server. "Sit down for a second, Cindy." Cindy reluctantly did as she was told, and when the server approached, they both ordered apple martinis.

McKenzie pulled the lime wedge from the edge of her glass and squeezed the juice into her drink. "So, how long are you in town?"

Allison sent her a dazzling smile. "I'm not sure. Back in the day, I couldn't get out of this one-horse town fast enough, but now that I'm back, I can appreciate its charm. My parents want me to move home to run the business side of their tire shop. You know, the one on the edge of town?"

"Oh, yeah. That belongs to your folks?"

"Yes. At first, I balked at the idea. It isn't a very glamorous job, for sure. But we'll see."

Cindy kept her gaze on the table while Allison talked, but when there was a lull, she looked up and asked, "What do *you* do, McKenzie? I feel like I've seen you around town, somewhere."

"Probably. I've been here for almost a year now. I work at the café. But the reason I came here in the first place was to help Caitlyn train her dog for K9 police work. I used to train K9s back in Florida."

"You're from Florida?" Allison gaped. "Why on earth did you agree to come up here to the middle of BF nowhere? If I lived in Florida, I'd spend all my time on the beach." Then her eyes took on a knowing glint. "But then again, if *I* had wrangled Dylan Reed, I would have never left Moose Creek in the first place."

Her barb struck its mark and heat flared behind McKenzie's eyes. "I thought it was Colt you had a thing for, not Dylan." The words flew out before she could stop them.

Allison stared at her for a second before a Cheshire grin slid across her pretty face. "Colt was always my *first* choice, but I would never have turned down either of the Reed brothers." A whisper of a laugh escaped her high-glossed lips. "Has Colt been telling tales out of school about us? No wonder he's been acting so nervous around me."

Crap. McKenzie had stirred a pot she had no business sticking her spoon into. "Colt didn't say anything, you did. By the way, has anyone told you that Colt and Caitlyn are engaged?"

Allison merely waved her off and reached up to accept her cocktail from the server. "Guess I'm just in time."

COLT SUCKED in a full breath of air as soon as he and Dylan were outside. He gripped his friend's shoulder. "You have to know I had nothing to do with Allison showing up here tonight."

"Maybe. But it sure seemed like she knew right where you'd be. Did you mention to her you were coming to the Tipsy Cow? I mean—how else would she know?"

Colt briefly closed his eyes and willed his temper to stay in check. "I haven't talked to her since she showed up at the café. I didn't say anything to her. I don't want to have anything to do with her." He jammed his hands onto his hips and took a step away before turning back. His jaw ached from clenching it so hard. "How stupid do you think I am? You seriously believe I'd risk everything Caitlyn and I have for," he flung a hand in the direction of the bar, "that?"

Dylan studied him with hooded eyes before finally shrugging. "Well, you are kind of stupid." He grinned and shoved Colt's shoulder. "Get outta here. I gotta go get my woman." Dylan offered Colt his hand.

Relief swam through Colt's body as they shook. "See you tomorrow, then?"

"I'll be there." Dylan clapped Colt on the back and returned to the bar.

11

Caitlyn waved to Sam as he raced into the steakhouse parking lot with red and blue lights flashing. He rolled down his window when he pulled up next to her and Renegade. "You going after the shooter?"

"We're going to try. It's already been fifteen minutes since the incident. That's an eon in tracking time."

"I'll go inside and work the case from there."

"Good. I'll call if I find anything."

Sam gave her a short nod. "Stay vigilant."

"You, too." Caitlyn and Renegade dashed across the main road and up a rocky incline to a vacant field. She estimated the lot was approximately ten acres in size. The light of dusk disappeared as soon as the sun dropped behind the foothills, and a pitch-dark night seeped in behind. Caitlyn unclipped a flashlight from her utility belt and swept the beam over the grass, looking for a matted-down area where a shooter might have positioned himself to fire. "*Find 'em*, Ren,"

Renegade dropped his nose to the ground and ran in a seemingly erratic serpentine pattern, searching for a human scent. Without better lighting, it wasn't likely they'd find the shooter. Caitlyn turned to face the restaurant, attempting to gauge the trajectory of the bullet. She couldn't be precise, but in this size of a field, the possible shot range was significantly narrowed. Keeping her eye on the broken window, she moved to her left.

Twenty feet further, her beam tripped on an outcropping of boulders. "Ren! *Kemne*!"

Renegade left his hunt and, with huge strides, was by her side in seconds. He sniffed around the rocks while Caitlyn searched with the light. There, behind the boulders, was a circle of flattened grasses. Adrenaline surged through her system, spurring her on.

"Ren!" She pointed to the spot, and Renegade smelled it. "*Stopa!*" Caitlyn commanded her dog to track the scent. He wandered four feet out from the spot searching for the scent. Meanwhile, Caitlyn felt between the rocks and around their base. When she stood, her light reflected off something metal. Rushing to the object, she found a shiny brass cylinder—a thirty-ought-six casing. Her pulse rocketed, and she reached for an evidence bag she kept in a leather pouch on her belt.

She bent to retrieve the brass and at the same time Renegade took off toward the back of the open space. She used the bag as a glove to pick up the casing and once she had it, she jammed the whole wad back into the pouch and sprinted after Renegade. "Good boy, Ren! I'm right behind you!"

They ran full out, leaping over the rugged terrain in

the bouncing flashlight beam. At the back of the lot, Renegade bolted onto a gravel road. With his nose to the ground, he circled and searched. By the time Caitlyn caught up to him, he was sitting down and whining. The look in his eyes held the anxiety of an unfulfilled search.

"It's okay, Ren. Good boy," Caitlyn panted. "You did your job." With his eyes glued to her face, he whined again. Caitlyn rubbed his sleek head and shoulders. "Good dog, Ren."

She stared down the road as far as she could see in both directions, but there was no sign of anyone. The shooter must have fired the weapon, then raced back to his vehicle and escaped. "So much for those threatening letters not meaning anything."

Caitlyn looked back across the field, the way she had come from the restaurant. Warm light glowed from the outside of the building and parking lot behind the harsher flashing lights of Sam's car and the sheriff's Bronco. She released a frustrated sigh. "Come on, boy. There's nothing more we can do out here tonight."

Renegade trotted to her side and licked her hand. "Thanks, boy. Don't worry. We'll get him, eventually." *Please let that be before he murders the judge.*

The pair made their way back to the steak house. She opened her truck door for Renegade, who leaped up to the seat. "You've got to stay in the cab while the sheriff investigates the crime scene, buddy." Caitlyn opened her glove compartment and pulled out Renegade's favorite Kong chew toy. "I'll be back soon."

She ducked under the yellow tape printed with *Sheriff's Line - Do Not Cross*. Inside, the sheriff was searching for the round that broke the glass. It could have ricocheted in any direction. Stepping carefully around the sea of glass shards, Caitlyn approached him.

"Didn't find the guy, huh?" The sheriff pressed his hand against his lumbar and stretched his back.

"No, but I did find this." Caitlyn held up the plastic bag holding the thirty-ought-six casing. "I located the spot the shot came from, but by the time we got there, the shooter had escaped through the field to the road behind. He must have had a vehicle parked back there. We should canvas area businesses. Maybe one of them has a security camera that caught something. Does your intersection have a camera?"

The sheriff paused to look up at her. "This is Mammoth. The intersection definitely does *not* have a camera, and I doubt any of the businesses have anything filming outward."

"It's worth a try. I can—"

Sam interrupted her by pulling her elbow. "I'm sure the sheriff can handle the investigation." He winked at her.

Realizing that she was trying to lead the investigation again, she released the tension in her shoulders and smirked. "Right. Sorry. Where's the judge?"

Sam led her to the kitchen. A sheriff's deputy was interviewing the staff, and the judge sat in the manager's office drinking a whiskey. He looked up as Caitlyn entered. "Did you catch him?"

"No, sir. But now we know that whoever is threatening you is serious about it. When we're finished here, we'll drive you home, and one of us will stay with you overnight."

Judge Hughes's usual smarmy attitude had vanished. Fear haunted his eyes as he stared at Caitlyn. "Do you think they'll try to come to my house tonight?"

"I don't know, but we'll be there in any case."

Sam backed out of the office and pulled Caitlyn with him. "Would you mind guarding the judge's residence tonight? I'd do it, but Laurie and Caleb are leaving first thing in the morning, and it's my last chance to spend some time with them."

"Yeah, of course. No problem. But you're spelling me tomorrow. I'll escort Hughes to the courthouse in the morning, and Renegade and I will do a building search, but then you're taking over."

"Deal. You should go soak in the Boiling River near the hot springs. You can sit in the water and adjust the temperature just by moving rocks around. It's awesome."

"That sounds fantastic. I just might do that."

As soon as the sheriff released everyone, Caitlyn and Renegade followed the judge to his house. They entered first and cleared each room. When she returned to the living room, she asked, "You set the alarm, right?"

"You bet I did." Hughes went to the bar and poured himself another whiskey. "I'm having a hard time grappling with what happened tonight." His hand trembled as he raised the glass to his lips.

"I know you're feeling shaken. That's normal, and you might have trouble sleeping tonight, but rest assured, Renegade will alert me to anyone coming near the house, and I'll be right here keeping an eye on things all night."

"I appreciate that, Deputy Marshal Reed." He swallowed a slug of scotch. "I feel I owe you an apology. I haven't shown you the respect I should have. I hope you'll forgive me."

"Don't give it another thought. Why don't you go on up to bed?"

He nodded and took his whiskey with him as he climbed the stairs. He stopped midway up the flight. "Oh, there are blankets in the hall closet."

"No need, sir. I won't be getting much sleep tonight."

He nodded. "Thank you."

Caitlyn turned out all the lights on the lower floor and pulled a dining room chair against the wall where she could see both the front and back doors. The chair would be uncomfortable enough to help her stay awake, and though Renegade curled up at her feet, she knew he wouldn't sleep either. Together, they sat in the darkness listening to the clock on the mantle tick-tocking the minutes away. Caitlyn pulled out her phone and texted Colt.

Caitlyn: **You up?**

Colt: **Yeah. Missing you.**

Caitlyn: **Me too. No injuries, but there was a shooting up here tonight.** She described the events of the evening.

Colt: **Are U confident in the local sheriff?**

Caitlyn: **Yeah. He's sharp. Plus, Sam's up here too.**

Colt: **Good.**

Caitlyn: **I doubt the shooter will try again tonight. So, I'll just sit here thinking about you.**

Colt: **Nice to know. Pick a date yet?**

Caitlyn set her phone face down on her thigh. She hadn't had any time to think about it. Honestly, they couldn't expect her to plan a wedding while guarding a judge, could they? Frustrated at the pressure, she flipped her phone over and typed: **No. Have you?**

Colt: **Yes. Tomorrow. LOL**

Caitlyn smiled at the words: **I wish.**

Colt: **Hurry up and catch the bad guy.**

Caitlyn: **Doing my best.** A clicking sound came from the kitchen, and Renegade jumped to his feet. A low rumble vibrated from his throat. **Gotta go.**

Caitlyn didn't see Colt's text wishing her sweet dreams.

12

The next day, Dylan yanked open the passenger door of Colt's Jeep. He and Larry barely got in before he slammed the door shut behind them. Colt eyed him, waiting for an explanation for Dylan's agitated behavior. When none came, Colt shifted into drive and headed down the gravel drive.

"Everything okay?" Colt finally asked as they drove out of town traveling south toward Chugwater.

"Fine." Dylan stared out his window while he tapped his fingers rapidly against the armrest. Larry stretched forward from the backseat to lick his ear, but Dylan wiped the wet kiss off on his shoulder.

"What's McKenzie up to today?" The question earned Colt a dark-eyed glare. "May as well spit it out. We have a long drive."

"She's pissed because I'm spending the day with you."

"Ah." Colt merged onto Highway 85. "Did you have plans with her?"

"Not really. If I wasn't here with you today, I would

have been branding calves. But somehow, taking the day off to spend with you instead of building her dog kennel was the wrong move."

Colt laughed. "You know, there's a secret feminine hierarchy code of priorities. You can never anticipate it or understand it, but you sure will get in trouble if you're not in sync with it."

"Laugh it up, Chuckles. Seems to me that Caitlyn is the one who puts work first in your relationship."

The truth of the comment stung, even though Colt understood the life of law enforcement officers was often dictated to them by criminal activity. Dylan was right. Caitlyn had been elated to go back to work, even when the job sent her on some boring guard-duty in the middle of nowhere. But Colt didn't want to talk about that. "Why does McKenzie want you to build a kennel?"

Dylan shook his head with fast evaporating irritation. His humor won the fight, and he grinned. "She's starting a K9 training business."

"That's awesome. She'll be great at that. But even if she gets her first puppy next month, it will be a couple of years before she can start breeding. What's the rush for a kennel?"

"That's the thing. She went to meet the breeder and found out the woman needed to get rid of all her dogs, including the mother of her puppy and a pregnant Rottweiler. The pups are all due soon, so McKenzie agreed to purchase the pregnant dogs, and now she needs a kennel for them and their litters."

"Where? At the ranch?"

"Yes, my mom offered a place in the backyard."

Colt laughed. "You're being double-teamed."

"Don't I know it?"

"So? Since you know you can't beat them, when are you going to cry uncle and give McKenzie your last name?"

"When I'm damn good and ready." Dylan's edge returned in a snap.

Shaking his head, Colt smirked. "You better get ready soon, or your mom will just adopt her. Then she'll be your sister."

"Ha-ha. I have a plan—I just don't like being pressured."

"You and Caitlyn both. A definite Reed trait."

Dylan side-eyed him. "What do you mean?"

"Catie's resisting setting a date, too."

"That has more to do with my mom than with not wanting to get married. You should see what's going on at my house. Mom's taken over my dad's office with all sorts of fabric samples and picture boards." Dylan chuckled. "Everything Caitlyn would hate."

A COUPLE OF HOURS LATER, Colt and Dylan bounced into the lumpy dirt parking lot of the Chugwater stockyards. They parked near the pens and climbed the metal stairs of the catwalk that looked down over the cattle waiting for the auction. Larry barked happily, clearly hoping for an opportunity to chase the big beasts. There were several groups of Herefords among a sea of Black Angus, Red Angus, Wagyu, and other breeds. So many cattle made finding the stolen cows an almost impossible venture.

"We've got our work cut out for us here," Colt said as he propped his forearms on the railing. "Let's go down and get a closer look at those Herefords."

Dylan nodded and slid dark glasses over his eyes. They clambered down the stairs to the dirt walkway below where two pens held Hereford steers. One of the steers lowered his head at the panel, staring at Larry. He scuffed his hoof in the dirt. Larry lunged forward, barking, and the small herd trotted to the back of their pen.

"Larry," Dylan growled in a voice that meant business and his dog backed off.

"This isn't them. Harbor said his missing stock are calves and cows, not steers." Colt moved on.

Three pens down from the steers they discovered a group of young Hereford calves. "Check it out, Colt." Dylan pointed. "Look at that brand. It's a double bar A."

Colt leaned over the rail for a closer look. "Those bars are thick." His heart skipped. "Do you think the bottom bar could cover a rocker?"

"Yep. It looks like somebody took a bar brand and covered the rocker and added a bar to the top of the A."

"We've found them!" Colt slapped Dylan's shoulder.

"Maybe, but there's no way to prove that's what happened."

Colt turned and jogged toward the auction office. "Come on, Dylan. Let's go see what the officials have to say."

They squeezed into the office behind a line of cowboys waiting to register their stock. Colt pushed his way to the front of the line and held up his badge. "I need to see whoever is in charge here."

The woman on the other side of the counter nodded and rushed out through the door. Within minutes she returned, followed by a slender cattleman who had the appearance of a life lived outside in the weather. Thin lines bunched around the man's eyes as he narrowed them at Colt.

"I'm Denny Barker. How can I help you, Sheriff?"

Colt shook the man's hand. He explained why he and Dylan were there and what they suspected. "I need you to hold off selling those Hereford calves you have out there, pending a DNA test. I think they may have been stolen from a ranch up near Moose Creek. I also need the name and address of the registered seller." Barker hesitated, so Colt pressed on. "I can get a warrant for the information, but that will slow us down and could mean closing the auction for a day or two. And I'm sure you don't want it getting out that you stood in the way of finding stolen cattle."

The auction manager considered Colt before he slowly nodded and motioned for Dylan and him to follow. "I'll get you copies of the paperwork, Sheriff, and in return, I'd like to keep our name out of it."

"If it gets out, it won't be from us. We just want to catch the thieves."

Colt, Dylan, and Larry followed the man down a hallway of offices. The building must have been built in the fifties and never renovated. Black scuff marks on the ancient tile showed its wear, and the cream paint covering the cinderblock walls was so thin he could see through to the cement.

Barker opened the door to an administration office

behind the registration counter. Four army-green metal desks occupied the space, and all were covered with stacks of auction paperwork. Barker spoke to a woman sitting at the closest workspace. He interrupted her as she carefully wrote numbers into a column on a paper financial record.

Colt tilted his head close to Dylan's ear and murmured, "You think they'll ever join the twenty-first century?"

The woman nodded at Barker and then stood, smoothing her plaid western blouse down over her jeans. "All of this information is double recorded in the computer database, Sheriff. Handling the paperwork manually is merely a double check."

Heat flushed over Colt's cheeks. "Sorry."

"Don't be. It's an honest mistake. We get a lot of paperwork coming through the front office. I'll try to find what you're looking for now."

While they waited, Colt called Greg Harbor. "We may have located your calves, but we'll need DNA proof. Can you have the vet come out to draw a blood sample?"

"I can do that myself."

"It's better if the vet does the draw, in case this whole thing ends up in court."

"Okay, will do. How about the cows?"

Colt shifted the phone to his other ear. "We haven't found them yet. But we'll keep looking."

Not long after, the woman returned with the original paperwork from the sale of the Hereford calves. She handed Colt a copy of the originals.

"Will you keep the copies for your records so I can have the originals?" Colt asked. "They're evidence."

The woman shrugged. "Sure. Let me get you a folder."

"Do you know if any other cattle came through here with an inspection done by this same brand inspector?"

"I can check, but that may take some time."

Colt handed her his business card. "Call me if you find anything." He thanked her and entered the address from the sales receipt into his Google Maps app. With the paperwork in hand, Colt, Dylan, and the dog ran back to the Jeep. "The address is up in Moorhead, just across the Montana border."

"You don't have jurisdiction in Montana, do you?"

"No, but I'll call the Sheriff there and have him go with me to the location tomorrow morning."

Colt's phone pinged, alerting him to a text. He glanced at his screen and closed his eyes against a cold foreboding. Clenching his teeth tight, he swiped the message away and searched for the phone number of the Moorhead Sherriff's Department.

13

McKenzie purchased two kennels from the Mercantile to transport her new dogs' home, and she lined the bottoms with thick moving blankets to cushion the ride. Dylan loaned them his F350 dually for the trip, but he went with Colt to find stolen cattle instead of going with her. She could have used his help and was deep in thought, trying to solve the challenge of getting a couple of very pregnant large dogs up into the bed of the truck on her own, when Stella appeared next to her at the tailgate.

"So, today's the big day?" Stella closed the latch on one of the kennel doors. "John and Dylan haven't completed the shelters and whelping boxes they're building yet, but I think the mamas will be very comfortable until they get it finished."

"I think so too, but I'm feeling a little nervous for some reason. Are you busy? Is there any way I could talk you into coming with me?"

"That's what I came out to ask, and I'd love to. I'm not surprised you're on edge. This is a big, new beginning for you."

"True. Thanks for sharing it with me."

"I'm excited for you. Besides, you're the only one who will talk with me about Caitlyn's wedding, and that includes Caitlyn. I swear, that girl." Stella winked.

"She'll come around when she's not so busy."

"I suppose." Stella helped McKenzie shut the tailgate, and they climbed into Dylan's huge truck. "When I was a young bride-to-be, my wedding was all I could think about."

McKenzie turned the key and the big diesel engine roared to life. "Did you have a job at the time?"

"No, I was still in school, studying to be a teacher." Stella gave a soft laugh. "Needless to say, I didn't do very well on my grades that final semester."

They rumbled down the dirt road. "Did you grow up here, in Moose Creek?"

"I did. Oh, land, that was so long ago. So much has changed in the town."

"So, you and John met in school?"

"Yes," Stella beamed, closing her eyes as if to focus on her past. She blinked and glanced at McKenzie. "Just like Caitlyn and Colt, only it took them longer to realize they were meant to be. And now, Caitlyn acts as though she has all the time in the world."

"I think it's just that she's at the very beginning of a new career and wants to do well. Colt understands."

"Hm." Stella gazed out the window.

When they arrived at the dog breeder's home, the woman who owned the place stepped out on the front porch wearing a baggy, faded house dress. She waved as they pulled up. McKenzie was glad to get the dogs away from the place. It almost felt like a rescue, even though the dogs were well cared for.

"Glad you made it." The woman called out as McKenzie and Stella got out of the truck. "The girls are all ready to go. I've put their bowls and toys in a bag for you."

"That's great. Thank you. Do you happen to have any of their food left? I'd like to take some home with them to mix in with the new, so they gradually get used to it."

"Yes, I'll show you where the bin is. You can have it all. I won't be needing it, since these are my last two."

McKenzie handed the woman a check in the amount they had agreed upon and went to open the tailgate and kennel doors.

The woman pointed to her porch. "If you want to back up to the steps, the dogs won't have too far to hop to get in the truck."

"Great idea, but..." McKenzie grimaced. "Stella, would you mind placing the truck. I am terrified of backing that thing up."

Stella gave McKenzie's hand a quick squeeze. "Of course, but you'll have to learn someday." She climbed into her son's truck and maneuvered it around like she'd done it all her life—which of course, she had.

The woman brought the dogs out of the house by their collars. "Athena moves around much easier than my Rottweiler mama. Her pregnancy is going smoothly." She led the Belgian Malinois into her kennel, and McKenzie latched the door. "Miss Ember here, however, is moving a bit slower." The woman gave the Rottweiler's butt a boost as she struggled to get up onto the tailgate. "Her pups are bigger and heavier."

"And both dogs are due in a month or so?"

The woman glanced away, not meeting McKenzie's gaze, and nodded. "That's about right." She held out a bony hand. "I want to thank you for taking these girls. I'm relieved they and their babies are going to good homes. I gave you the list of the people that made deposits for the pups, right?"

"You did. I have all their paperwork at home, so I think we're all set unless there is anything else I might need to know?"

"No. You'll be fine. I'm sure of it."

McKenzie's nerves had blossomed, carbonating her blood. She couldn't remember being so excited since she was a little girl and got her first puppy. "They'll get all the love they can handle." She shut the tailgate. "You take care, and I hope your move goes smoothly."

McKenzie and Stella climbed back into the crew cab, ready to transport the precious cargo. "I won't want to leave the ranch at the end of the day." McKenzie giggled. "I might need to borrow a sleeping bag so I can spend the night out in the dog yard with my new girls."

"You're welcome to stay over." Stella patted her hand.

"I'm just teasing but thank you for the offer."

By mid-afternoon, McKenzie was introducing Athena and Ember to their yard. She carried their empty kennels to a spot next to the house for shelter. They could sleep in them for the time being. "I can't wait for the whelping boxes and shelters to be built. Dylan promised to make them cozy like a den they could go in and out of easily." She filled a bucket with fresh water, then stood back to watch the new members of her family.

John came up from the barn and leaned on the fence rail. "Letting the dogs get accustomed to their new digs?"

"Yes." McKenzie couldn't stop grinning. "They have the rest of the afternoon to get used to things before Dylan gets home with Larry. Then they'll have to work out their pecking order."

John nodded his agreement as the dogs checked out the unfamiliar space. "Dylan told me you were getting a Rottweiler. She's a pretty girl. Have you decided to breed Rotties too?"

"I don't know yet, but I couldn't leave the poor girl behind."

John chuckled. "You sound just like Stella." He watched the heavy-bellied dogs sniff around the yard and find places to lie down. Ember pulled the blanket out of her kennel and dragged it to the corner where the porch met the house. She scratched at the fabric. "That Rottie looks ready to go. When did you say she was due?"

McKenzie joined John at the fence. "I was told another month."

"Nope. I think you've been hoodwinked." He pointed. "See how she's panting?" He came through the gate, and they approached the Rottweiler together. John spoke to her in a low, calm voice. "Hey there, mama. Is it okay if I check your belly?" He smoothed his weathered hand over Ember's distended abdomen. "She's as tight as a drum. I'd say you were lucky you got her home in time. You're going to have a litter tonight or tomorrow, I'd guess."

"I thought she looked big, but I believed what the woman said. Why didn't she tell me the puppies are due now?"

Stella knelt next to them and placed her arm around McKenzie's waist. "She seemed desperate to me. Perhaps she was worried you wouldn't take Ember if you knew she was ready to deliver."

"Maybe, but I could have been more prepared." A strange concoction of fear, anticipation, and excitement brewed in McKenzie's stomach. "Stella, do you have any old towels or blankets we could use?"

"I'll get some and make us some sandwiches while I'm at it. We might be in for a late night."

John pushed himself to his feet. "Dylan has an extra heat lamp down at the barn. Anything else you need?"

McKenzie beamed up at him. "I don't think so. This is exciting. I hope Dylan gets home in time to see the puppies born."

"Did you say the pups are already spoken for?"

"Yes. They'll need to stay with their mama for at least six weeks, and I'll have to pay for shots and food, but after that, the proceeds from this litter will give me a good start in my business." Her mind raced over the items she still needed to care for all the puppies. "I'll have to get some different colored collars to help us tell the babies apart."

Later, when Colt dropped Dylan off at the house, it was close to nine. He called out from inside asking where everyone was, and John hollered for him to join them out back. By the time Dylan and Larry made their way down the back steps, a third little black and brown bundle was born. Once Ember cleaned him off, McKenzie proudly held the little guy up for Dylan to see. A broad smile filled his face and warmed her heart.

"What do we have here? I thought the puppies weren't coming till next month." He ran his finger over the small dome-shaped head.

"That's what we were told, but here they are! Aren't they adorable?" McKenzie exclaimed. She placed the pup up to his mama's belly. Ember licked her newest baby clean before she pressed her head against the blanket. "Here comes another one!"

Dylan put Larry back inside the house and then squatted down beside McKenzie. "How many did her vet think she'd have?"

"This is her first litter, and with palpating her belly he thought she'd have four." McKenzie resisted an overwhelming urge to gather all the puppies into her arms. But she'd wait until tomorrow. Ember needed to bond first.

Stella carried out a tray of mugs filled with hot cocoa for everyone to sip on while they waited. Two hours later, after Ember left the birthing blanket to relieve herself, McKenzie proclaimed Ember had finished delivering her litter of four perfect darlings.

"I need to get the paperwork in order right away. I know the new owners will want photos and a visit with their puppies." She leaned back against Dylan. "Isn't this the most amazing thing? Rottie pups are so adorable. They look like little bear cubs."

He encircled her with his arms and kissed her hair.

"Every birth on the ranch is incredible. It's my favorite part of ranching." They watched Ember care for her newborns, occasionally nudging a misaligned pup to find an open teat. She finally fell asleep, though her hungry pups suckled on.

Stella stood and stretched. "Time for me to hit the sack, too. Come on, Mr. Reed." She held her hand out to John, and he clasped it, love shining from his eyes. "See you two in the morning."

McKenzie and Dylan said goodnight and watched his parents go inside. When the door closed, Dylan took McKenzie's chin and turned her to face him. "I missed you today." He brushed his lips across hers.

"I'm glad you were here to see the puppies being born."

"Mm-hm," he murmured as he kissed her again, shifting for a better angle. Dylan raked his fingers through her hair, getting them caught in her long braid. He pulled the band from the end and combed out the plait before easing them both down to the grass.

McKenzie's pulse tumbled over itself, and she placed her hands on either side of Dylan's face, returning his ardor. He trailed kisses across her jaw and nibbled her earlobe, causing her to suck in her breath. His rough chuckle tickled her tender skin as he nuzzled and kissed his way down her neck.

A whine and yelp from Ember had McKenzie sitting up and pulling away. "Dylan. She's having another puppy!"

He sat up behind her and draped a curtain of her hair over her shoulder so he could see. His cheek bunched against hers in a grin. "Look at that. You have an extra pup!"

"My business is starting like gangbusters. I'll have to advertise him."

"Really? Do you have to?"

McKenzie canted her head to look at Dylan. "What else would I do?"

Pleading eyes bore into hers. "Can't we keep him?"

14

In the morning, when the judge came down the stairs, Caitlyn sat on the living room sofa petting a long-haired cat. Renegade sniffed the white, fluffy fur. "I thought when you said you turned off the alarm to let the cat in that you were using a metaphor for Una."

Judge Hughes laughed. "I was, in a way. I was letting them both in." He wandered into the kitchen and rummaged in a cupboard. "Coffee?" he called.

"Yes, please, if you've got plenty." Caitlyn finally dozed on and off during the night after she realized the kitchen noise came from a curious kitty, but still, she needed a good jolt of caffeine to get moving. She set the puffball on the floor and stretched. Finding her phone scrunched down between the couch cushions, she texted Sam.

Caitlyn: **How soon can you get to the courthouse?**

Sam: **Does 11 work?**

Caitlyn: **I guess, but you owe me.**

Sam: **Next round of drinks is on me.**

Caitlyn: **You're on.**

She was tired, but she could hold out until 11:00. She understood. After all, if Colt were here, she'd want to spend time with him too. *In fact, if Colt does come up to visit, Sam can't complain about working overtime for me.* The thought buoyed her mood, and she took Renegade with her into the kitchen to feed him and search for the promised caffeine buzz.

Judge Hughes poured her a steaming mug. "Cream or sugar?"

"Neither, thanks."

"I'm not going into the office this morning. I have a meeting over in West Yellowstone."

"Montana? Why is this the first I'm hearing about it?" Caitlyn wilted inside. She'd have to accompany the judge there and back—she and Renegade would need to clear his meeting space. There was no way they'd be back before late afternoon. Why couldn't the meeting be on Sam's time?

Hughes swallowed a bite of jelly toast. "Honestly? I didn't take the threats seriously until last night, so I didn't bother telling you. But now I admit I'd appreciate your protection."

"When do you plan to leave?"

"Half hour?"

Thank heavens she kept a go bag in her truck. "I need to change and clean up, and you have to feed me. I didn't get dinner last night, and I'm starved."

"Toast?"

Caitlyn raised a brow. "Sure, with a couple of scrambled eggs and one of those bananas." She pointed to the fruit bowl on the counter. "And another cup of coffee."

. . .

THE JUDGE EXPLAINED he wanted to drive by himself in his own car so he could make several confidential phone calls during the trip. Caitlyn agreed and she and Renegade followed the Chrysler down Highway 89 toward Jackson. The scenic drive made up for the inconvenience, and she relaxed to enjoy the ride.

The calm was short-lived. "What the hell is he doing?" Caitlyn asked Renegade. Her dog lifted his chin from his paws and cocked his head at her. She stroked his ears but kept her eyes on the car in front of her. The judge was swerving all over the road. When he increased his speed, Caitlyn punched his number on her phone. He didn't answer.

They were traveling downhill on a two-lane highway. Cars coming the opposite direction were few, but the judge's driving was erratic. "Is he having a heart attack?"

The judge waved his hand frantically out the window. He honked his horn, and his speed increased.

"I don't think he has any brakes!" Caitlyn's body revved to full alert, and she checked her rearview mirror. No cars behind her, and none that she could see in the oncoming lane. But there was a set of curves coming up. If she didn't do something fast, the judge would lose control and crash. "Hold on, Ren!"

Caitlyn crossed the double yellow lines and surged forward. She was almost parallel with the judge when another car rounded the bend, racing toward her in the same lane. Forced to brake hard, she maneuvered behind the Chrysler, narrowly avoiding a collision. When the oncoming vehicle passed her, the driver honked and flipped her off. Caitlyn sucked in a breath and swerved once again into the opposite lane. She gunned her engine and sped past the judge. His face was a ghostly white.

Another car appeared in the lane. She could slow down and get behind the judge again, or risk it, and race forward. Without thinking, she gassed her power-stroke and with a mighty growl, the truck surged ahead of the Chrysler and flew into the right lane with seconds to spare. Ren lost his balance when she swerved back to her lane, and he fell to the floor. "Sorry, Ren. Hold on!" The oncoming car swerved to the shoulder on his side, barely missing her.

Caitlyn's heart slammed against her sternum and echoed in her head. She held her breath—taking stock of Judge Hughes's car from all her mirrors. Caitlyn did her best to match his speed. When she estimated they were both traveling at the same pace, she slowed down by a mere three miles per hour. She pointed to the floor. "Lehne!" Renegade obediently laid down and watched her every move with absolute trust gleaming in his eyes.

Caitlyn braced for the impact she wanted, hoping it would be fairly soft. When the Chrysler hit her back bumper, the truck jolted forward, slamming Caitlyn against her seatbelt. She glanced at Renegade, but he seemed to take the impact in stride. The judge's face in her mirror wore a terrified expression, and she imagined her face looked the same.

"Easy does it, Your Honor." Slowly, Caitlyn downshifted her engine, not wanting to wear out her own brakes. Their speed gradually slowed, and to the judge's credit, he maneuvered the curves in the road without breaking contact with the truck. Before long, Caitlyn stopped them both. She pulled off in a spot that advertised a scenic view. Once both vehicles were at a complete standstill, she released her imprisoned breath and sucked in a fresh gulp. She mentally ordered her fingers to release the steering wheel, and Renegade leapt onto the seat beside her to lick her face and neck.

"I'm okay boy. We're okay." Caitlyn's breath came fast as she embraced her dog briefly before she jumped out of her truck and ran to check on the judge.

Judge Hughes mopped his brow and stared straight ahead. Caitlyn opened his door. "Judge, are you hurt?" He shook his head, but his expression was shell-shocked. She gave his shoulder a squeeze to reassure him while she studied his pallor. "I'm calling an ambulance."

"No, don't. I'm fine. I just need to catch my breath." He shuddered and wiped his face with a handkerchief before looking up at her again.

"I'm still calling 911."

"You saved my life, Deputy Marshal Reed. I don't know how to thank you."

Caitlyn patted his shoulder and smiled. "You did a great job of maneuvering through those curves. What happened? Did your brakes go out?" she asked as she dialed.

Her road-side service provider sent a tow truck which arrived first. It seemed like forever before the emergency vehicles got to the scene. Caitlyn directed the paramedics to the judge before she spoke with the sheriff. "So, do we know what happened?"

The lawman kept his voice low so no one would overhear. "The brake fluid reservoir in the car is empty. One of the lines was probably crimped or worn through enough for the fluid to leak out."

"Are you sure they were just worn through? Could they have been cut?"

He raised a hand to the tow truck driver to hold off, and he led her to the car to see for herself. "I didn't look that close. I just figured..."

Caitlyn unlatched the hood. She pulled a pen from her pocket and bent down. "Look." She lifted the brake lines with the pen. "These splits are precise and in line with one another."

The sheriff removed his sunglasses to get a better look. When he stood back up, he nodded. "You might be right."

Caitlyn closed the hood and made a circular motion with her hand, telling the tow truck driver he could pull the Chrysler 300 onto his flatbed.

"I'm having the judge's car towed to your impound lot, Sheriff. I need you to follow behind and stay with the car to maintain a clear chain of custody until it's signed for and sealed pending a thorough investigation." Caitlyn brushed at a clump of hair that had loosened from her braid. After securing it behind her ear, she reached inside her pocket and pulled out a business card. "I have to drive with the judge back to Mammoth. Will you please call me with any updates?"

"Yeah, but are you okay to drive?"

"Yes." She smiled at his concern. "I was a little shaken up, to be sure, but I'm fine now. Thanks."

Caitlyn inspected her truck's tailgate and bumper. She

ran her fingers over a few minor scrapes and dents. Thanks to her trailer hitch, the judge's luxury car suffered the worst damage. *I sure hope the Marshals Service has good insurance.*

When the paramedics were finished checking the judge, Caitlyn helped them secure Hughes inside the ambulance. Renegade sat in the middle of the bench seat and Caitlyn indulged in some much-needed cuddle time with him before she started the engine and pulled a U-turn to drive back to Mammoth. On their way there, she called Sam to tell him what had happened.

"Sounds like you're the hero of the day."

"Honestly, I wasn't sure what to do. Getting in front of his car was the only thing I could think of."

"You saved his life, Caitlyn, and probably the lives of other drivers coming the other direction. Good job."

"Thanks. I'm headed to the hospital behind the judge's ambulance, but I need to get something to eat. I'm feeling pretty shaky."

"I bet. Why don't I meet you there, and I'll take over? You deserve your afternoon off. Laurie and I found some good trails up near the hot springs. You and Ren could go on a hike and have a nice, long soak in the river."

"Oh… that sounds amazing. I may do that after I crash for a couple of hours. I'm wiped out. I'll see you soon."

15

Doctor Moore, the local veterinarian, stopped in the Sheriff's Office first thing in the morning while Colt poured himself a cup of coffee. "Hey Sheriff, I wanted to let you know I got the blood sample from Harbor's bull yesterday. I'll take care of talking to the vet down at the sale barn and find out if we have a match."

"Thanks, I appreciate it. Wes and I are headed up to the Montana border this morning to talk to the people who dropped the calves off for market. Call me as soon as you know. If it's a match, we'll definitely be making some arrests."

"I'll call you right away."

Colt and Wes followed Doctor Moore out of the Sheriff's Office. The vet waved as they climbed into Colt's Jeep. "We're meeting the Moorhead Sheriff at his office first, then we'll follow him out to this address. When I spoke with him yesterday, he told me the address is for a trailer home parked by itself out on a vacant plot of land. Nothing else around and easy to find."

"Are we going to arrest the people, whether or not we have the DNA information?"

"Hopefully they'll be home, but we might have to wait for the proof. I don't want to tip them off beforehand, but there's no harm in doing a little recon."

Colt removed his hat when they entered the Moorhead Sheriff's Office. "Good morning, Sheriff Munson. I'm Colt Branson and this is my deputy, Wes Cooper. We appreciate you helping us out today."

Sheriff Munson reached a work-worn hand out and shook Colt's with a firm grip. "Not a problem. You'd do the same. I know the address in question. Why don't you follow me?"

"I'd like to scout out the location before we approach. See what we're in for. Besides, I'm hoping to get a positive report on the cattle's DNA. Then we can make the arrests while we're up here and get the remaining calves back to their owner."

"Good plan. There's a ridge about a mile away from the trailer where we can park our vehicles and remain unseen."

"Perfect. Lead the way."

The two sheriffs' SUVs bounced along a barren stretch of prairie, turning only to avoid an occasional rock outcropping. When the lead car pulled over, Colt parked behind it and reached into the center console for his binoculars. The three lawmen hiked up the side of the small ridge and laid down on their bellies, careful to avoid patches of barrel cactus. Sharp stones jabbed into Colt's elbows as he propped up his magnifying lenses and peered over the top of the hill to spy on the trailer below.

A late model truck hitched to a stock trailer was parked behind the mobile home. Another nondescript compact car sat in the sun in what was probably once a yard. The only movement at the scene came from three buff chickens pecking and scratching in the dirt.

"You see anything?" Wes whispered next to Colt.

"You don't have to whisper, Wes. We're too far for them to hear us. But no, I can't tell if anyone's home. There are two vehicles parked in the yard, but no other signs."

Colt's phone buzzed in his pocket. He handed the binoculars to Wes and read the text from Doctor Moore.

Doctor Moore: **We have confirmed the DNA match. The calves are absolutely Harbor's. Still no leads on the location of the cows. Barn office searching for paperwork.**

Colt texted his thanks. "We've got 'em. We have DNA proof, falsified brand inspections, sales papers, this address given for payment, and a stock trailer to boot."

Sheriff Munson stood up and stretched. "Let's go round 'em up."

The law enforcement officers drove the remaining mile to the trailer. Colt directed Wes to watch the back exit for runners while he and Sheriff Munson approached the front door. His heart battered the inside of his ribcage as they prepared to arrest the rustlers. Theme music from Jeopardy blared from a TV inside while the sheriffs positioned themselves on either side of the doorframe. Colt pounded on the flimsy entrance.

The TV clicked off. Muffled whispers and shuffling sounds came from the other side of the thin wall. "Moorhead Sheriff's Department. Open up," Munson yelled.

A loud boom rocked the structure, and a gaping hole blew through the front door. The shotgun blast barely missed Colt and the force sent Sheriff Munson flying from the rickety porch. Colt dropped to his knee and yelled, "Drop your weapons! You're surrounded!"

The trailer shook as the inhabitants ran across the flimsy floor inside. Colt peered around the edge of the gaping hole. Three men were trying to squeeze through the narrow back door at one time. He glanced at Munson. The sheriff was uninjured and motioned for Colt to leave him and back up the deputy. Colt nodded and darted to the rear corner of the feeble structure. Wes knelt on the dirt, peering around the next corner, and Colt joined him there.

When the three cattle rustlers finally got through the backdoor, they ran toward the old truck.

Colt commanded, "Freeze! We've got you covered. Drop your weapons. Do. It. Now!"

The men, one muscle-bound and two slighter of frame, stopped in their tracks and raised their hands. The big guy held a shotgun in his hand above his head.

Jacked up on adrenaline, Colt yelled, "I said drop your weapons!"

Slowly, the man brought his arm down and bent at his waist. Without warning, in a smooth twist, he spun and dropped to his knee, releasing another shot in Colt and Wes's direction. Colt fired in return, hitting the man square in the chest. The man flew backward, landing at the feet of his compatriots.

"Don't shoot! Don't shoot! We don't have any guns!" The smallest man cried.

With his pistol at the ready, Colt maneuvered toward the shotgun lying on the ground. He kicked it away from the body, bleeding out before him and growled, "Get down on your knees and lace your fingers on top of your heads."

The men complied while Colt held them at gunpoint. "Wes, cuff them and search them for weapons."

Wes, looking stunned, ran toward them. Munson joined him, and they patted the prisoners down and bound their wrists. Colt pressed his fingertips against the big man's neck. It did not surprise him to find no pulse. He shook his head at Munson.

Sheriff Munson reached for his phone. "I'll call it in."

"Get a warrant while you're at it." Colt turned to his deputy. "Wes let's go check the trailer. We have to be sure no one else is in there." Colt felt for the kid. It was a horrible thing to see a man's chest explode.

They started toward the house, but Wes stopped and stretched his jaw. He gripped his waist, blinked at the ground, and clamped his mouth shut. His Adam's apple bobbed in his throat and the color drained from his face.

"You gonna puke?"

The young man shook his head, but Colt wasn't so sure. These kinds of bloody scenes were depicted over and over on TV and in the movies, but when a shooting happened in real life, dealing with the aftermath was a whole other thing.

"Meet me inside when you're ready." Colt entered the back door. He had cleared each of the small, cluttered rooms by the time Wes joined him. There were no other people, but they did not come up empty-handed.

"Sheriff. Look at this." Wes pointed to the coffee table. Along with an array of dirty dishes and trash, there was a lighter, some wrinkled tinfoil, and a grungy syringe.

"Well, now we know what they wanted the cattle money for. Let's go outside and wait for our warrant, then we'll see what we can find."

Sheriff Munson strode across the grass with his phone held in the air. "I've got the warrant. Go ahead and search the place, and I'll watch these idiots."

Colt scanned the tiny living room. His gaze narrowed in on the floor by the couch. "What do we have here?" He pulled a rubber glove from a pouch on his belt and snapped it on. Lifting several small plastic packets off the floor and into the light streaming in the window, he read, "*rockeT*."

Wes bent in for a closer look. "That stuff is showing up all over the place."

Colt's gut knotted. "Yeah, and we have to figure out where it's coming from."

They returned to Sheriff Munson and the cattle rustling druggies out back. Munson stared at him over the rim of his sunglasses. "Find anything?"

"Sure did." He held up a packet and addressed the captives. "Where did you get this?"

"It's not ours. I swear," one of the men cried. "It came from some Indian at the casino."

His partner kicked at him. "Shut up. We don't have to say nothin' till we see a lawyer."

Colt smirked at that. "That's true." He glanced at the other sheriff. "Did you read them their rights?"

Munson nodded. "Sure did. Let's take 'em in."

They waited for the local coroner and an ambulance to arrive before taking the junkies to jail. Wes wrote up the report while Munson helped Colt search the trailer. When they were satisfied they'd seen everything, they drove the two suspects to the police department. There, while they waited for the requested public defender to meet them, Colt texted Caitlyn.

Colt: **I've had a hell of a morning. How are you?**

CAITLYN'S PHONE buzzed from her pile of her clothes, but she ignored it as she eased down into the Boiling River's hot mineral water. This was just what she needed. Renegade napped in the shade of a nearby bench where Caitlyn had left her things. Gradually, she let her mind play back the events of the morning.

Whoever was trying to hurt the judge must have cut those brake lines in the middle of the night. She'd had Renegade sweep his car before he got in that morning, but he was sniffing for explosives. She tried hard to remember if she'd seen any liquid under the car, but the driveway was constructed of two long strips of cement for the tires, and natural grass filled the gaps. Even if she had looked, which in all honesty she hadn't, she wouldn't have noticed any fluid.

Her phone buzzed again, and not wanting to miss an important call, she dragged herself out of the hot water. When she realized it was Colt, she called him back. "Hey. Is everything alright?"

"Yeah, but you'll never guess what I came across this week." Colt told Caitlyn all about the cattle rustlers and the packets of *rockeT* he'd found at the high school and at the rustler's trailer home.

"It's got to be Ray Burroughs. Don't you think?" Caitlyn stood dripping water in the dirt.

"I'm betting it is. He's certainly still in the area, but where?"

"Have your suspects said where they got it?"

"I haven't been able to talk to them yet. They lawyered up."

"Maybe you can offer them a deal for information. Burroughs is a much bigger fish."

"Especially if he's hooked in with Trova from New York."

Caitlyn's skin prickled with apprehension. "The mob boss's tentacles seem to reach everywhere."

"Yeah. Are you on lunch?"

"No, actually I was soaking in the Boiling River." Caitlyn laughed.

"Tough duty. Where's the judge?"

"Sam's here in Mammoth now and he's finally taking a shift. I had a crazy morning, too."

16

After catching up with Colt, Caitlyn toweled the remaining dampness from her swimsuit and pulled on her cut-off jeans shorts. "How about a hike, Ren?" Renegade sprang to his feet, wagging his tail.

It had been far too long since they had a day off and time to play. And after their crazy morning and a decent nap, they could sure use it. For the rest of the afternoon, they adventured around the multi-colored terraced rocks of the hot springs, taking in the steaming crystal blue and aquamarine pools captured in white and copper-stained stone. Caitlyn's nose adjusted to the sulfur smell of the springs, but even if it hadn't, she would have stayed. The sights were incredible, and Renegade's sensitive nose didn't seem too bothered by the scent either.

Caitlyn finally gave up the day when the gold-tinged salmon sun nudged its way into the purple horizon. "Come on, Ren. We better get back to the truck while there's still enough light to see." Her dog scampered down the wooden walkway that led to the cars. He turned to wait for her and graced her with a wide canine grin. His long pink tongue draped over his molars and hung out the side of his mouth. Her love for Renegade swelled in her chest and pricked at her eyes.

"I bet you're thirsty, aren't you, boy?" She caught up to him and ruffled the fur between his pointed ears. He answered with a happy yip.

Caitlyn's phone buzzed and when she held it up, McKenzie's smiling face beamed up at her from the screen. She swiped her thumb across the glass. "Hey, Kenze. What's up?"

McKenzie's quiet laughter echoed through the speaker. "Just thought I'd let you know Dylan and I are in the Mercantile with your mom. All I have to say to is, you'd better start directing your mother's energy, or you're going to have a wedding that has nothing to do with anything that you want."

Caitlyn's belly sunk with a cold weight. "Can't you guys convince her to wait until I get home?"

"I don't think anything will convince her to wait. After a long winter of worrying over your dad's health, wedding shopping is bringing her a ton of joy."

"Maybe she should become a wedding planner then and bother some other couple." Caitlyn grumbled. "Colt and I should have never said anything."

"Yeah, right." McKenzie giggled.

"I don't know why you think this is funny." Caitlyn resented the pressure from her mom ruining the relaxed feeling she had garnered from her half-day off. And it didn't help that her best friend thought her mom's antics were so hilarious. "I'd like to have some say in my own wedding."

McKenzie gasped. "Oh no! Caitlyn, you'd better come up with a color scheme soon. Your mom is looking at baby-pink taffeta for bridesmaids' dresses."

"What bridesmaids? Whose wedding is she planning?" Caitlyn's neck and shoulder muscles bunched tight, and she rubbed an ache forming at the base of her skull.

A distant female voice sounded in the background of the call. "Hello, Dylan. Fancy seeing you here. Seems like we keep running into each other." Her brother's deep voice rumbled in response, but Caitlyn couldn't make out his words.

"Oh, no," McKenzie murmured.

"Hello again, McKenna," the woman said.

Caitlyn tried to place the voice, but it wasn't familiar.

"It's McKenzie." The laughter had dissipated from her friend's tone, and Caitlyn pressed the phone hard against her ear, trying to hear.

"Kenze? Who are you talking to?"

A muffled noise preceded McKenzie's lowered voice. "Guess who's back in town?" Without waiting for Caitlyn to answer, she blurted, "Allison Snow."

McKenzie's words punched Caitlyn deftly in the solar plexus, and all the air rushed from her lungs. "Allison?" The name skidded across her tongue.

"Yeah, and if she rakes her fingers down your brother's arm once more, I might have to break off her bright red acrylics."

Caitlyn blinked and drew in a sulfur-infused breath. *When did Allison show up in Moose Creek? And why didn't*

Colt tell me? "When did she come to town?" Her words wobbled, and she cleared her throat to cover it.

"A couple of days ago. Didn't Colt mention it? She's been throwing herself at our men like it was pitching practice. She's a trip."

Caitlyn forced her lungs to draw air and she held on to the breath like it was her last. Her mind raced over the brief conversations she'd had with Colt over the past couple of days. He had said nothing at all about Allison. *He should have warned me. He should have said something... right?* She pressed her fist into her stomach to quell the sudden nausea.

"Caitlyn, are you still there?"

"Yeah, but I gotta go. Let's talk later." Caitlyn slid the phone from her ear, but she heard McKenzie call her name right before she tapped the red hang-up button. Staring at the phone, she wondered if she should call Colt and ask him why he never said anything to her about Allison being in town. The woman had obviously been there long enough to become an irritant to McKenzie.

Caitlyn crouched down next to Renegade and rested her forehead against his shoulder. At a complete loss as to how to handle the situation, she imagined different scenarios. She could confront Colt on the phone or ask Dylan to challenge Colt in person. Maybe she should show up in Moose Creek unexpectedly and have Renegade chase Allison out of town. When her thoughts veered to fantasizing about punching Allison in the face, she drew herself up short.

She trusted Colt. He'd earned that. But the scars left on her heart from his past betrayal burned and flashed warning signals to her self-protective nature, making it hard to reason. She drew in a fortifying breath and stood. In the end, Caitlyn knew she would let Colt tell her in his own time—if he decided to tell her. And that decision would inform everything she needed to know about the success of their future together.

She nearly dropped her phone when it buzzed in her hand. The new call was from Sam. "Yeah?"

"Have a relaxing day?"

"Yep." Her answers were clipped and so she swallowed hard and forced her mind into work mode. "How's the judge?"

"He's fine. He has no physical injuries, just a serious case of nerves. We're back at his house for the night now."

"Okay, good. I'm just leaving the hot springs. After I grab something for dinner, I'll be in my hotel room."

"Okay. Hey, I heard from the forensic mechanic where the judge's car was towed. He told me he is absolutely certain the brake lines were sliced. He said if they were worn through, there would be thinning and wear on the rubber, but the cuts were clean."

Caitlyn released her breath. "We better figure out who's trying to kill Hughes before it's too late."

In the morning, Caitlyn waited in the courthouse parking lot for Sam and Judge Hughes to arrive. It was her turn to take the dayshift. A black Lincoln rolled in and parked in the judge's spot, followed by Sam in his SUV.

Sam waved at her and she raised her chin in greeting. "Come on, Ren. Time to go to work."

The judge climbed out of his shiny rental car. "Good morning, Deputy Marshal Reed." He beamed at Caitlyn.

"Judge," she responded.

Sam remained in his car but waved her over. When she approached his window, he said, "I was thinking we could alternate in twelve-hour shifts, if you want?"

"Fine with me, if you don't mind taking the night shift. Renegade and I have to guard the courthouse during working hours."

Sam gave her a thumbs up. "Eight to eight, then?"

"Sure. Go get some sleep."

Caitlyn and Renegade followed the judge inside through his private entrance and up the back stairway to his chambers. "Renegade and I need to clear your office before you go inside, sir. Then we'll search the courtroom. What time is the first trial?"

"Not until this afternoon."

"Good. We'll have the whole building swept by then." Caitlyn asked Renegade to search the judge's chambers. He sniffed the edges of the room before turning his attention to the desk and other furniture. He found nothing but continued sniffing until Caitlyn directed him to move to the outer office. Renegade didn't understand he was finished unless he actually found something so Caitlyn often had to simulate success to keep him motivated. At the end of his daily hunt, if he found nothing, Caitlyn would stage a find, then drop his favorite toy over his head onto the decoy so he would think the reward came from finding the scent itself.

Judge Hughes entered his office, carrying two steaming cups of coffee. He offered one to Caitlyn. Stunned, she sputtered a thanks. He patted her shoulder. "You saved my life. It's the least I can do."

"I was just doing my job, Your Honor."

"Well, I'm grateful." He sipped from his own cup. "I was told someone severed my brake lines. I can't imagine either of my ex-wives even knowing there *are* brake lines, let alone sneaking around my car in the middle of the night to cut them."

"No, but one of them could have hired someone else to do it. From now on, your car gets parked in a locked garage."

"Yes. I'll do that, but…" Caitlyn waited for him to continue. "I was thinking it might have been my neighbor. We've never gotten along. Not since I sued him to remove a monstrous tree that hung over my fence."

"How long ago was that?"

The judge shrugged. "Over a year ago, I think."

"I'll look into it but having to cut down a tree doesn't seem like enough of a motive to kill someone." Caitlyn's thoughts wandered back to the morning she found Una at the judge's house. Caitlyn *had* seen the neighbor's drapes rustle that day. She chewed on her lower lip as her mind replayed the scene, but then she shook her head. Curiosity was one thing. Harming someone was another. "What was the outcome of the lawsuit?"

"The court ordered him to remove the tree and pay me a thousand dollars in damages."

"What kind of damages did you incur?"

Hughes raised one shoulder. "The fence had some scrapes and my lawn…"

"So, the judge awarded you more than necessary—what, as a professional courtesy? What about doing what's right?"

The judge had the decency to look sheepish. "Maybe my neighbor is just trying to scare me."

"I'll talk to him this evening, after I follow you home." Caitlyn lifted Renegade's lead and started toward the office door.

Judge Hughes called out, "By the way, I should probably tell you that Una is moving in with me. She'll be living at my house starting tonight and moving the bulk of her things in this weekend."

"Judge…" Caitlyn turned to face him. "Are you sure now is a good time for that? You might be putting her in danger by adding her to your household."

"Nonsense." Hughes waved her away with his meaty hand. "You and Deputy Marshal Dillinger are already guarding my house. Now Una will be safe there, too."

"Do you have reason to believe she is in danger?" Caitlyn's nervous system went on alert, sending pinpricks to her scalp. "Have you had any more communications from whoever is threatening you?"

Judge Hughes shook his head and sat behind his desk. "No. Nothing like that. It's just the right time for us."

Caitlyn bit her lip, hard. It was unethical for the judge to move his court reporter into his house… wasn't it? Either way, what the judge did in his personal life wasn't Caitlyn's business. She wasn't the moral police. Her job was purely to protect him. That was it.

Una chose that moment to enter the judge's chambers. "Good morning." The smile she sent Caitlyn bordered on smug, and Caitlyn drew her brows together wondering what that was about. Renegade positioned himself in front of Caitlyn's feet, supremely sensitive to her reactions.

"Good morning, Ms. Murphy." Caitlyn murmured in response and tilted her head to the side. "Murphy. That's an Irish name, isn't it?" Una bobbed her head. "What kind of name is Una? I've never heard it before."

Una studied Caitlyn but didn't respond. The judge answered for her. "It's a native name. Crow, to be precise. Una's father was Irish, but her mother was full-blooded Crow. Isn't that right, sweetheart?" He reached for his girlfriend's hand and pulled her close for a quick kiss.

When the afternoon trial adjourned, Caitlyn waited for Judge Hughes to gather his things so she could escort him home. Una followed Hughes out to his car, dragging a roller-board suitcase in tow. Caitlyn pressed her lips together to keep from sharing her unwelcome opinion and opened her truck door for Renegade.

Sam was waiting for them in front of the judge's house, and he stepped out of his car when they arrived. His eyes darted to Una's suitcase and raised a sandy brow at Caitlyn. She shrugged with a smirk.

Sam rolled his eyes and jogged up the walk, beating the judge to his front door. "Let me go through your house before you enter, Your Honor."

"Get to it then. I don't want to stand out here forever."

Caitlyn raised her hand in farewell. "I'll see you in the morning, Sam," she called. "But I'm going to talk with the judge's neighbor before I call it a day." After nodding to the judge, she parked her truck across the street and hopped out. She and Renegade walked up the path to the house of the nosey neighbor and Caitlyn knocked.

The curtains at the window moved and seconds later the front door opened to the extent of a chain lock. A small man with glasses and thin brown hair peered through the crack. "Yes?"

Caitlyn introduced herself and held up her badge. "I'd like to ask you a few questions."

"What do you want?" The man asked without moving to open the door any farther.

"I noticed you watching the judge from your window the other morning and I wondered if you've seen anything unusual going on. Have you seen any strangers, or unfamiliar cars around?"

"I've seen you."

"Yes, I'm here to make sure the judge is safe."

The man's eyes shifted to look beyond Caitlyn. "What does that have to do with me?"

"I thought maybe you could help me by reporting anything unusual."

"Okay." The door edged closed.

Caitlyn stopped it with the toe of her boot and reached for her pocket. "Wait. Here is my card. Call me if you see anything, will you?" She slid her business card through the slit.

"Yeah, okay."

"Thank you," Caitlyn said to the now-closed door. *Strange guy. I wonder what he's afraid of—or what he's hiding.*

Caitlyn and Renegade drove to the hotel and within minutes, she was sitting on the bed enjoying an ice-cold malty brew. She checked her messages and texts. Her mother left one of each wanting to discuss wedding plans. She deleted them and chose to call Colt instead.

Colt's phone rang six times before it sent her to his voicemail. Sighing, Caitlyn clicked off without leaving a message. She moved to the table and opened her laptop. Renegade shifted so he could lie on top of her feet, and she searched through Judge Hughes's recent court cases. It was killing her not to have any idea who was terrorizing him.

Caitlyn wasn't convinced the person was actually trying to kill the man. Both incidents had been absolute failures if injury or death was the goal. If the restaurant shooter had wanted him dead, he would have taken a second shot. And the judge decided on the morning of the brakes incident to drive to West Yellowstone. If he'd have stayed in town, the severed brake lines wouldn't have caused more than a fender bender. *Is his enemy just hoping to intimidate him? If so, why?*

She scanned the court docket for the month before the judge received his first threatening letter. Nothing stood out, so she increased her search a month at a time. Her phone buzzed, and she answered. "Hey, Sam. What's up?"

"So… Una Murphy is moving in with the judge?"

"It appears that way. I tried to explain that now was not the best time, but Judge Hughes wouldn't listen to me."

"This guy is something else."

"No kidding." Caitlyn put Sam on speaker so she could continue scrolling down the court docket. "I'm looking through Hughes's recent court cases to see if anything stands out. We need to find out who's threatening him."

"That's not our job, Caitlyn. Let the FBI do that. We're just here for guard duty."

"They're taking too long. No one from the FBI has talked to me yet about the failed brakes."

"It's still their job. Not ours. I'm sure they've received all the reports from forensics."

Caitlyn grumbled, and Renegade got up and rested his chin on her leg. "Renegade agrees with me."

Sam laughed. "I'm sure he does. Still, don't kill yourself trying to investigate this thing on your time off. You should get some food and have a good night's rest."

Caitlyn swiped through to the end of the year's worth of cases but found nothing that stood out. "I suppose you're right. See you in the morning?"

"I'll be here."

After hanging up with Sam, she rifled through a stack of to-go menus and ordered a deep-dish pepperoni pizza for delivery. While she waited for her supper, Caitlyn slowly scrolled back up through the year's docket until she was staring at the past month's calendar. When she still found nothing suspicious, she opted to look one year farther back. Perhaps Hughes had made a judgment that angered someone *before* he became a federal judge.

The pizza arrived and Caitlyn changed into the flannel shorts and t-shirt she wore for sleeping. She pulled on a sweatshirt and settled in to read through hundreds more cases. An hour later, she still remained empty-handed, but couldn't shake the feeling that she was on the right track.

Caitlyn returned to the tab displaying the judge's current caseload. With blurry eyes, she stared at her computer screen. At the time the judge received his first threatening letter, he was presiding over a trial that involved the murder of a Native American high school student. The federal prosecutor had attempted to convict three teenage boys of an alleged hate crime. The prosecution contended their bullying had resulted in a fourth boy's murder. However, the case ended in a mistrial due to lack of solid evidence and a hung jury. Something about the case niggled at the edges of her mind.

Caitlyn mowed the rest of her way through the entire cheese-laden pie while she read the full transcript of the trial.

COLT TOSSED a couple of frozen burritos in his microwave and pressed the cook time. While he waited, he checked his phone. Two missed calls. One was from Caitlyn, but she hadn't left a message. The other was a voicemail from an unknown number, so he listened.

"Hi Colt. It's Allison. It's been so good to see you." He rolled his eyes and rubbed the back of his neck. "I—well… I'll be at the Tipsy Cow tonight, if you want to stop by. We could have a drink, play some pool… or… whatever. I'd love to see more of you—you know, maybe walk down memory lane. Besides, I have something I need to talk to you about. Okay, well, this is my phone number, so you don't have any excuse not to call me. I can't wait to hear from you."

Colt released a long sigh and stuffed his phone into his back pocket. The timer beeped and he burned his fingertips, yanking his scalding hot meal onto a plate and removing the plastic wrappers. After drowning the cardboard flavored burritos with salsa, he grabbed a beer and collapsed on his couch in front of the TV. Finding a baseball game, Colt settled back to scroll through his phone while he ate dinner. He checked his texts to see if Caitlyn left a message for him there, but the only text was from Principal Nestor with the time of their morning meeting. Tomorrow, they had an appointment with the kids who were caught with the *rockeT* and their parents.

Colt dialed Sheriff Munson. "Have those dirtbag rustlers given up any information about where they got their drugs from?"

"Not yet. They're not talking about anything."

"Well, keep me posted. I have a meeting tomorrow with the local high school principal and several boys on the baseball team who were caught with those same packets. I want to know where that meth is coming from."

"Let me know if you learn anything, too."

"Will do." Colt's phone beeped and he glanced at the screen. "I've got another call. I'll talk to you tomorrow." He clicked on the incoming call. "Sheriff Branson, here."

"Hi there, Sheriff." Allison's smooth voice flowed over the line. "I'm so glad I caught you."

17

Colt walked with Wes through the school building toward the administration office. He nodded to the secretary, and she led them down a short hallway.

"They're back here in the teacher's lounge. Mr. Nestor's office was too small to fit everyone." She tapped on the door before opening it wide. "Sir, the sheriff is here."

"Thank you," Colt said, before entering the room. A tray of donuts sat next to a coffee machine on the counter heating fresh smelling coffee. Three young men sat, each with their parents behind them, facing Principal Nestor. The administrator perched on the edge of a long table but stood when Colt and Wes came in. He introduced them to everyone.

Colt recognized most of the parents, but he addressed the boys. "Gentlemen, I know that your parents and teachers have all done their best to teach you how dangerous using drugs can be. But methamphetamine is deadly. It is highly addictive, and it destroys your body and mind from the inside out." He glowered down at them. "You are all athletes and I'm certain that isn't what you want for yourselves. Is it?"

The boys, each studying something—a shoelace, a tiny rip in a pair of jeans, fingernails—all shook their heads no. Colt noticed the shame permeating the faces of the parents but continued. "This is an extremely serious crime. If you were over eighteen, you'd all be headed to jail. As it is, you will be required to attend drug counseling, and if you are cooperative and help me find the person who is dealing the meth, I'll recommend that the judge assign you parole rather than send you to juvey. Are you willing to help yourselves?"

The teens side-eyed each other and fidgeted until Ben thrust his chin toward Zach. "Zach's the one who brought it to school. That's all I know."

Zach's mom gasped and covered her mouth with her hand, but his dad nudged the boy's shoulder. "Zachary?"

Two angry spots flared up on Zach's peach-fuzzed cheeks, but he remained silent.

"Zach," Lane, the third boy, implored. "You gotta tell them. Otherwise, we're all going down."

Zach sent Lane a fierce glare, but after a moment of consideration, he mumbled. "I got it from Pete."

Zach's dad gripped his son's arm and pulled him around until they faced each other. "Pete?" He stared hard into Zach's eyes. "As in your *cousin,* Pete? My brother's son?"

Zach stared at his hands in his lap, and the red spots

on his face deepened. He nodded. His dad turned away to face the wall for a few seconds before he swung around and stared at Colt. "I'll get you my brother's address. They live in Montana, on the Crow Reservation. His son has been in trouble for a long time. I had hoped it wouldn't bleed over into my family, but obviously, that was just wishful thinking."

"Thank you, sir. And Zach, I'm proud of you for telling us. It's not too late for you to clean up your act and recover from this mistake. You may even have saved your cousin's life. I suggest you take this opportunity seriously."

Zach kept his face down until his dad gripped his shoulder. "Yes, sir," the kid whispered.

COLT CALLED Sheriff Munson as he made his way north toward Montana. "Do you have any connections in the Crow PD?"

"I know a few guys. Why?"

"Apparently, the meth is coming from someone on the Reservation. I have the name and address of the boy who allegedly sold it to some kids at our high school, but I want to know where that kid got ahold of it in the first place."

"They won't appreciate us trying to investigate drugs on the Reservation, but I'll see what I can do. Why don't you swing by here and we can drive the rest of the way together? You never know, the Crow PD might be feeling friendly today."

"On my way."

Colt's radio crackled. Static laced the broken words. *Did I just hear something about an explosion in Mammoth?* The blood drained from Colt's head, and he shuddered with a sudden chill. He pressed Caitlyn's number, but his call was sent immediately to voicemail.

IN THE MORNING, Caitlyn waited for Judge Hughes and his girlfriend to arrive at the courthouse, but in their usual fashion when they arrived together, they zipped through the judge's private entrance, leaving Caitlyn and Renegade to walk around the building to the front door.

She greeted the CSO with a wave, and the guard smiled in return. Caitlyn commanded Renegade to search the first floor, since they were already there. She'd go up to the judge's chambers next and counsel him once again on waiting for her and Ren to clear his space before he went inside.

Renegade sniffed the perimeter of the entrance before they checked both restrooms and all the meeting rooms of the lower floor. They were taking their time on the main stairway when Caitlyn's phone rang.

"Deputy Marshal Reed. How can I help you?"

Judge Hughes's voice boomed through the receiver. "Marshal. I need you up here right away."

"I'm almost finished down here. I'll be up in a few minutes.

"No. I mean right now!"

Her body snapped with instant clarity and alarm. "Is everything okay?"

"No!" The judge clicked off. Caitlyn checked her phone to be sure she hadn't lost the connection. "Ren, *kemne*!" She dashed up the stairs with her faithful dog by her side. Rounding the ornate, hand-carved newel post on the second floor, she bolted down the tiled hallway toward the judge's chambers. She and Renegade raced as fast as they could, her dog's claws scraping and scratching across the high gloss floor.

The judge's door stood ajar, and Caitlyn slowed down. She unholstered her handgun and crept up to the opening, peering inside. In the middle of the room, sat Judge Hughes, tied to his chair, wearing only his underwear. His face was bathed in sweat and fear.

With a gurgled cry, he uttered, "Help me!"

Caitlyn took in the full scene. Judge Hughes trembled as he stared at a dark egg-shaped object clutched in his hands.

Her mind screamed, *grenade!* Adrenaline surged through her veins and her body prepared to bolt, but she forced herself to stand still and breathe. As calmly as she could, she asked, "What's going on, Judge?"

"It's Una! It's been Una all along." He shook his head and looked up at Caitlyn. Dismay filled his eyes.

"Okay," Caitlyn held her hands up as though to stop him or calm him down. "First, let's deal with the grenade in your hands." She curled her fingers into a fist and silently gestured for Renegade to sit. Opening her palm flat, she commanded him to stay. She wanted to run and take Renegade with her, but Caitlyn edged herself forward to get a better look at the explosive device clutched in the judge's fingers. "Where is the pin?"

"Una pulled it." Hughes stared at the corrugated bulb in his fist. "If I let go, we'll all blow to hell."

"Where is Una, now?" Caitlyn asked as she dialed 911 and briefly explained the situation to dispatch.

"I don't know. She pulled a gun on me and told me to take off my clothes." His eyes rolled up in his head. "I thought she was being funny. Playing—you know?"

"Then what happened?" Caitlyn kept the judge talking while she studied the grenade. If the judge released the pressure of his fingers, the small bomb would explode. His skin glistened with sweat, and his grip could slip at any moment.

"She told me to sit, then she tied me to the chair. I'm such an idiot. I still thought she was playing, so I went along. I told her the rope was too tight, and she laughed." A frightened sob escaped his throat. "She forced me to hold this." He raised his hand as far as the rope allowed. "Before I realized what it was, she pulled the pin."

"Did she say why she was doing this to you?" Caitlyn searched the top of the desk hoping to find the discarded pin. It was nowhere to be seen.

"She said it was revenge for Paytah."

"Paytah? That name sounds familiar… who is Paytah?"

Hughes broke down in tears. "A native kid murdered a while ago. There wasn't enough evidence to convict the boys who probably killed him, and we had to let them go."

"And she blames you?"

The judge nodded in rhythm with his sobs. "Paytah is her nephew. Her last name is Murphy, so I never made the connection. She was there in the courtroom when it all happened. I never suspected. This whole time I thought she wanted to be with me, but really, she just wanted to get close to me to… to kill me!"

Caitlyn opened the desk drawers, looking for something that might help the judge hold on to the grenade until help arrived. She had no idea how long it would take to get the bomb squad here, but the guys at the fire department would know what to do. "Where is she now? Do you know?"

"She grabbed her purse and ran. I don't know where she went."

The top drawer of the credenza was filled with office supplies, and Caitlyn rummaged through them. *Packing tape!* She snatched up the roll.

Sam ran through the door. "What's going on, Reed? I heard the emergency dispatch on my radio. When I got here, the CSO told me you received a call from the judge this morning and ran upstairs, and that he hadn't heard from you since. Is everything okay?"

"Things are definitely not okay." She stepped aside so he could see. "Judge Hughes has a live grenade in his fist, and the pin is missing. I'm going to wrap tape around his hand so he can relax his grip. Will you go down and point the firefighters up here?"

Sam rushed in and grabbed the roll of tape from Caitlyn. "I'll tape his hand. You and Renegade evacuate the rest of the building. Pull the fire alarm in the hallway. That will get people out of here the fastest."

Caitlyn glanced up at him, unwilling to leave Sam to deal with the grenade on his own. He pointed toward the door. "Go!" he ordered.

She swallowed. "Renegade, *kemne*." They bolted out the

office door and ran toward the stairway where Caitlyn pulled the red fire alarm lever. Bells screamed through the halls and faces peeked out of doorways. Caitlyn yelled, "This is not a drill. Everyone must leave the building. NOW!"

Caitlyn and Renegade ran through the offices and checked all the bathrooms on the upper floor to make certain no one was left behind. People scrambled down the stairs and out to the lawn. Together, she and her dog confirmed no one remained upstairs besides Sam and the judge. They sailed down the marble flight and searched through the lower-level offices, conference rooms, and restrooms. When she was certain no one else remained inside, she found the sheriff and told him all she knew about the situation.

Emergency vehicles skidded to a stop at the front of the building. Caitlyn ran toward them to apprise them of the grenade, when a flaming blast of heat hit her from behind. She flew off her feet as a deafening *BOOM!* rattled the sky. Renegade's body slammed into hers midair, and they fell together onto the pavement. Caitlyn rolled sideways to cover Renegade with her body, sheltering him from a shower of bricks, cement chunks, broken glass, and other debris. She whipped her head around to see what had happened and her vision swam at the sight of the missing upstairs corner of the courthouse.

Jagged bricks, like broken teeth, framed what used to be Judge Hughes's office. Black smoke billowed from the hole, and papers floated with it in the air. Caitlyn blinked, and terror clogged her throat. "No!" she screamed. She spared half a second to check on Renegade and then, together, they sprinted toward the building. "Sam!"

The arm of a burly fireman caught her around her waist. The giant man swung her off her feet and held her firmly as she kicked and clawed at him. "You can't go in there, ma'am. You must stand back while we do our jobs."

Caitlyn pushed away from him. "I'm a federal marshal. My partner is in there! Inside, with Judge Hughes." Her voice teetered on hysterical. "I have to find him!"

"Stand down, Deputy Marshal. You won't be any help if you get yourself killed. We'll find them." The fireman nodded to someone inside the red truck.

A younger man leapt down from the rig and, brooking no objection, escorted Caitlyn back to a safe distance. Standing with his hand on her shoulder, he said, "It would be best if you stay here until the paramedics arrive." A siren wailed in the morning air. "The ambulance is on its way."

Caitlyn gave herself a hard mental shake. She couldn't afford to lose control out of fear for what might have happened to Sam. That would have to wait. For now, she had a job to do. When the dust settled, she'd find Sam and then together they could hunt down Una Murphy. She shoved away all foreboding that insisted Sam wouldn't be joining her. Ever again.

Images of Sam's beautiful wife and son stormed into to her thoughts, but she ignored them, stuffing them into a locked compartment in her mind. Caitlyn held her hands up and yelled, "Everyone, please remain behind the emergency vehicles. We must stay out of their way. Is anyone hurt?"

A handful of people raised their hands or pointed. A man with a scraped and bleeding face stumbled from the crowd. "Over here!" He pointed to the ground where a co-worker lay on the grass holding her bloody arm.

Caitlyn gathered the people who were wounded from the fall out together in a spot several feet from the larger crowd and ran to flag down the paramedics. A man in his early twenties jumped from the back of the ambulance and ran toward her. "Easy, ma'am. I've got you. Slowly lower yourself to the ground."

"I'm not waving at you for myself. The injured people are this way." Caitlyn turned to lead the way, but the paramedic gripped her wrist. Barking, Renegade maneuvered in front of her, blocking her path. Caitlyn narrowed her eyes at him. *What is wrong with you, Ren?* "Renegade, *knoze*. Get out of the way!" Something flew into her eye, and she wiped her face to clear her view. Dizziness washed over her, and the paramedic's grip tightened on her waist.

"Ma'am, we'll get to everyone, but it looks like you need the most help right now. I need you to sit down so I can take a look at your head wound."

"My head wound?" Caitlyn fell to her knees, and the man eased her the rest of the way down. Renegade whined and bumped his cold nose against her chin.

The first responder yelled, "Someone get this dog out of here!"

"No!" Caitlyn shoved the man's hands away. "He stays. He's a federal K9—my partner."

Renegade sat next to Caitlyn but instinctively gave the paramedic room to work. "Okay, you're bleeding a lot, but that's normal with head wounds. It appears that you may have been hit with flying debris." He pressed something on her wound at the back of her head that felt like liquid habanero fire. Caitlyn yelped. She gritted her teeth and squinched her eyes shut. "You'll need a couple of stitches."

"Can you do that now?"

"I'd rather take you to the clinic where we can sterilize the wound and give you an anti-biotic."

"I'll do that later. Stitch me up now. I have to help."

The paramedic hesitated. "I really think—"

She grabbed a handful of his shirt. "On a regular day, I'd agree with you. But there is nothing regular about today. Stitch it up now, or I'll go without. Either way, there are still two missing people I need to help find."

He sighed and helped her back to her feet. "Come to the ambulance." She sat on the edge of the back entrance while he clipped her hair to the side and cleaned her scalp. He shaved an inch wide patch around the wound, and saturated the cut with antiseptic, before opening a field suture kit and going to work. "When this is all over with, you need to go to the hospital and have this checked out. Do you understand?"

"Yeah, got it."

He held up a syringe and tapped it. "This is an antibiotic. Hopefully, it will keep your laceration from becoming infected." The paramedic pressed the injection site with a cotton ball and stuck it to her arm with band-aid. "There you go."

Caitlyn bobbed her head and winced at the pounding in her brain. "Ren, *knoze*!" Ignoring the throbbing pain,

Caitlyn sprinted with Renegade by her side to her truck to get Renegade's protective boots. Then they ran back to the crumbled building.

18

McKenzie arrived at the Reed Ranch early, excited to check on the litter of Rottweiler puppies. She parked by the backyard gate. Dylan was in the yard, sitting by the whelping box.

"Good morning!" she called out as she climbed out of her car.

Dylan grinned at her. "Morning. These little guys are starving." The puppies squealed for their mother, who was taking a much deserved, momentary break.

Lariat lay next to Dylan, wagging his tail. When the puppies squirmed over each other, Lariat barked and jumped to his feet. He pawed one of the pups.

"Dylan! Get Larry out of there." McKenzie rushed through the gate, and Dylan gave her a patronizing smirk. "I'm not kidding. The puppies are too small to be introduced to other dogs."

"He's not going to hurt them." Dylan stroked Lariat's back.

Holding the gate open, McKenzie called, "Larry,

come." The dog looked at Dylan, but when his owner didn't object, Larry trotted toward her. She led him through the gate and closed him out of the yard. "Good boy."

"I think you're overreacting. Besides, you don't want Larry to feel jealous of the new puppies."

Ember climbed back into the box with her babies and laid down. McKenzie and Dylan helped the pups to latch on for their next meal. "You're right about not wanting Larry to feel resentful, but it's still too early to introduce him to the puppies. He could carry germs they can't handle yet. Besides, the best way to assure he feels secure is for you to spend more time with him than you do ogling these cuties."

"How long before their eyes open?"

"Ten to fourteen days."

Dylan ran his fingers over the little bodies. "I think they've already grown."

"They have. They'll double in weight during this first week."

"Wow. When do you start supplementing their mama's milk?"

"Not for three or four weeks. Probably three with these hungry pumpkins." McKenzie stood and stared down at the darling litter. The impact of what these puppies meant to her dreams and goals filled her with hope and pride. "Let's let them be for a little while. They'll nap as soon as they're full." She reached out her hand to help Dylan up. "How's Athena doing?"

Dylan swung his gaze to the Belgian napping in the shade. "She seems fine to me. Getting her sleep in now."

McKenzie knelt in the grass next to the pregnant dog and ran her hand over the dog's silky coat. She smiled up at Dylan. "She's so beautiful, isn't she? Ren is going to fall head over heels for her."

"Can you spell personification?" Dylan teased. "Come on, want a cup of coffee?

"Please." She followed him into the house. "I don't care what you say. I know Renegade will adore her."

"What did Caitlyn say about breeding them?"

McKenzie pulled the kitchen door closed behind her. "I haven't had a chance to talk with her about it yet."

Stella pulled a tray of fresh-baked blueberry muffins from the oven as they came through the door, and McKenzie breathed in the scent of the sweet, warm bread. "Am I in heaven?"

"Good morning, dear." Stella smiled with pleasure. "Perfect timing. The bacon is done. Now all I have to do is scramble up some eggs."

McKenzie nudged Dylan with her elbow. "You are so spoiled."

"Don't I know it." He planted a kiss on the top of his mother's head. "Need any help?"

"I've set the table, but you can pour the juice." Stella cracked farm-fresh eggs into a bowl.

John wandered into the kitchen, kissed Stella's cheek, and poured himself a mug of coffee. He held the pot up and raised his brows at Dylan and McKenzie.

"Yes, please." McKenzie pulled two more mugs from the cupboard. Sipping her coffee, she looked on as the Reed family went through their morning routine. Within minutes, Stella was serving the eggs and bacon. McKenzie carried the basket filled with warm muffins. She took her place at the table with Dylan's family, feeling a deep sense of belonging. *This really is heaven.*

They lingered longer than usual until Dylan groaned. "Okay, I've got to get going. I've already missed one full day this week and lounging around over breakfast isn't getting my chores done."

John stood with him, and they gathered their dishes. McKenzie motioned for Stella to remain seated. "I'll help with the rest of the dishes. You enjoy your coffee." She took the remaining plates into the kitchen but dropped one when Dylan yelled for her from the backyard. Her nerves cut across her like the shards of glass on the floor. She set the remaining plates on the counter and ran outside.

"One of the puppies is gone!" Worry framed Dylan's dark eyes.

McKenzie counted the puppies sleeping together in their cozy pile. Only four of the five were there, so she knelt and lifted the puppies off each other to be sure they hadn't miscounted. But still, there were only four. Ember slept in the corner of the box, unaware that she'd lost a pup.

McKenzie glanced frantically around the backyard. Athena was now sleeping peacefully inside her kennel. "Where's Larry?"

"You closed him out of the yard. He's probably down at the barn." Dylan jogged toward the gate. Placing one hand on the rail, he swung his legs over the fence. "I'll find him."

McKenzie's belly tightened at the thought of Lariat sneaking off with one of the puppies. *Surely not.*

John and Stella came outside and helped her look around the large backyard. Stella asked, "How could the puppy get out of the box? They're not big enough to climb over."

"Ember could have moved him, or," McKenzie swallowed hard, "Larry..."

Dylan ran up from the barn toward them. "I found Larry. He was harassing the chickens, but I found no sign of the puppy."

A sick sense pressed down on McKenzie's chest, and she hurried back to the whelping box. "Ember!" she called. "Ember, get up!"

The Rottweiler lifted her head and regarded McKenzie with sleep-glazed eyes. McKenzie slid her fingers under the mother dog's shoulder and shoved her up. Her fear was realized. Ember had fallen asleep on top of the puppy. McKenzie lifted the limp body and tears sprang to her eyes, blurring her vision. She dropped to her knees and, holding the small mite in one hand, she rubbed his little form firmly with the other.

"Come on. Come on, little one. Breathe!" she cried.

Dylan skidded to his knees by her side, and John and Stella hovered over them. McKenzie ran her thumb across the tiny nose and mouth, then she felt the little chest for a heartbeat. There was no pulse. A sob rose in her throat, but taking a firm mental grip on herself, she forced herself to remain calm. McKenzie slid her thumb and forefinger behind the puppy's front legs and pressed rapidly against his chest. Every five seconds, she cupped her hand into a cone over his mouth and puffed air into his mouth.

She shouted for Stella to bring her a towel, and Dylan's mother dashed inside. McKenzie continued the puppy CPR until she felt the little heartbeat stutter and then pulse under her fingertips. She went on helping him breathe until he managed on his own, and she wrapped him in the warm towel.

"You did it, Kenze!" Dylan gripped her shoulders. She glanced at him, and her heart melted at the tears brimming in his eyes. Times like these moved her beyond words. This rough and tough man she'd fallen in love with was all soft and gooey under the surface. He hid his tender heart from the world, and in that moment, she was honored he'd shared his true self with her.

"I think he'll be okay. I'm going to sit out here with him for the rest of the morning to keep an eye on him. Sometimes mamas are so tired, they don't realize they are on top of a baby. I can't believe I didn't think to look there, first." McKenzie let her own tears flow as she held the puppy up to Ember's nose. The dog covered her puppy's head with one long lick, and the little guy whined for a teat. Laughter bubbled up inside McKenzie, and she laid the puppy at his mama's belly. "That was a close call."

Dylan put his arm around her shoulders as they watched the puppy suckle. "He's the one we're keeping, right?"

McKenzie looked up at him and grinned, loving the boy inside the man he let her see.

19

"Damn it!" Colt waited to leave a message on Caitlyn's phone. "Catie, I just heard something about an explosion up near you. Just checking to be sure you're alright. Call me." He pressed the button on his steering wheel to hang up, and then he called Wes. "I'm about halfway up to Moorhead. I need you to look into an incident I heard about on the radio. See if you can find anything about an explosion over in Mammoth."

"Hold on." Wes clicked on some keys before answering. "No news reports so far. Maybe Munson will know something when you get there."

"Maybe." Colt ended the call, gripped the steering wheel with force, and pressed harder on the gas. He knew Caitlyn would be busy with whatever happened in Mammoth, but whether it was reasonable or not, he wished she'd at least text him to let him know she was safe. *God, please let her be safe.* His radio must have intercepted a small part of one of the emergency calls, but Colt wished it hadn't because now he'd worry until he heard Caitlyn's voice. She had to know he'd hear about the incident and fear for her. Though, to be fair, it sounded like it had just happened. He tried to push his anxious thoughts aside, but it was impossible.

Wes rang back ten minutes later. "I found something. This report says there was an explosion at the courthouse and that people are being treated for minor injuries." Wes paused his scroll. "It says two men are still unaccounted for."

"Does that mean everyone else is safe?" Colt coughed at the sound of desperation in his voice.

Wes silently read the information. "That's what it looks like to me."

Colt eased his grip on the steering wheel, though the tension in his neck and shoulders continued to tighten like a vise. "Thank, God. Call me if you hear anything else." He tried Caitlyn's phone again, gritting his teeth when her recorded voice brightly asked him to leave a message.

Sheriff Munson was waiting for him in his squad car when Colt pulled into the Moorhead Sheriff's Department parking lot. Munson waved and called out the window, "Follow me."

Colt fell in behind the Moorhead Sheriff and they drove the long distance to Crow Agency, hoping to find the local meth dealer. When they finally arrived, their first stop was the Tribal Police Department. Munson entered the parking lot, but Colt was forced to wait for a blue Civic speeding by before he could turn. *Ballsy to drive that fast in front of the police department.* He considered chasing the car but ticketing a speeding driver was low on his list of priorities right now. Not to mention, he had no authority up there.

Four black-and-white Chargers painted with "Crow Nation Police" and two Chevy Tahoes with "Apsáalooke Police" blazoned across their doors sat side by side in front of the building. Munson drove past them to the far side of the lot, but Colt parked in the visitor's parking. He waited for Munson, and together they went inside. Sheriff Munson asked to speak to his friend in the department, Officer Squallie. The receptionist smiled politely, and though she continued to click away on her keyboard, said, "Albert Squallie isn't in today. I'll tell Sergeant Long Feather that you're here, though. He'll be right out."

The two sheriffs waited in the lobby for half an hour before the sergeant sauntered out from his back office. "Sheriff Munson, how can I help you today?" Long Feather's eyes held no warmth.

"We're up here hoping to find a kid who's been dealing meth." He nodded at Colt. "This is Sheriff Branson from Moose Creek, Wyoming. He caught some kids at the local high school down there with meth and one of them said he got it from someone who lives up here. It's being distributed in plastic packets with the word *rockeT* printed on it. Have you seen anything like that anywhere on the rez?"

"You find drugs in Wyoming and decide it must be a Crow kid's fault? Typical." A sneer joined the sergeant's unfriendly gaze.

Colt stepped forward. "That's not it, Sergeant. One of the kids confessed he got it from his cousin who lives on the Reservation." He pulled out a notepad from his front shirt pocket and flipped up the cover. "A boy named Peter Hawk." He looked the sergeant in the eye. "Have you heard of him?"

"It's a big Reservation, Sheriff." Long Feather answered. "I don't know everyone who lives here."

Colt flexed his jaw. "Mind if we look around? Try to find him?"

"Damn straight, I mind. You don't have any business up here." The sergeant crossed his arms over his broad chest. The man was not as tall as Colt, but he was built like a tank. Clearly not a guy to mess with. "You're not even from Montana. Let alone the rez."

Munson mirrored the sergeant's stance. "Sheriff Branson is with me. I'm good friends with one of your fellow officers, Al Squallie, and we hoped your department might help us out. No one wants kids doing meth—here or down in Wyoming."

"So, you two think you can come in here and point the finger at a native kid? How do you know it isn't white kids dealing meth up here?"

This was going nowhere fast. Colt perched his hands on top of his utility belt. "We don't. You could be right, Sergeant. The drugs could be coming up here from the kids in Wyoming. I don't know, but I want to find out. I'd like to put a stop to the stream of drugs wherever they're coming from. We need to do what we can to protect all our kids. Regardless of where they live. Don't you agree?"

Sergeant Long Feather studied Colt for a time, and gradually he nodded his head. "Yes, I agree. But I'm still not going to allow you to chase down any Crow kids on the rez. Give me the name and description of the boy you're looking for, and I'll take it from there."

Colt's muscles bunched. It was difficult to believe, and even harder to swallow, that this police officer refused to let them apprehend a drug pusher. Didn't he realize that if the drugs were coming from somewhere on the Reservation that all the Crow kids were in danger? Families were destroyed by addiction to this drug. It ate away at a user's body from the inside out. Where was this man's sense of compassion—of wrong and right?

Sheriff Munson shook his head. "Okay. But we're not leaving. We'll wait here for Albert, then we can see what he has to say about it."

"Be my guest." Long Feather swept his hand toward the double glass doors. "No doubt you'll be most comfortable waiting in your car."

20

Keeping Renegade on his shortest leash, Caitlyn commanded, "Find 'em, Ren." He dropped his nose to the ground and sniffed. She knew instantly when he caught a scent because he yanked her hard. "Good boy." Caitlyn watched his body language carefully as he pulled her forward into the midst of the rubble. Crumbled concrete and broken brick lay strewn over the lawn. Pieces of computers, furniture, and personal items compiled the rugged terrain, and papers fluttered in the slight breeze. Caitlyn's heart throbbed, causing a dull, heavy ache to lodge in her throat, and she coughed at the dust suspended in the air. With each step she prayed she'd look up and see Sam grinning at her from the crowd or, at worst, pushing himself up from the dirt and making some wisecrack about how hard his job was.

The grenade blew the judge's chambers clear out of the building. The bottom floor remained mostly intact, if you didn't count the snapped wires and broken glass, as did the walls of the second floor, minus the blasted corner. Renegade pulled harder and Caitlyn kept her eyes on the debris littering the ground, maneuvering around the crumbled concrete so she wouldn't trip. Her dog stopped and barked earnestly. On the ground before him was a torn and bloody section of human forearm.

A cry broke free from Caitlyn's throat, and she covered her mouth with her hand. "Oh, God." Nausea roiled in her belly, threatening to erupt any second. *Where is the rest of the body? Please, please, don't let it be Sam.*

Caitlyn whistled to a deputy sheriff working to keep the crowd behind the yellow crime tape he'd strung. "Deputy! Get a crime scene investigator over here. Now!" The young man gave her a thumbs up and ran to do what she'd ordered.

Trying to keep her gaze away from the partial limb, Caitlyn knelt next to Renegade. "Good boy." She buried her face in his fur for a quick second of reprieve before she stood and commanded him to search again. He took off at her command and sniffed through more of the fall-out. He paused, sniffed, and bolted forward, straining Caitlyn's shoulder. Bounding over a large boulder-sized chunk of concrete, he sat and barked, staring at his new find.

When Caitlyn caught up, she released a groan of agony. "No! No! Sam! No!" She fell to her knees before the broken and bloodied body of her partner and friend. The explosion had shredded his midsection. Gore and blood matted his button-down shirt. Strangely, his face, though smudged with soot, captured an expression of peace. Tears blurred Caitlyn's vision as she stroked his cheek and felt his neck for a sign of life she knew was long gone. "Oh, Sam," she cried. Renegade nuzzled her with his cold nose and licked her face. Caitlyn remained kneeling by Sam's body until she heard a fireman yell that he'd found Judge Hughes's body under a splintered desk and chair.

Paramedics approached and gently helped Caitlyn to her feet. They walked with her and Renegade back to the ambulance, where she'd received her stitches. Her ears rang, and she gagged on the thickening lump in her throat. "I've got to call—"

"Right now, you need to sit down." One of the paramedics steadied her as she lowered herself to the step at the back of the ambulance. "I'm going to get you a blanket, okay?"

Caitlyn stared at him. He spoke, and she heard the words, but she couldn't make sense out of them. "I have to call Dirk. And Laurie—oh God. Poor Laurie! And what about Caleb? How will I ever tell them?"

"Deputy Marshal, you're in shock. I want you to lie down." He waved at his partner and together they set up a gurney and eased her on to it.

"Can you lower this thing so I can see my dog?"

They did as she asked and then propped her feet up on a pillow. "Here's a blanket. Rest here for a few minutes. I'm going to put you on oxygen to help you feel better."

Caitlyn shoved the blanket away. "I'm fine. *I* wasn't the one who stayed inside and got blown up!" Her voice bounced with hysteria. "I have to call Deputy Marshal Sterling!"

"I've got this." A low growling voice sounded from beyond Caitlyn's immediate view, and the paramedic stood and moved aside. "This man is just trying to do his job, Reed." Quick-silver eyes glinted at her from a face chiseled in stone.

"Dirk! Sam—Sam is..."

"I know." He pressed her down onto the gurney with a firm hand.

"It should have been me. I should have made him leave the building. It was my shift! The judge was my responsibility!" Her stomach rebelled, and she leaned over the far side of the cot to vomit. Bile singed the back of her throat. Her head swam and her nose and eyes ran. The paramedic was quick to wipe her face with a cool cloth.

Dirk knelt next to Caitlyn and held her hand. "Look at me, Caitlyn. Dillinger was your superior, and I know he ordered you to leave the courthouse. You followed his orders, and by doing so, saved all the other people in the building. You cannot blame yourself for this. What happened is horrible. It truly is. But it is not your fault."

Droplets trembled at the edges of Caitlyn's eyes. She blinked and she bit down on her lip, wanting to be strong. She shook her head and the rogue tears escaped, washing over her burning cheeks. "He has a little boy, Dirk."

He patted her shoulder. "I know. The chief dispatched a bereavement team to talk to Laurie. They'll take good care of her... and Caleb."

"I should be there." She searched his eyes for the blame she deserved.

Dirk shook his head. "No. The best thing for us to do, as soon as you catch your breath, is find the son of a bitch who did this."

A sharp stabbing pain pierced Caitlyn's heart. "I know

who did it, and we have to catch her!" She tore the oxygen mask from her face, and gripping Dirk's arm for leverage, she sat up.

"Easy does it. Sit for a minute so you don't pass out when you stand." He adjusted her blanket by wrapping it around her shoulders. Renegade sat at her feet, looking up at her with soulful eyes, and whined.

"I'm okay, boy." She stroked her dog's head, then shifted her gaze to Dirk. "I know who killed the judge… and Sam." Caitlyn's chest constricted as she rehashed the events of the day, most importantly what Judge Hughes told her about Una when he called Caitlyn to his office.

"So, this Una Murphy wanted to kill the judge to avenge her nephew?"

"Yes. That's what Judge Hughes told me Una said to him before she left him holding the grenade. The boy's murder case ended in a mistrial, and she blamed him. She believed it was his fault that the boys who beat her brother's son to death were let go. This was her way of getting justice for her nephew. Una started up a relationship with the judge so she could get close enough to him to kill him."

"When did you figure this out?"

"Not until the judge told me this morning. She had me fooled, too." Her stomach clenched, threatening to heave again. *How could I have been so naïve? If I would have realized it was Una sooner, Sam would still be alive.* "Evidence pointed to one of the judge's ex-wives as the culprit. But now I see that was Una's plan all along. She's the one who suggested the ex-wives to me. How could I be so stupid, Dirk?"

"First of all, it wasn't your job to investigate where the threat originated from. You and Sam were here purely to guard the judge."

"Fine job I did of that."

"Reed. Stop blaming yourself. If this happened to anyone else, you would see clearly that there was nothing they could have done. Sam was your superior, and he ordered you to leave the building. That's all there is to it." Dirk stood and held out his hand to Caitlyn.

She rubbed her nose on her sleeve and nodded. She hauled herself to her feet. "Ren, *kemne.*"

Dirk dug around in his bag. He pulled out a grape Gatorade and handed it to her. "We'll never know exactly what happened in the judge's office, but by the look of things—with the judge's arm blown off and all—it's likely he was still holding the grenade when it exploded. I think Sam knew it was going to blow and tried to cover the blast with his body. It was an incredibly brave act." His eyes moistened, and he hid them behind mirrored sunglasses. "Now, let's go find this Una Murphy and get our friend the justice he deserves."

21

Colt didn't know for sure, but he figured that the place the cattle rustler claimed he got his *rockeT* from was the casino on this Reservation. It was certainly the closest casino to where the cattle thieves were holing up when they found them. So, instead of sitting around waiting all day for Munson's friend, he decided to check it out.

"Hey, Munson. I'm going to see if I can stir up some information about whoever sold the meth to the rustlers up at the casino. Call me if your friend shows up."

The older sheriff's mouth slid into a lopsided grin. "You won't get very far asking questions if you go in there dressed in your uniform."

Colt glanced down at his shirt and badge. "I suppose you're right. I think I've got another shirt in my Jeep." He rummaged through his car for something else to wear, but all he found was a jeans jacket. So, Colt pulled off his khaki work shirt and wearing only a white undershirt, he slid the jacket on over it. "This ought to do."

Munson nodded. "I'll be here."

Colt waved and drove north toward the local gambling establishment. The one-story, wood-sided building located at the edge of a neighborhood didn't look like any casino he'd ever seen. The structure could have passed as a community lodge or a church. There were no flashing lights on the outside of the red- trimmed building that called customers in to try their luck. The only lights were on a pizza delivery marquee.

In the middle of the afternoon, the lot was mostly full. Colt drove past the parked cars looking for anyone loitering, but no one was outside. He edged his Jeep into a makeshift spot at the end of a row and went inside. For a casino, the interior was dingy, though bulbs strobed from slot machines. Dimly lit signs pointed to the roulette and craps tables brightened the place a little.

Colt hoped his change of clothes would help him blend in, but he was wrong. At this time of day, he was the only white guy in the place. To cover, he acted like he'd been there before. He walked across the blue and red floral carpet to the Blackjack table and sat down next to two other players. He nodded to the dealer and set down a twenty-dollar bill.

She took his money and gave him four chips in return. "Good luck."

Colt picked up three chips, leaving one in place for his bet. He waited for the woman to deal the cards. He held a jack of diamonds and a six of clubs. The dealer had a two of hearts showing, so when it was his turn, he motioned for another card and turned up a three of diamonds. Next, she pulled an ace of spades. In the end, his nineteen lost to her twenty-one, and she took his chip. He tossed another down.

Colt won the next two hands, and on the fourth, he ventured his question. "Know where a guy can score some ice?"

Not meeting his eye, the dealer shook her head and shuffled the card deck. One of the other players picked up his chips and thanked the dealer and moved on to play roulette.

As the next hand was dealt, the man beside him leaned a little closer. "You look like a cop."

Cold fingers of apprehension trailed down Colt's spine as he tipped up the corner of his cards. But he gave the man half a grin. "Maybe I am when I'm on the clock. But right now, I'm just a guy looking for a tweak."

The other player studied him for a minute before turning back to the card game. Colt lost again, and the man set his cards face down on the felt. "Follow me." When the guy stood, he was an easy six-foot-four and looked like he'd won a bar fight or two in his time.

Glad for the pistol resting under his arm in its shoulder holster, Colt rolled off the chair, tipped the dealer a chip, and followed the man. The situation didn't feel right. Too bad he hadn't asked Munson to come with him. He trailed the big man to the back of the building and down a dark hallway where his guide rapped on a flimsy hollow door before opening it. Colt peered over the man's shoulder into a brightly lit room. As they entered, a man in a shiny gray suit left through a door that led to the parking lot. Colt didn't see his face, but when he looked out the window, he noticed the man driving away in a dark blue Lincoln Sport. Something about the man's gait and the type of car triggered a memory. The last time he'd seen a car like that was when Tito Garza drove his Lincoln to Moose Creek, the day he came to identify his wife's body. Colt had suspected him of murdering his wife, but it ended up that the murder was a form of punishment from the crime family Garza was connected to in New York. The man who left could be Tito Garza. He lived on an estate somewhere outside of Billings. *If that was him, what was he doing in the casino office?*

Three other men occupied the office besides the blackjack player who led him there. A well-dressed, middle-aged man with a long nose and neatly trimmed black hair sat behind the desk. The guy in a leather jacket, hovering in the back corner, was obviously a bodyguard. Colt presumed the skinny, pock-marked man standing before the desk was a pusher. Maybe even the one he was looking for.

His fellow card player tapped him on his elbow. "Raise your hands. I need to pat you down."

Shit—there goes my gun. "I'm armed. Left side," Colt confessed, hoping the admission would keep the goon from checking for his secondary weapon. Fear flooded his mind, but adrenaline fueled his courage. He drew in a deep breath.

The bodyguard moved out of the corner and pulled a pistol from his back holster. He pointed it at Colt while the man patting him down took Colt's Glock.

The boss leaned back in his chair, narrowing his dark eyes. With one hand, he smoothed the side of his slick hair. "I have to ask myself why a cop would come into my casino looking for illegal drugs." He spread his hands wide and smirked. "We have nothing like that here. This is a decent, family game-center."

Colt shrugged and settled into his role. "That's not what I heard, man. But even if it's true, I still need to score." He scratched his arm for effect.

The guard who took Colt's gun shoved it into the waistband of his jeans. "But you're a cop. You even admitted it."

Colt darted his eyes around the room in what he hoped was a sketchy fashion and dragged his fingernails over his cheek. "That's true, but I was undercover for a couple of years and picked up a... a taste for a little gunk now and then." He made a squirming movement. "No big deal if you don't have it. I'll just be on my way."

"I don't think so." The man at the desk chuckled. "It wouldn't be very hospitable of me to let you leave without what you deserve. Sit down."

Colt shifted his weight back and forth to stay loose, his muscles tensing in preparation for what he knew was coming. "I'm good."

The dark-haired man nodded, and the guy who took Colt's weapon rushed him, drawing his fist back at the same time. Colt blocked the powerful blow aimed at his face with his forearm and pushed the guy backward. The fighter temporarily lost his balance, but quickly sprang at Colt again, and clutching his jaw in an iron grip. He cocked his fist again, this time landing the punch across Colt's face. Colt's nerves erupted as their electrical impulses lit up and his eyes and nose watered, blurring his vision. The abundance of adrenaline surging through his blood stream kept him from feeling the pain right away—but experience told him that wouldn't last. Colt chopped his arm away and twisted it backwards, raising the limb with both hands and pressuring his elbow to bend the wrong way, forcing the man to drop to his knees. Colt pressed his hand against the back of the man's head and held him down.

"Let him go." The second bodyguard aimed his handgun at Colt. Colt yanked his captive up, holding him as a shield. The guard fired anyway. He hit the man in Colt's grasp. His heavy body went limp, and he fell. Colt shoved his bulk toward the gunman. Bracing against the man's weight with both hands, the guard exposed his throat. Colt was quick to jab his knuckles square into the man's windpipe. Both guards fell to the ground and Colt scrambled to retrieve his Glock.

The tweaker skittered away from the action like a cockroach. He disappeared through the exit. The boss zipped around the desk and jumped onto Colt's back. He slung his arm around Colt's throat. Colt rammed his head back into the man's face. A loud crack told Colt he'd smashed the guy's nose, which forced the man to release his grip. Colt spun, trapping the bleeding man's neck in a chokehold. He jammed his pistol under the man's jaw as his guard untangled himself from his dying partner and climbed to his feet.

"Hands up!" Colt shouted. "Do it now!"

The boss bobbled his head, and the bodyguard raised his hands above his head. With the muzzle of his Glock pressed into the boss's flesh, Colt reached for his phone and thumbed 911. He was going to have hell to pay for the way this whole thing fell out.

22

After the ordeal with the puppy, it was long past time for Dylan to get to work. McKenzie slipped her arm through Dylan's as she walked with him down to the barn. When he shoved open the big wooden doors, she breathed in the mingled scent of hay and leather. "What's on the ranch agenda today?"

"It's time to wean the calves. Dad and I will spend the rest of the day separating them." He opened Sampson's stall and slid a halter over the large horse's head. "Be fore-warned, we're in for a couple of weeks of listening to the calves bawling for their mothers."

"That's so sad." McKenzie sat on a bale of hay that poked her legs even through her jeans and watched Dylan groom and tack Sampson, preparing him for the workday. "Why can't you leave them together?"

"We need to breed the cows again for next year, and the calves are old enough now to graze and drink water on their own. They don't need their mother's milk anymore." Dylan swung his saddle onto Sampson's back and tightened the cinch. "If we let them, those calves would nurse forever. It's time to put the bulls in with the herd to breed and it helps when the calves are away from the cows. We don't want the mamas trying to grow new calves while nursing their older ones at the same time. That would be hard on the cows and besides, we want all their energy going toward next year's stock."

"That makes sense, but don't you feel bad for the babies when you separate them?"

Dylan grinned. "Maybe for about an hour. Then the bawling gets old. You'll see." He held Sampson's bridle up and waited for him to accept the bit before sliding the headstall over his ears and buckling the leather straps. Guiding Sampson by his reins, Dylan reached for McKenzie's hand and pulled her to her feet. They walked together up the drive.

McKenzie leaned against Dylan's arm. "I'm going to stop in and see Dr. Moore today. I want to talk to him about the puppy we almost lost this morning and see if he thinks I need to do anything else for the little guy. I also need to make an appointment for the puppies to get a checkup. Do you want me to pick anything up for you while I'm in town?"

"Well, since you're offering, if you want to take my truck, you could swing by the feed store and pick up my standing grain order. All you have to do is back up to the loading dock and Jim will load it up for you."

"Jim?"

"The owner of the feed store."

"Okay, sure. I'll also see if your mom needs anything from the store before I head in.

Dylan tilted her chin up and kissed her. "Will you be here for dinner?"

McKenzie leaned into him. "Is that an invitation?"

"I thought you had a standing invitation." He winked and kissed her again.

Warmth flowed through her veins as she reached her arms around Dylan's neck. "Well then, yes. I'll be here. See you tonight."

BUMPING along in Dylan's Ford dually long bed, McKenzie drove into Moose Creek on her errands. She hadn't considered the challenge of maneuvering the gargantuan truck inside the feed store's parking lot or backing it up without smashing into other vehicles. The two men waiting for her on the loading dock laughed at her behind their hands as she performed an awkward five-point turn.

With heated cheeks, McKenzie hopped down from the cab. "Hey, no laughing, guys." She jogged up the steps to join them. "I've never had to back that thing up before. I'm just learning."

"You'll get the hang of it." Jim shook her hand when she introduced herself and told them why she was there.

The two men loaded the bed of the truck with twenty bags of grain. McKenzie signed for them and waved as she drove away, thankful she only had to pull forward from there.

Her visit with the vet was quick. Doctor Moore assured her she had done all the right things with the puppy and told her all she had to do now was keep a close eye on him. The doctor jotted down the name of the food he recommended for the puppies, and McKenzie scheduled an appointment for the litter to come in for a checkup.

Next on the list was the mercantile where she beelined for the pet section. They had a big selection of puppy collars, and she picked a different color for each puppy. She found a pair of hemostats to take care of the dewclaws and tossed them into her cart, along with two bags of puppy food and several toys. The brood wouldn't play with them for a while, but she couldn't wait. Joy sparkled up her spine as she thought of her precious puppies.

McKenzie had a short list of grocery items for Stella, so she steered her shopping cart to the food side of the store. On her way to the produce aisle, she passed by the cash registers at the front of the shop. Allison Snow entered the Mercantile through the automatic doors with her parents and a younger boy who was probably her brother or a nephew. Though she didn't want to engage her, McKenzie waved, but Allison widened her eyes and, with an expression of surprise, shuffled her little group away in the opposite direction. *So much for trying to be friendly.*

Later, when McKenzie returned to the ranch with her purchases, the calves in the pasture behind the barn were bawling like crazy. She found Stella in the kitchen. "What is going on with those calves? Is everything okay?"

Stella rolled her eyes. "The cow-song of weaning season. Be thankful Dylan herded the cows out to the north pasture. Otherwise, we'd have to listen to the cows calling back."

"That must be what Dylan was talking about this morning." McKenzie helped Stella put away the groceries. "Do you know who Allison Snow is?"

Biting her lower lip in concentration, Stella looked just like Caitlyn did when she was thinking. "Oh, she must be Myrna and Alan Snow's daughter. I think she went to school with my kids, but she moved away somewhere after graduation. Why do you ask?"

"She's back in Moose Creek visiting her parents. I've met her in town a couple of times."

"Oh?"

"I saw her at the Mercantile with her parents and little brother this morning. I waved, but she pretended she didn't see me. I wondered why she'd do that. I don't think I've offended her in any way."

"It's hard to say. I never knew her. She wasn't close friends with any of my kids... but I always thought she was an only child. I don't think she has a brother."

McKenzie shrugged and set a box of elbow noodles in the cupboard. "I don't have to work until tomorrow, so I'll be here with the puppies all afternoon. Dylan invited me for dinner, if that's okay."

Not one to be subtle, Stella gave her a mega-watt smile. "Of course, it's okay."

23

Caitlyn and Dirk began their search at the small house in Mammoth that Una had been renting for the past year. If they had any doubt of her guilt, they found all the evidence they needed to confirm it inside her closet. Una had taped maps of the town and a hand-sketched floor plan of the judge's house to the wall. On a small table, Caitlyn found a frame holding a photo of a young boy, whom she figured was Paytah, standing next to an older man with the same eyes and nose.

"Holy shit, Dirk. Here's another one." A cold flush of anxiety flooded from Caitlyn's head down over her shoulders. She pointed to a sturdy box on the closet floor filled with straw and holding another grenade with a handwritten instruction sheet lying next to it. Propped up in the corner was a Winchester model 70 Super Grade. "This must be the rifle she used to fire at the restaurant. It never occurred to me it was a woman who fired that shot."

"Look for any clues about where she could have run to."

"I'm betting she's headed to the Crow Reservation in Montana. That's where her brother lives."

Dirk looked over his shoulder at her. "Isn't Murphy an Irish name? And didn't Paytah go to school in Gardiner?"

"Yes, and yes, but the name Una is a Native American name. The trial documents said Paytah lived in Gardiner with his grandfather, but I think his dad lives on the Reservation." She studied the picture in the frame. "I bet this is a photo of Paytah and his dad."

"Why didn't the boy live at home?"

Caitlyn shrugged. "I don't know, but I think we ought to find out."

"Okay, well, let's finish looking around here first. If we don't find anything hinting that she went anywhere else, we'll head up to the Reservation."

Caitlyn opened the nightstand drawer, where she spotted miscellaneous bills and notes. She emptied the contents onto the bedspread and sorted the papers. She scanned through the piles until she came upon a personal letter. *Dear Una, your heart is good, but what you're doing is dangerous. You'll never get the justice you seek. Come home. Ben.* "Dirk, look at this." She handed him the letter, and he read it while Caitlyn looked closer at the envelope. "The postmark is from Billings and check out the name on the return address. Kanoska. That was Paytah's last name."

"That's evidence enough for me. I'll call it in and add arresting Una to the warrant."

"Let's also get her driver's license number and a description of any cars she has registered in her name. We can check if any traffic cameras have picked up her car in the past two hours—especially along I-90 headed toward the Reservation." Caitlyn tapped a number on her phone. "I'll have the sheriff send a deputy to guard this evidence until investigators can get here."

Dirk bobbed his chin, and they waited for the scene guard. As soon as the patrol car parked, Dirk ran toward the door. "Come on, Reed. We can call all this in while we're on the road and also request back-up. We'll stop along the way to see if anyone saw Murphy drive through, but I'm convinced you're right. She's probably running back to her brother on the Reservation."

They took Dirk's SUV, and Renegade stretched out in the back. Dirk stopped to fill his gas tank while Caitlyn dashed inside the convenience store to get sandwiches and water for the trip.

Once on the road, Caitlyn's heart broke at the breathtaking scenery of the Mammoth Hot Springs and surrounding hills as they headed north on highway 89 up into Montana. It was the last place Sam had spent a few hours of fun with his family. Had the bereavement team told Laurie about Sam's death yet? Caitlyn's gut wrenched in pain for the young widow and her son.

She and Dirk had several hours of drive time ahead of them, unless they caught up with Una Murphy on the way. Once they were traveling east on I-90, the miles zipped by. They stopped for to-go cups of coffee in Greycliff and on a whim, Caitlyn showed the barista Una's photo. He said he recognized her and told them the woman had come through the drive-up window a couple of hours ago.

"We're on the right track, Dirk. Let's go!" Caitlyn grabbed her hot cup and dashed back to his car. The knots knitting together in her belly tightened. "How much farther to the Reservation?"

"We'll have to go through Billings, and when I-90 turns south, we'll take it to Crow Agency, where the police department is. After a quick check-in with them, we can hunt Una Murphy down. You have her brother's address, right?"

"Yeah." Caitlyn felt the outside pocket of her cargo pants and the envelope bearing Ben Kanoska's address crinkled inside.

Dirk glanced at his watch. "We'll be there in a couple of hours."

"Step on it. Let's shave some of the drive time off."

He pressed the gas and his SUV surged past two other vehicles in the right lane. A mostly silent hour and a half later, Dirk followed his car's navigation map to the police station in Crow Agency. They pulled into a lot full of Crow Police cars and a Moose Creek Sheriff's jeep. Caitlyn bolted straight up and squinted her eyes at the man in the driver's seat. Sure enough, Colt sat inside the Jeep holding something against his face.

"Stop!" Caitlyn barked. Dirk slammed on the brakes, furrowing his brows at her in question. "That's Colt! What is he doing here?" She opened her door, jumped out of Dirk's car and ran to the Jeep.

Caitlyn ran toward him. Colt's jaw slackened when he saw her, and he dropped the instant cold-pack he'd been holding to his cheek. He stepped out of his car. "Catie?"

"What are you doing here?" She reached up and gently touched his bruising eye socket. "What happened?"

He grabbed ahold of her and squeezed her tight to his chest. "Never mind about that. Thank God you're alive."

"You heard?"

"Only that there was an explosion. Did the judge survive?"

Caitlyn's legs wavered. "No, he didn't. And—" she stared into his eyes. "Neither did Sam."

"Oh Christ, Catie. I'm so sorry." She nodded, giving her throat a minute to loosen up, but Colt continued, "We're waiting for Sheriff Munson's friend to show up so he can take us onto the Reservation. The sergeant here isn't the welcoming type." A ghost of a smile haunted his lips. "But the real question is why are *you* here? As soon as I heard about an explosion in Mammoth, I tried to call you." Caitlyn sagged against him at the mention of the morning's incident and Colt held her close. "Are you sure you're alright?"

"Yeah, but..." She swallowed hard and sucked in a breath before meeting Colt's gaze. "The explosion happened at the courthouse I was supposed to be guarding. I was supposed to protect the judge and Sam."

Colt's eyes roamed her face and searched her eyes before he pulled her into his arms. "I'm so sorry. Tell me what happened."

"I'll tell you about it later. We're in a hurry to catch the bomber." Caitlyn stepped back, and Dirk approached them.

He held out his hand and the two lawmen shook.

"Looks like you're working on quite a shiner there, Sheriff. What brings you to Montana?"

Colt explained about the drug trail. "We're hoping to talk to the cousin of the kid who had the drugs. I'm sure he has a lot to do with the recent influx of methamphetamine down in Moose Creek. Our problem is the sergeant in charge here is not inclined to let us onto the Reservation in any official capacity. We have no jurisdiction up here, but I went to the casino to poke around and ask a few questions." Colt grinned. "The black eye is my reward."

A slow smile spread across Dirk's swarthy face. "Maybe as a sheriff you don't have jurisdiction, but as a temporary Deputy US Marshal, you will. We're chasing a killer—a domestic terrorist, in fact, and we need help. Raise your right hand, Sheriff." Colt did as Dirk asked, and Dirk swore Colt in as a temporary Special US Deputy Marshal. "There, now you have jurisdiction. I'll go in and tell them why we're here, then we can go. When our backup gets here, these guys can send them in." He ran into the small police department.

Sheriff Munson grinned. "Pays to know people. I'll stay here and wait for Squallie and give directions to your backup. Keep me posted as to what you find, and I'll meet you there as soon as I can."

Colt nodded before trailing his fingers down Caitlyn's arm. "Who exactly are you after?"

"Her name is Una Murphy. It's a long story, but she's the one who killed the judge. It's her fault Sam is dead." Caitlyn looked away to take a couple of steadying breaths.

"We think she ran up here to hide out at her brother, Ben Kanoska's, house."

Dirk jogged out of the building and opened his car door. "Let's go!" Renegade barked and wagged his tail when Colt got into the backseat with him, and as soon as Caitlyn shut her door, they took off.

24

McKenzie checked on the litter of puppies bundled together, napping in a pile near their mama. She needed to nip their dewclaws. It was best to take care of the procedure while they were sleeping and then place them with their dam for a comforting meal, but she'd wait until she had help.

"McKenzie, I have an idea." Stella came out through the kitchen door and joined her in admiring the lump of black and brown fluff. "Instead of here, how does dinner in Spearfish, sound?"

McKenzie grinned. "Fine with me."

"Wonderful. Will you also join me at the Bridal Bonanza while we're there? Dylan has to drive over there to do some business with another ranch. I thought we could shop while he does his thing. Then we could all have dinner together before we come home."

McKenzie was sorry for Stella. The woman was desperate to plan a wedding for her daughter who was preoccupied with her job and resisted organizing the event. But the Bridal Bonanza? Seriously? Stella dreamed of planning a glorious ceremony, but the bride was unavailable and hadn't set a solid date. "I'd love to come with you." McKenzie slid her arm around the older woman's shoulders and gave her a gentle squeeze.

"Good. I'll be ready to leave as soon as Dylan gets back from checking on the herd. Maybe fifteen minutes or so? Will that work for you?"

"Sure. The best thing right now is to let this mama take care of her pups."

DYLAN DROVE and Stella insisted they all ride in the front seat, so he pushed up the center console to make a bench, and McKenzie sat in the middle next to him. They listened to a country-western radio channel and sang along when they knew the words. At a pause between songs, the DJ read a breaking news report informing listeners that there had been an explosion at the courthouse in Mammoth.

"That's where Caitlyn is working." Stella cried and pulled out her phone. She pushed some buttons and waited. "There's no answer." A deep line furrowed between Stella's eyes. "I'll text her. Hopefully she'll let us know what happened and if she's safe."

McKenzie searched her own phone for news of the explosion but couldn't find anything. She glanced at Dylan, whose face looked drawn. He stared hard at the road before him. "Call Colt."

Stella dialed again. Colt's phone went straight to voicemail, too. "Who else can I call?"

"I'll try Wes." McKenzie tapped on her screen.

"Deputy Cooper here. How can I help you?"

"Wes, it's McKenzie Torrington. What can you tell us about the explosion up in Mammoth? Have you heard from Caitlyn? Is she okay?"

"I know there was an explosion, but I've heard nothing else. Sheriff Branson is on his way up to Montana. Let me see what I can find out, and I'll call you back. Is this a good number?"

"Yes, call this number as soon as you know anything. I'm here with Caitlyn's mom and brother."

"Will do." He ended the call.

They rode in silence. McKenzie grappled with her fearful imagination and prayed that Caitlyn was safe. When her phone rang, McKenzie jumped, and the device slid to the floor. She reached for it and set it on speaker. "Hello? Wes?"

"Yes, it's me. I couldn't find out much, but apparently there were only two casualties—both male."

"Oh, thank God," Stella cried and instantly looked abashed. "I mean, I'm not thankful about the two men, just that Caitlyn is safe."

"Of course." McKenzie gripped Stella's hand and swallowed her own tears of relief. Dylan flexed his hands. He'd been gripping the steering wheel hard, but now his white joints returned to their normal color.

"Did you speak with Caitlyn?" Dylan asked.

"No, sir. I called the local Sheriff's Office and spoke with them. I'm sure Caitlyn will call in as soon as she has a minute, but I imagine the scene will be hectic for a long while."

A deep sigh left Dylan's chest. "Okay. Good. Thank you."

McKenzie leaned against Stella's shoulder. "Well, at least we can be sure Caitlyn is safe. She'll call when everything settles down, but that might not be until tonight. So, let's try to enjoy the evening."

Stella's smile wavered. "You're right." She leaned forward and spoke to her son. "You can just drop us off at the Bridal Bonanza and pick us up again when you're finished with your business."

"Bridal Bonanza? Priceless," Dylan chuckled. "Well, I suppose if you're looking for wedding stuff for Caitlyn, this is the place to go." He pulled up to the curb of an elegant-looking shop that defied its western-sounding name. "Looks expensive."

"I only have one daughter," Stella said as she climbed down from the truck.

McKenzie kissed Dylan's cheek. "See you soon, and I'll call if I hear anything more about Caitlyn." Before she could get out, he slid his hand behind her head and kissed her properly.

Smiling, she slid across the seat to the door. She almost said *I love you* but stopped herself. They weren't at a place where they said that in front of his parents yet. Still, he grinned and winked at her as though he'd read her mind.

Inside the shop, the owner greeted them and took their jackets. She led them to a set of white velvet chairs and offered tea. The woman's assistant went to get the refreshments while she sat with McKenzie and Stella. She smiled at McKenzie and interviewed them about the ceremony. "When is the wedding day, my dear?"

"Oh!" Startled, McKenzie's hand flew to her throat. "I'm not the bride. I'm just the friend." She gestured at Stella. "And this is the bride's mother."

"I see. Will the bride be joining us?"

"Not today," Stella answered. "She's working out of town for the time being. We're just helping her get a start on the planning. I thought perhaps McKenzie here could try on a selection of gowns and I could send pictures of them to my daughter to help her define what she's looking for."

"That's a wonderful idea. What type of designs are we thinking?"

The assistant approached with a tray ladened with a silver teapot and china cups. The offering included wafer-thin sugar crisps. "Here we are." She set the tray on a tufted ottoman.

The women discussed styles and what they thought Caitlyn would most like. Stella gravitated toward layers of bejeweled tulle. "I would have loved to have a gown like this when I was a bride."

McKenzie pressed her lips together and gave herself time to construct a response. "It is beautiful, Stella, but when we think about who Caitlyn is... well, I can't see her wanting to wear something so... fancy." She turned to the assistant. "Can you show us some dresses that have a simpler elegance?"

The woman brought out six gowns and hung them in various places around the mirrored room. McKenzie had never seen such beautiful dresses in her life. She blinked at them in wonder.

Stella pushed her to stand. "Try each of these on, and I'll take pictures."

McKenzie followed the assistant into a large dressing room, the size of a small bedroom. Mirrored walls reflected every angle of the elevated platform in the center of the room. She shook off her clothes and the woman helped her step into the first gown. McKenzie stared at herself in the mirror. She felt like Cinderella must have when her fairy godmother turned her torn dress into a glistening ball gown. Her hands spread from her ribcage down over her hips to the tops of her thighs. The fabric was rich and smooth.

"Beautiful. Let's go show your mother-in-law."

"My mother-in-law?"

"Oh, I'm sorry. I just assumed. I saw you getting out of the truck, and if you're not the bride—"

McKenzie's face flamed. "No, I..." She didn't bother to finish as she stepped out of the changing room to show Stella the first gown.

"That's nice," Stella commented. "But don't you think a wedding gown should be lacier?"

"When was the last time you saw Caitlyn wearing lace?" McKenzie tittered while Stella snapped photos on her phone.

The assistant nodded. "Perhaps we can try something with more detail that isn't necessarily lace." She turned back to the dressing room, and McKenzie followed.

They repeated the dress and photo experience four more times before McKenzie slid into the final gown in the selection. When she looked at her reflection, her breath caught in her throat. The woman helping her finished fastening the long string of buttons up the back and gathered McKenzie's hair up into a mock up-do. "This gown looks like it was made for you. I don't know about the woman you are shopping for, but when your special day comes, you ought to wear this dress."

McKenzie's breath was rapid and shallow as she stared at herself in the mirror. "Oh—" was all she could say. She went out to show Stella, who was also dumbstruck for a minute.

"McKenzie, you…"

A deep voice sounded from behind Stella. "Are stunning." Dylan finished his mother's sentence. He took one more step toward them, his eyes roaming over McKenzie in the gown. Her cheeks grew warm under his intent perusal. The moment lengthened and no one spoke. Finally, Dylan gave a little shake of his head. "Is—," he cleared his throat and started again. "Is that dress for Caitlyn?"

A little smile played on Stella's lips as she watched her son. "Maybe. I've taken photos of several gowns, and we'll see what she thinks."

"Are you ladies ready to go to dinner?" Dylan looked like a rhinoceros in a lingerie shop, wearing rugged western clothes and black felt cowboy hat. He shoved his hands into his jeans pockets and stole another glance at McKenzie.

"I'll just change." She hurried toward the dressing room door.

Through the thin wall she heard Stella say, "I'm not

hungry, and I'd like to look at mother-of-the-bride gowns. Why don't you and McKenzie go to dinner and pick me up when you're through?"

"Sure, Ma. Whatever you want."

When McKenzie emerged in her street clothes, Dylan continued to stare at her like he had when she was wearing the gown. His intensity made her feel giddy. He opened the shop door for her and, as she passed by, she asked, "Is everything okay?"

He blinked at her and his cheeks flushed. "It's far better than okay."

25

Caitlyn's phone buzzed, and she glanced at the screen. A texted photo of McKenzie modeling a hideous dress made from a mess of frothy, sparkling layers of tulle appeared. "Oh, my God."

Colt leaned forward. "Who is it?"

Without a word, Caitlyn held up her phone. Colt barked out a laugh. "Well, at least they're trying to get our wedding planned."

"Don't laugh. You haven't seen what my mother thinks you should wear yet. It could be even worse!"

Colt gave her shoulder a squeeze. "I don't care what I'm wearing, as long as you say, 'I do'."

Caitlyn smiled and touched his fingers, glad for the short but meaningful reprieve on her otherwise hellish day. "Let's get Una behind bars first." Her heart stung with sudden pain at the mention of her name. "And I want to help Laurie put Sam to rest. Then we can talk about the wedding."

"Right. What is Una's brother's address? I'm looking at

my GPS, but the houses are far apart and not in any sort of order."

Caitlyn read off Kanoska's address, and Colt punched the information into his phone. "Take a left on the next road," he said to Dirk.

They sped along on the rough dirt road and Caitlyn glanced over her should at Colt. "You said you think the meth that the high school boys had, came from someone on the Reservation?"

"Yeah. The kid who confessed said he got it from his cousin who lives up here. Did I tell you the meth we found was packaged in those plastic packets with *rockeT* printed on them?"

Caitlyn turned in her seat to face Colt. "No kidding? Do we know if Burroughs is connected to anyone on the Reservation?"

"I haven't come across anything that indicates that, but nothing would make me happier than to capture Ray Burroughs and Elaine Woodrow."

"It's too much to be a coincidence, don't you think?"

"I don't know. The drugs could come from anywhere along the supply line, but we're closer now than we were yesterday."

Dirk's gaze sought Colt's in the rearview mirror. "As soon as we apprehend Una Murphy, we'll help you round up your drug pushers."

Colt nodded. "Deal."

They pulled to a stop in the dirt yard of a small house constructed of weathered plywood that someone had painted gray but never finished. A rusty compact sedan sat in a clump of weeds baking in the sun, but Una's blue car wasn't there. Of course, that meant nothing. Caitlyn slid Renegade's Kevlar vest on and clipped a lead to it. "I'll cover the back in case we get a runner."

Dirk and Colt unholstered their pistols and ran to take positions on either side of the front door. Dirk pounded on the thin entrance. "US Marshals! Declare yourselves and come out of the house with your hands up. If you do not, a police dog will be released. He will find you and bite you." Dirk announced the K9 presence three times to allow the people inside a chance to cooperate before giving Caitlyn the order to release her dog.

Renegade strained against his leash, barking with excitement when he heard the announcement. He knew it was time to go to work. He and Caitlyn waited by the back exit and, just as she'd suspected, two young men bolted through the crooked screen door. One of them turned and fired his gun wildly in Caitlyn's direction. Fortunately, the shot was wide. Caitlyn's endocrine system rocketed into overload and her muscles trembled as she deployed Renegade. He darted after the men in a flash. The dog sprang forward, biting down on one of the men's hamstrings. The apprehended runner fell to the ground, screaming.

Caitlyn steadied her breath to slow her heart rate. She held her Glock in both hands, and aiming at the men, yelled, "Freeze! Get your hands up where I can see them." The second man came to a halt and raised his hands above his head. As she walked toward them, Renegade held his runner pinned to the dirt. She heard Colt and Dirk clearing the inside of the house behind her. In less than a minute, they emerged from the back door to assist

Caitlyn with the arrests. Dirk took care of the man still standing, and Caitlyn held Renegade's collar until Colt handcuffed the man on the ground. When he'd locked the silver bracelets, Caitlyn called, *"Pust"*, releasing Renegade from the bite. "Call an ambulance. This guy's leg is messed up."

Colt held up a plastic packet. "Look what I found on the coffee table."

Caitlyn raised her eyebrows and pressed her lips together in a flat line. Colt slid the packet into an evidence bag and called for the paramedics.

While they waited, Dirk leaned into his suspect's face. "Where is Ben Kanoska?"

The young man, whom Caitlyn guessed was probably seventeen, glared defiantly at Dirk, but when his friend with the torn-up leg cried out in pain, his bravado slumped.

With a low, growling voice, Dirk leaned closer. "You better tell me where he is."

"I think he's at work," the teen faltered.

Dirk tightened his grip on the boy's shirt. "Where is his work?"

"He owns the excavating company down the road."

"How far down the road?" Dirk pulled out his phone and held up a map. "Show me."

With another glance at his friend, who was writhing on the ground, he pointed the way.

Caitlyn squatted down next to Renegade and touched the boy's good leg. "Where did you get the meth in that *rockeT* packet?"

He shrugged, and Caitlyn murmured, *"Stekej,"* the

command for Renegade to speak. Her dog barked at the suspect, baring his fangs and flinging drool into the boy's face.

"Okay, okay," he cried out and raised his hands to block the dog. "Our teacher sells it to us."

"Your *teacher*? Here on the rez?"

"Yeah, but she's a white lady."

"What's her name?"

"Mrs. Smith." The boy's wide eyes convinced Caitlyn that he believed that was truly her name, even though Caitlyn doubted its authenticity.

Sirens sounded in the distance, and they waited for the ambulance and accompanying patrol car to arrive. As soon as they passed the suspects over to the local first responders and Caitlyn shared the information she'd gathered about the teacher with the Crow police officer, the team climbed back into Dirk's SUV and headed toward Kanoska's excavation company.

In the car, Caitlyn opened a bottle of water for Renegade. She poured some into his travel bowl to drink and used the rest to wash the drying blood from the fur around his mouth. A radio call came in from the backup contingent of DEA agents and she answered. After informing them of their destination, she shouted, "Meet us there!"

26

A mile down the dusty dirt road, a steel-sided building glinted in the sun. Two dump trucks and a backhoe were parked on the left side of the building that bore the Kanoska Excavation logo on the front.

"There it is!" Caitlyn pointed, and Dirk sped toward it. He skidded to a stop in the gravel parking lot next to five other cars.

"Do you think Murphy is there?" Dirk rose from his car and unholstered his pistol.

Caitlyn stepped out of the SUV and checked Renegade's vest clip. "It's as good a guess as any. This is her brother's business. If he's here, it makes sense she'd run to him for refuge. I bet this is where she got ahold of the explosives, too. Her brother would have a license to buy them."

Colt climbed out of the back seat and pointed up the drive in the direction they had come. "I think our backup is here." A line of four black SUVs raced along the road and skidded to a stop in front of them. A man wearing a blue DEA windbreaker and ball cap emblazoned with the same large block letters jumped out of the passenger's side of the first car.

"What's the situation?"

Dirk shook his hand and introduced himself and the others. "We're after a dangerous fugitive who we believe is hiding out inside the building. We could be up against both firearms and explosives." Caitlyn pulled up a photo of Una on her phone and passed it around to the backup team.

After a quick strategy discussion, Dirk took command of the scene. "We'll cover all exits, but I must announce the police dog before we breach. I'll yell out three times that we have a dog. If the people inside don't come out, we'll send him in. Hopefully, they'll be smart and come out with no trouble. Renegade has already shredded one hamstring today."

One of the DEA agents turned to Caitlyn. "What if someone shoots the dog when he enters?"

Her gut clenched. "We're hoping that since this is a place of business, the workers will simply evacuate the building. If not, Renegade wears a vest and knows his job, just like the rest of us do." She felt Colt's eyes on her, and she figured he was shocked at her response. He knew how much she loved Renegade and that it would kill her if someone shot him. But the truth was, they were all in danger. Any one of them might get shot. That was the job. They all knew the inherent risks. Caitlyn pushed the thought away. She couldn't afford to freeze up worrying about the risk to either Colt or Renegade.

The DEA chief assigned his agents to their locations, and once everyone was in place, Dirk tried the entrance door. It was locked, so he pounded on the metal entry. Movement from inside stilled, and silence echoed from within. "US Marshals! Declare yourselves and come out of the building with your hands in the air. If you do not, a police dog will be released. He will find you and bite you."

Shuffling and running footsteps sounded through the walls, but no one answered Dirk's command. He banged on the door and shouted the same words again.

Before Dirk had a chance to yell the orders a third time, a bullet pierced the door from the within and whizzed out past them as they stood off to the sides of the entrance. Dirk called for the door ram. He pointed the two armored DEA agents carrying 'the Enforcer' to the entrance. They bashed the door twice before it crumpled and swung inward. Members of the DEA Special Response Team breached the building in a well-choreographed sequence.

With her weapon at the ready, Caitlyn followed them in with Renegade, whose whole body was flexed like a high-tension spring, strained to bolt into the space. They made their way through a front reception area into the back warehouse space.

Thirty or more people covered from head to toe in yellow plastic suits and wearing blue rubber gloves stared at the busted door through filtered breathing masks.

It took a second for Caitlyn to dicern what they were seeing. The scene before them made it look like they'd just landed on a different planet. Renegade lunged forward, excited to chase someone, but Caitlyn held him back. The last thing any of them needed was to run, unprotected, into a frickin' meth lab! She swung her gaze to Colt. His brows were scrunched over his determined face and set jaw. He looked as ready as Renegade to run inside after the fleeing yellow-clad people.

Dirk thrust out his arm, unnecessarily holding Caitlyn back, but she knew better than to run in. He called out to Colt. "Wait here. I have respirator masks in the gearbox in my car." He ran to retrieve the protective face coverings, joining the many DEA agents hustling after the same safety gear from their vehicles.

Colt adjusted the respirator Dirk handed him and entered the building before and other law enforcement officers cleared the lower floor of the warehouse of people. His unit found six people huddled behind racks of large, stacked cardboard boxes. They ordered the meth cookers to put their hands on their heads and ushered them outside.

Rather than joining Colt's search inside and risking Renegade's hypersensitive nose, Caitlyn ran with her dog around the back of the building. Several agents had positioned themselves there to catch runners as they attempted to escape through windows and doors. As people raced from the lab, agents forced them to remove their masks and hoods. They ordered everyone to kneel and put their hands on their heads.

Renegade sniffed the lines of suspects who were on their knees, searching for firearms and other weapons. She approached one chemist who had not removed his headgear, and a DEA agent yanked it off. Caitlyn's breath caught in her throat. Right there, on her knees before her, knelt Elaine Woodrow—the woman whose husband and son had been killed by Burroughs and his brother in their home last spring.

"Elaine?" Caitlyn squawked. "What are you doing here? Are you here with Burroughs?" The methamphetamine puzzle pieces were snapping into place. She glanced around for Colt, but he was attending to another row of kneeling suspects. He would be as shocked as she was to see Elaine here.

Colt commanded the suspects in his charge, "Keep your fingers interlaced on top of your heads and kneel down in a straight line." Two Reservation cops took over searching them for weapons and binding their hands behind their backs, so Colt went to assist with the line Caitlyn and Renegade were working. When he saw the woman at Caitlyn's feet, he gawked at her and then met Caitlyn's gaze with a stunned expression.

Elaine glared up at Caitlyn with unfiltered hate. "I'm teaching at the Reservation High School."

Caitlyn's mouth dropped open. "*You're* the one selling drugs to children? You're a mother! How could you?" As soon as Caitlyn said it, she realized Elaine was not the kind of mother who cared for other people's kids. Hell, she didn't even care about her own. "Never mind. Why would I think you'd show any concern after abandoning your only surviving daughter to run off with Burroughs—the murderer of your family?" Elaine turned her face away from Caitlyn.

Renegade growled and went into a fury of barking. He tugged Caitlyn so hard, she stumbled. Renegade's razor-sharp canines were millimeters from a masked man's face.

"Renegade! Lehne!" Caitlyn yelled for her dog to lie down. Colt pulled the man's mask off and pushed back his hood.

Ray Burroughs's black eyes shot arrows at Renegade. The dog obeyed Caitlyn's command, but his body trembled with rage.

Caitlyn took hold of Renegade's collar. "He remembers you, Burroughs. If I were you, I'd sit perfectly still."

Spit sprayed from his mouth as Burroughs cursed. "I should have shot that dog twice for good measure."

"You probably should have." Burning anger flared in Caitlyn's chest. She wanted to slap the man's spiteful glare from his face. "Because now he'll have his revenge."

Dirk rested a calming hand on Caitlyn's shoulder. "Colt, the DEA, and the Reservation cops can deal with all these people. Don't forget, you and I are here to find Una Murphy."

Thankful for the redirect, Caitlyn shook her head and took the filtered breathing apparatus that Dirk handed her. She secured Renegade inside Dirk's SUV before following her partner into the building. Long stainless-steel tables stood in rows across the cement floor. Three of them held Bunsen burners, beakers, and all sorts of science lab paraphernalia. Two other tables looked like cutting and packaging stations, and at the end of one were boxes filled with small plastic packets. Next to the boxes were ink pads and stamps.

With a gloved hand, Caitlyn pushed one of the wooden stamps onto a pad, then pressed it against the side of the cardboard box. She was elated, but not surprised, to find that the red ink spelled *rockeT*. "Looks like we've found the producer of the meth that's been spreading through the schools." Caitlyn's voice echoed inside her breathing apparatus. "Elaine has been selling it to her students up here, and I'm guessing one of those kids is the cousin of the boy in Moose Creek."

"No doubt." Dirk bent the flap of the box back and reached for a packet. "She must have been building a network of kids to push the drugs for her. It was probably one of her students who sold the *rockeT* packets to Colt's cattle rustler in the casino parking lot, too. This is a profitable bust. We're cleaning up." Dirk's words were muffled. "If we locate Una, we'll have captured three fugitives in one swoop." He turned toward the stairs that led to an office space overhead and motioned for Caitlyn to follow him.

"Let's find her!" Caitlyn's body thrummed with adrenaline. She knew if they caught Una, Dirk would likely have to hold her back from strangling the woman.

They were halfway up the steps when a figure slipped out from behind a wall of barrels stacked two by two at the back of the warehouse. The runner had a respirator on, but it did not cover her long black hair. *Una!* An agent outside saw her too and yelled for her to freeze. As she ran, Una turned and raised her handgun. She aimed at the man who ordered her to stop and fired twice into the team of law enforcement who was busy arresting the drug makers.

Caitlyn yelled from across the room, "Drop your weapon!"

Una had fired her gun into the crowd where Caitlyn had last seen Colt. She then pivoted and aimed at Caitlyn and Dirk on the stairs. Caitlyn's heart slammed against her ribs. In one fluid movement, she pulled her Glock from its holster, leveled it at the woman, and squeezed the trigger. Una's pale pink blouse burst with a red blossom. Return gunfire spit into the building from the agents Una had shot at, and Dirk unleashed several rounds too.

Una's body hit the cement floor, and the breathing mask fell from her face. Her body was swallowed up by a blinding white light as a searing wave of heat lifted Caitlyn off the step. A deafening *BOOM!* vibrated through her body and she flew like a crash dummy through the air. Searing flames nibbled at the edge of her face, singeing her hair. She slammed backward into a metal wall. Her head and shoulders smashed into the corrugated steel. The image of Una firing into the crowd where Caitlyn last saw Colt flashed through her mind. His name, her last conscious thought, screamed through her brain. *COLT!*

27

At first, Colt was stunned to see Elaine among the suspects. He'd been searching for the woman and her boyfriend ever since Elaine's husband and son were murdered months ago near Moose Creek. Renegade sniffed his way down the line and went ballistic when he came upon a particular suspect. Caitlyn struggled to hold him back. Colt pulled the man's mask and hood off. "Burroughs!"

Dirk interrupted the scene and pulled Caitlyn away. The last time Colt saw them, Caitlyn and Dirk had entered the building and were making their way up the stairs. Renegade was not with her, which was smart. The chemical fumes in the building were toxic for anyone without breathing protection.

Colt continued down a line of suspects, zip-tying each person's wrists behind their backs. A DEA agent followed him patting them down and pulling them to their feet. Gunfire erupted from inside the building. Police officers and DEA agents scrambled to take cover, and the suspects scattered.

Colt instinctively responded by pulling his gun and dropping to one knee. He aimed his weapon into the building Caitlyn and Dirk had disappeared into minutes ago. Bald fear gripped his chest. A Crow police officer fell to the ground next to him, clutching his torso. Blood oozed between the man's fingers.

Colt yelled, "Keep the suspects together!" But it was too late. They had dispersed in the chaos. They wouldn't get far. Conflicted rage coursed through Colt's body. He dragged the downed officer behind a vehicle for cover and applied pressure to his chest wound. Caitlyn was inside the building, and he was desperate to know if she was injured. But first, he had to help the cop and secure his prisoners before he could look for her.

Agents responded to the gunfire by launching a multitude of rounds into the building. The shooter fell to the ground. As soon as an EMT took over for him with the fallen officer, Colt rushed to round up the suspects. Before he had a chance, something inside the warehouse exploded.

"Catie!" Her name tore from his lips as he was knocked to his knees by the force of the blast. He got up and shoved his captives toward a local cop, then ran back to the building. He drew his weapon and peered around a blown-out edge in the metal siding. Thick, black smoke billowed through the opening. His respirator allowed him to breathe—barely—but he couldn't see anything.

Firefighters yelled for everyone to get back, but Colt ignored them, until a hulk of a man in fire-fighting gear grabbed him by the shoulders and shoved him away. Colt regained his footing and charged toward the opening again.

The firefighter tackled him to the ground. "Stay behind the safety line, Sheriff. We'll get everyone out."

Terror clawed at Colt's throat. "There are two Federal Marshals inside!"

The huge man looked him directly in the eye. "We'll find them." He pulled Colt to his feet and pushed him toward the barricade line. The fireman clicked the visor on his helmet closed and ran into the flaming building, disappearing into the thick smoke.

Colt paced behind the barricade trying to see through the billowing blackness. *Catie and Dirk went in there minutes ago. There's no way they had time to get out before the explosion. The gunfire must have ignited the explosive chemical compounds. Even if they weren't blown up, Catie could be shot.* His pulse ricocheted through him.

Caitlyn could be bleeding to death right now, and there was nothing he could do. Every cell in his body demanded he race inside to find her, but he'd be engulfed by the toxic fumes within seconds, and only become more of a liability.

He approached Dirk's SUV. Renegade barked and frantically scratched at the window to get out. Colt jerked the driver's door open with all his might. The action did nothing to ease his fear or frustration. His desperate emotions aligned with Renegade's, and Colt had to restrain the dog to keep him from bounding out of the car. "She'll be okay, Ren. She has to be." Colt poured Renegade another bottle of water before he closed the car door. He then ran toward the triage station to lend a hand and keep himself out of the burning building.

"REED!" Caitlyn heard Dirk calling her name. Her cheek stung when he slapped it and her eyes fluttered open. "Reed! Are you okay?"

Her vision was dim. She pulled in a breath through the respirator filter and the image of Dirk staring down at her cleared. She slowly moved each of her limbs, checking for broken bones. Though sore, everything seemed to be in working order. However, her head screamed with pain, and she reached up to feel the back of her skull. "My head is killing me."

"No doubt. You're bleeding, but not too bad. You probably have one a hell of a concussion, though."

"Are you okay?"

Dirk gave her a sheepish look. "Yeah, unfortunately, you cushioned my landing. I'll be sore tomorrow, but I'll be alright."

"What the hell happened?"

"Something in the lab blew up. Firefighters are on the scene, and it looks like they have things under control, but we need to get out of here before anything else blows." Dirk stood and pulled Caitlyn to her feet. He held her arm as they stumbled down the metal stairs. Together, they ran outside into the bright sunlight. They ripped off their masks and gulped in fresh air.

Caitlyn fell to her hands and knees before she scanned the immediate area. Renegade was barking wildly inside

Dirk's car, but the sight of him only gave her a second of relief before her intestines wound into a knot. "Where's Colt?"

Dirk coughed. "I'm sure he's helping with the arrests."

"No! He'd be trying to find me. Is he in the building?" Panic surged up from her tightened belly and flew out of her mouth. "Colt!" she screamed. Caitlyn pushed herself to her feet and rushed toward the opening of the burning building, but Dirk caught her by the arms and held her back.

"You're not going in there. If he is inside, the firefighters will get him. Don't make more work for them by becoming another casualty. There is nothing you can do."

Caitlyn fought him like a wildcat. She jerked and flung herself, trying to escape his grasp. "Let go of me!"

"Caitlyn!"

Caitlyn stilled. Was that Colt's voice?

"Catie, thank God!" It was him. She twisted around in Dirk's hold as Colt ran toward her.

"Let me go!" She pushed at Dirk's hands. He released her, and she flew to Colt, jumping into his outstretched arms.

"I thought… I knew you and Dirk were inside!" Colt held her back at arm's length. "You're bleeding."

Caitlyn touched the cut at the back of her head. "I'll be fine." She searched Colt's face, running her fingers over his jaw and down his neck. Her intense appraisal lingered on his shoulder where he'd been shot months ago. "Where were you? Una fired out the door and—"

"I was still with the suspects when the shots were fired, and the explosion happened."

"I was scared I'd never see you again." Caitlyn touched the bruise on his soot-covered face.

"Me too. I thought..." Colt pulled her into his chest and held her tight without finishing his sentence.

Colt's legs had wavered when he saw Dirk holding the bristling fury that was his fiancée. She bucked and screamed, "Let me go!"

Colt yelled, "Caitlyn!" She didn't hear him. He called again, "Catie, thank God!" She stilled in her partner's grasp and turned slowly to face him.

She shook free and ran toward him. He caught her as she threw herself into his arms.

He had seen her go inside the building right before the explosion, and the memory caused a deep shudder to course through him. Colt set her down and pushed her back a step so he could check her over for himself. The fear he'd held back broke free and flooded his mind. With a trembling hand, he smoothed his fingers over her face, brushing a lock of hair behind her ear. Her hair was sticky with blood. "Catie, you're bleeding."

Caitlyn reached around and touched the bump on the back of her head. In typical fashion, she shrugged off her own injuries, more concerned about him. After pulling her close to reassure himself she was truly safe, he assured her that he was uninjured. Together, they walked over to an ambulance to have the cut on her scalp stitched up.

The paramedic dabbed at the cut with an antiseptic

pad. "You only need a couple of stitches on this cut, but it looks like you already have some sutures in your head."

Colt scrunched his brows together. "Other stitches?"

"From the courthouse bombing this morning," Caitlyn smirked. "I think I've seen enough explosions for one day."

Colt swept aside a long strand of hair that had come loose from her braid to look at the first laceration. "Did you already have a concussion before you came here?"

"Probably."

"Caitlyn! You have to take yourself out of the action if you're hurt. This is not okay."

The paramedic finished his final stitch. "The sheriff here is dead on. If you want to keep doing your job, you've gotta take care of your brain. You have some bruising at the back of your scalp, and it's easy to presume you have a double concussion at this point. I need to take you to the hospital."

Caitlyn sighed. Colt knew she hated being fussed over and, worse, being taken out of the action. She smiled at the paramedic. "Listen. I feel fine, and I will not take up the time and space that others need who are hurt far worse than me. Sheriff Branson will drive me home and make sure I see our doctor there. Okay?"

The medic shook his head. "I can't force you to come with me, but you seriously must see your doctor. Tonight."

She held up her hand in a three fingered scout's pledge. "I promise."

CAITLYN RELAXED into Colt for a second before her addled brain filtered through the event. "Una's dead." She pushed back and looked up at Colt's face. "She was the person firing the gun from inside, and I shot her. She fell right before the explosion."

"Seems she got what she deserved. And we've arrested Elaine Woodrow and Ray Burroughs."

"I should be more excited about that, but all I can think of is how grateful I am that you're alive."

"Me too. And listen to me, Caitlyn Rose, I don't want to wait any longer to get married."

"Me either, Colt." A wave of love overtook her, and she couldn't breathe. When her lungs worked again, she said, "Let's just do it. No stupid ceremony. Let's just go to the Justice of the Peace on our way home."

Colt smiled, causing white creases in the soot around his eyes. "I'd love to do that, but I could never face your mama if we did. And neither could you."

Caitlyn shrugged. "You're right. But no huge ceremony. Is that okay with you? Just family?"

"That's good by me. You're the only one I care about being there. Well, you *and* your mom." He grinned and kissed her forehead. "She'd murder us both if she wasn't included."

It was as though they were their own private island amid all the chaos that surrounded them. People ran in all directions, emergency vehicles came and went, but she blocked all of that out. Caitlyn pushed up on her toes and pulled his head down to hers. She pressed her lips hard against his mouth. Her pulse surged, causing her head to throb. She tried to ignore it, but finally she lowered back down. "I think I need to have my head examined."

Colt chuffed. "That's probably a good idea."

Caitlyn grinned and smacked him in the arm. "Shut up." She peered around Colt and pointed. "Hey. Did you see that?"

28

Colt turned to look at where Caitlyn was pointing. "What? The firetruck?"

"No, the car that's leaving the parking lot."

Colt narrowed his eyes at a pair of red taillights speeding away in the dusk. "The Lincoln Sport?"

"Yeah. Does it look familiar to you?" Caitlyn stared up at him with a thoughtful gaze.

"Yes, and it's strange. I saw that same Lincoln earlier today in the casino parking lot, and I thought I'd seen it before somewhere. It's the same kind of car Tito Garza drove when he came to Moose Creek to identify his wife's body. Remember?"

Caitlyn rolled her lip between her teeth. "You're right. But why would he be here?"

"Garza lives near Billings, and if he's involved in the meth business, maybe the T in *rockeT* stands for Tito?"

"It sure makes you wonder. We should have the local cops look into it."

Colt took her hand and walked her toward Dirk's car

and Renegade. She opened the door, and her dog leapt out. He wagged his tail so hard he had a difficult time keeping his feet on the ground. Caitlyn knelt and threw her arms around his shoulders and buried her face in his fur. "Good boy, Ren. I'm okay. Colt's okay. We're all going to be fine." Her dog bathed her face and neck with his tongue, and she giggled. Colt's heart swelled with love for them both.

"Get in." Dirk called as he jogged up to the SUV. "The local first responders can manage the rest. We need to go to the Reservation PD before we can head home." Colt helped Caitlyn get in, and Dirk drove them back to the police department.

PANDEMONIUM WAS in full swing at the Crow Police Department. They did not have enough room or cops to deal with all the arrested suspects. Caitlyn approached the intake desk and asked about Elaine Woodrow and Ray Burroughs. The woman behind the counter confirmed that Elaine Woodrow had been processed and was in a jail cell, but there was no record of a Ray Burroughs.

After asking to interview Elaine, Caitlyn turned to Colt. "They say Burroughs was never processed. But he was arrested. I saw him. Is there any way he could have run into the building and been killed in the explosion?"

A furrow formed between Colt's brows. "I don't see how. I saw him too. I assumed he was brought to the jail."

"But he's not here. Do you think he escaped?"

"God, I hope not. Tomorrow, they'll do a thorough

forensic fire investigation, so if he was somehow inside the building when it exploded, we'll know." Colt led her to a chair and insisted she sit down.

She looked up at him from her seat. "And if he wasn't, we should assume he's in the wind. Again."

The muscles in Colt's jaw knotted. "What if he somehow snuck off in Garza's car? That would explain why the Lincoln was there."

Caitlyn closed her eyes and nodded at the probability.

"Excuse me, ma'am?" The intake officer approached. "Elaine Woodrow said she has nothing to say to any cops, and she wants a lawyer. Says she might want to make a deal."

Caitlyn slid to the edge of her chair. "Did she hint at what information she has to offer?"

"She said something about supply lines, and that she knew who was at the top, running the whole show. But then she stopped talking and demanded a lawyer."

"Damn." Caitlyn rubbed her forehead wearily. It had been a hell of a day. "Okay. Does she have an attorney?"

"Not yet. She's asked for a public defender."

"How long will it take to get her one?" Caitlyn asked as she tried to stand, but Colt pressed her back into the chair.

The Crow officer shook her head. "There are two public defense attorneys here and they're working their tails off to get through the long list of detainees. It could take all night."

"Can you do me a favor?" Caitlyn squeezed Colt's hand and stood, even though she knew he didn't want her to. She looked the fellow female LEO in the eye. "We believe

Elaine Woodrow is involved with criminals on a much higher level than this single drug bust. Can you please see to it that she's interviewed by one of those lawyers right away? She might consider telling us something useful in her plea deal. Her information could be critical."

"I'll see what I can do." The woman's long black ponytail swung as she returned to her desk.

COLT WATCHED the frustration play across Caitlyn's features and he took her hand. "Try to relax. Elaine isn't going anywhere. You'll be able to talk to her soon enough." Caitlyn leaned into him. She was obviously exhausted, and Colt wanted to get her home.

"Excuse me. Sheriff Branson?" The Crow sergeant he'd met earlier in the day approached. "I have Ben Kanoska in an interview room. I thought you might like to be in on the interview since you're up here chasing down a lead on drugs." Colt was surprised at the sergeant's new attitude. Maybe the guy had a new appreciation for the greater law enforcement family after they all worked together to take down the meth lab.

"Yes. Thank you." Colt eased Caitlyn into a chair. "I'll be right back." She nodded and, closing her eyes, rested her head back against the wall.

Colt followed the sergeant down the hall. Inside the interview room, Colt chose to stand. He listened quietly for the most part to the officer's questioning.

"Ben, I've known you my whole life, brother. I can't believe you're cooking meth." The sergeant reached forward and unlocked Kanoska's handcuffs. "Why? Is it the money?"

Ben dropped his chin to his chest. Colt watched Ben's every twitch. He wasn't comfortable with the man's free hands.

"Come on, Ben," the sergeant urged. "You can talk to me. I might be able to help. But if you don't tell us what this is all about, you've got a dead police officer on your hands and a warehouse full of meth. You'll be going away for a long time."

Ben spoke toward the table. "What difference does it make now, with Paytah gone?" He remained still for a long moment, likely considering his predicament. "I never meant for any of this to happen." He blinked up at the Crow officer and sighed. "They came to me. Said they knew I had a warehouse, and they wanted to use it for the operation. I said no—that I had a business I ran out of the shop. It went on like that for a while, but then they threatened my family. They said they'd hurt Paytah." Ben dropped his chin again, and his shoulders shook.

The sergeant clasped one of the man's wrists. "So, you went along?"

Ben nodded. "Yes. One night when Paytah was hanging out with some friends, a fancy car pulled up to them. A couple of thugs got out, grabbed Paytah and roughed him up. He came home with a black eye, a fat lip, and a message. 'Let us use your warehouse, or else.'" So, I sent Paytah to live with my father down in Gardiner and did what they said. At first, I made good money and I thought Paytah was safe." He paused. "But then, Paytah was killed anyway."

Filled with unexpected compassion, Colt pulled out a chair and sat down. "Do you know the name of the man who threatened you?"

Ben shrugged. "He drives a fancy blue Lincoln. I think his name is Goba… Goza… something like that."

An icy flush bloomed in Colt's face, and he sat forward. "Garza? Tito Garza?"

WHILE COLT WAS STILL in his interview, the intake officer returned to speak with Caitlyn. "Deputy Marshal? I thought you'd like to know; Ms. Woodrow told her public defender that she is willing to give up information having to do with Ben Kanoska's meth lab, and she's agreed to testify against the people higher up the food chain."

Caitlyn stood up, her pulse energized. "What does she want in return?"

"Protection, and a deal of some sort for less jail time. You'll have to talk to her lawyer tomorrow. For now, Woodrow is back in her cell. The public defender has thirty more people to see, at least."

Caitlyn reached into her breast pocket and pulled out a wrinkled business card. "Okay. Will you please have her attorney call me as soon as he can?"

The woman took the card. "Will do, Deputy."

"Catie." Colt called from down the hall as he hurried toward her. "The Lincoln does belong to Garza! Kanoska told us he'd been pressured into letting Garza use his warehouse for the meth lab. And he's willing to testify!"

Caitlyn's head swam at Colt's news, and she held onto

the back of the chair to steady herself. Colt gripped her shoulders and turned her to face him. "I want to get you home and have Blake check the cuts on your head and see if you have a concussion. Besides, we have a long drive ahead of us, and you need to rest."

"Okay. You're right. And Ben and Elaine won't be going anywhere."

THEY WERE ABOUT HALFWAY home when Caitlyn's pocket vibrated, and she reached for her phone. An unknown Montana number flashed across her screen. "Deputy US Marshal Reed, here," she answered.

"This is Sheriff Lowell over in Gardiner, Montana."

"Yes, Sheriff? How can I help you?"

"I have some information you might find interesting. You know the hate crime and murder trial that took place regarding that young Crow boy, Paytah Kanoska?"

"Yes?"

"I thought you might like to know that we caught one of the young men accused of his murder trying to destroy some missing evidence."

"What evidence?"

"The boy was attempting to burn a beaded knife scabbard that belonged to Paytah. When we caught him, the kid broke down and confessed to being a part of the murder. He's willing to roll over on the other two boys if he gets a lighter sentence. But it looks like all three of them will be going to prison for murder."

Hot tears spilled from Caitlyn's eyes. This news was the final drop that caused her emotions to spill over. She covered her mouth and shook her head. Colt clasped her hand, concern etching his eyes. She cleared her throat before returning to Sheriff Lowell's call. "Thanks for letting me know about the boys, Sheriff. I appreciate it. I'll be in touch."

Caitlyn blinked up at Colt and told him what she'd just learned. "Today we discovered that Una is Paytah's aunt. Paytah was sent to live with his grandfather to keep him safe from Garza and his thugs. But he was killed anyway, and Una bombed the courthouse to avenge her nephew after what she believed was an unfair court ruling." Tears spilled over the rim of her eyelids. "If Garza had never threatened Paytah, none of this would have happened. And if the prosecution would have had all the facts, Judge Hughes would have convicted those kids, and Una would have never tried to kill him." A sob broke her sentence. "And Sam would still be alive. But now he's dead—and for what?" Caitlyn leaned across the console and rested her head on Colt's shoulder. He lifted his arm and circled her shoulders, holding her until her body stilled. She sniffed and wiped her eyes.

29

After dinner, McKenzie and Dylan returned to the bridal shop to pick up Stella. Once again, McKenzie snuggled up against Dylan in the truck's cab for the drive home. Stella took up a lot more room than she did on the ride to Spearfish, insisting on keeping her shopping bags next to her on the front seat instead of setting them in the back. It was fine—McKenzie certainly didn't mind pressing into Dylan—but she giggled to herself at his mother's not-so-subtle nudging.

"Did you find a dress?" McKenzie asked.

"I found two, but I couldn't decide, so I got them both. I'll pick one and return the other." Stella flipped through a catalog she picked up at the shop.

Dylan pulled up to the log home's front steps and hopped out to help his mother down from the truck. McKenzie scooted over and started out of the cab after her.

"Where are you going?" Dylan gave her a half grin, and

something that looked like mischief danced in his eyes. The glimmer ignited a flame deep inside her belly.

McKenzie stepped onto the running board. "I thought I'd help your mom organize her purchases, and I want to check on the puppies."

"Okay. But after that, will you go on a ride with me?"

"A ride? As in horseback? At night?"

Dylan chuckled. "Yes."

"I guess." She looked down at the skirt she wore, and holding it out, said, "Actually, no. I can't ride a horse in this."

Without taking his eyes from her face, Dylan called to his mother. "Hey Ma. Does Caitlyn have a spare set of jeans in the house anywhere?"

Stella turned back from the porch. "I'm sure she does. She keeps extra clothes in her old room."

Dylan's grin stretched to include the rest of his mouth. "There you go. You can borrow something of Caitlyn's. Come out to the barn when you're ready." Larry scampered up to them from somewhere, his tail wagging so hard his whole body wiggled. "Hey, buddy. Want to go on a ride?" Larry barked happily in response, and Dylan reached down to scratch his neck. He glanced back at McKenzie. "See you soon."

Dylan had a look in his eye McKenzie had never seen before. He was up to something, but there was an earnestness behind the glimmer that she couldn't place. She couldn't wait to pull on a pair of Caitlyn's jeans and get down to the barn to find out what was going on. Dylan kissed her cheek and then pointed to the truck door and Larry leapt in. McKenzie's insides went warm and squishy as she watched her man climb into the cab after his dog and drive down to the barn.

McKenzie turned to find Stella grinning like a quokka. "Come on, Stella. Let me help you with your bags."

The women took the purchases into John's office, or the room that *used* to be John's office but was now Wedding Headquarters. Stella pinned the swatches of fabric she purchased from the bridal shop onto a cork-board. "What do you think, McKenzie? Which blue do you like best for the bridesmaid dresses?"

"Did Caitlyn say she wanted blue?" McKenzie didn't want to be rude, but she was eager to join Dylan in the barn.

Stella raised one eyebrow, and she looked just like Caitlyn, only with graying hair. "Caitlyn hasn't answered that question, but her favorite color is blue. Well, a light, greenish blue, so—what is your opinion?"

"I love this darker sea-blue, myself." McKenzie felt the silky fabric she preferred between her fingers. "But we really should ask Caitlyn." She moved her hand to Stella's shoulder and gave her a gentle squeeze. "I know you're excited, but if you go too far in the planning without Caitlyn, it will only make her angry."

"Perhaps, but if she doesn't get busy with this, July will come and go without a wedding."

"Well, let's wait a little longer. With what happened up in Mammoth this morning, she'll be coming home soon and will have more time."

Stella released a puff of air. "I guess. I hate Caitlyn's job. It's so dangerous. It was bad enough when Logan joined the Army. Then it was the FBI Bomb Squad. Now Caitlyn…"

McKenzie hugged Stella. "I know you worry, but Caitlyn wouldn't be happy doing anything else."

"She's always run headlong into danger when someone needed help. I guess her career shouldn't surprise me."

"You've raised three fine people who care about others, Stella. You should be proud."

Stella smiled up at McKenzie. "Thank you."

McKenzie rushed to unpack the remaining shopping bags while Stella hung both of her mother-of-the-bride dresses from the curtain rod. "What do you think?"

"I'm sure they are both beautiful on you." McKenzie glanced at her watch.

"That color looks best on me, I think, but I like the length of the other one." Stella folded the bags that her purchases came in. "Can you stay for a cup of tea? Dylan will be back from the barn in a few minutes."

"I'd love to, but actually, Dylan asked me to go on a ride, and I want to check on the puppies before we go."

"A moonlit ride? Oh—*that's* what you need the jeans for. Sounds romantic." Stella beamed at her. "You best get going, then. You'll find a pair in Caitlyn's room. Upstairs, first door on the right. Have fun."

After McKenzie changed clothes, she went to the backyard. A ball of puppies tumbled over each other for about ten minutes before they climbed back into their box, looking for another meal and a nap. Ember turned out to be an attentive and nurturing mother, which made the job of raising a litter so much easier. McKenzie hoped Athena would be just as caring with her litter. After snapping a handful of photos to send to the new owners, she lifted the smallest pup—the one Dylan wanted to keep—and snuggled him to her cheek and breathed in his distinct puppy smell.

Dylan was a gruff man, but when he asked if they could keep one, he had looked like a little boy. How could she refuse him? Besides… he'd said "we." "Can *we* keep him?" Did he mean him and his parents? Or him and McKenzie? She could only wish he meant her.

McKenzie set the little guy down and helped him find a teat before she made her way down to the barn to meet Dylan.

He came out of the building leading two horses: Sampson, his big quarter horse and another smaller, tawny-colored one. "This is Gucci. He'll take good care of you while you're learning to ride."

A breeze chilled McKenzie's skin, and she shivered.

"Are you cold?" Dylan pulled her close and rubbed her arm. McKenzie snuggled into his heat. "Let me get you a jacket." He jogged to the tack room.

She ran her fingers down Gucci's neck, and his white muzzle twitched in a nicker. Dylan returned with a coat and after she slid it on, he boosted her into the saddle and looked up at her with what she'd describe as wonder in his expression. "What? Are you so surprised I'm coming for a ride?"

"No." He shook his head and went around to Sampson's side. He swung himself up into the saddle without using the stirrup. Whenever Dylan was on Sampson's back, he and his horse looked like they were fused together—one fluid being—which made it McKenzie's turn to stare in admiration.

They rode side-by-side past the arena, out by the old tree swing, and the white-cross memorial marker of Logan's Army K9. She fell in behind Sampson when the switch-back trail narrowed and wound up the face of the mountain. The view of the valley and ranch below was a vision to behold in the moonlight. Dylan led the way to a meadow clearing that overlooked the ranch and he dismounted. He held Gucci's reins and McKenzie slid to the ground.

"This is the best view of the ranch, and personally, I think it's the best view anywhere." Dylan tied the horse's reins to some branches before he held out his hand to her. She took it and followed him to the edge of the steep drop-off. "What do you think?"

McKenzie agreed. "It's breathtaking, Dylan. Look, you can see the white peaks glowing in the distance."

"This is my favorite spot in the entire world."

"I can see why, and this is probably the most amazing time of day to view it."

"Yeah."

McKenzie felt a tug on her fingers, and she glanced at Dylan, expecting to find him standing next to her. Instead, he'd lowered to one knee and searched her face with obsidian eyes. Her breath caught in her throat.

Dylan removed his cowboy hat and set it on the ground next to his knee. He took her hand in both of his. "I had honestly come to believe I'd never be doing this. That I'd never find a woman I loved even more than my ranch. More than my life."

McKenzie held her breath and suppressed a cry, covering her mouth with her free hand. Her knees wobbled. *Can I stay on my feet? Or am I going to end up falling to the ground at Dylan's?*

"But, over the past year, I've come to know you, and I've come to love you that much." He swallowed, and the moon reflected the movement of his Adam's apple. "I don't have much to offer. I'll never have a ton of money, and ranch life is hard work. But there is great joy in it—if you love it. McKenzie, I want to give you all I have."

McKenzie's eyes filled with tears, and her chest constricted, trapping the air in her lungs.

"McKenzie Torrington, what I'm trying to ask you is—will you marry me? Will you make me the happiest man in the universe?"

Her tears spilled over and splashed down her cheeks. She clasped his hands with both of hers and dropped to her knees. "Yes! Oh Dylan, yes. I will marry you." She hiccupped, and they both laughed. The tenderness in his eyes engulfed her. He held her face in his fingers and kissed her as though she were as fragile as a gossamer butterfly wing.

He reached in his pocket and pulled out a simple diamond solitaire and slid in on her finger. When he gazed back into her eyes, his were filled with tears of his own. He pulled her close and kissed her again with a passionate promise of things to come. He drew back and gazed at her in wonder as a wispy cloud sifted away from the face of the silvery moon.

30

It was late when Colt pulled to a stop in front of the Moose Creek Clinic. He'd called ahead, and Blake was waiting for them at the automatic doors of the emergency room entrance. Blake held his arms crossed over his chest, and he tried to glower at Caitlyn, but with his handsome features, the effect was moot.

"Caitlyn Reed, your head can only take so much punishment."

"Nah, I'm hardheaded. Just ask Colt." She laughed, but neither of the men appreciated her humor.

Blake led the way to an exam room. "So, tell me exactly what happened."

Caitlyn explained how her day had started with the bombing in Mammoth and closed with the explosion on the Crow Reservation. "This morning, something from the explosion hit me in the head—part of a brick maybe—and this afternoon, I was blasted into a metal wall. Different places on my head, though."

"And two sets of stitches, I see." Blake asked her to

hold her arms out, one at a time. "See if you can resist me pushing your arms down." Caitlyn thought she did fairly well, considering how tired she was. "Now grip my fingers as hard as you can."

Blake had her stand on one foot then the other. He tapped on her knees and ankles with his little rubber hammer. "What did you have for breakfast today?"

"What? I don't remember."

"Don't or can't?"

Caitlyn tried to think back. A ton had happened between then and now. *Did I even eat breakfast today?* "Ha! A trick question. I didn't have breakfast this morning because I ate an entire pizza last night." She was pleased, and somewhat relieved, she remembered. "I can't believe that was only last night. It seems like a week ago."

"So, it appears I need to talk to you about your diet as well." A black eyebrow elevated over one of Blake's cerulean eyes. "I think the best thing for you is to get some rest. But I don't want you left on your own. Someone needs to check on you regularly through the night." His gaze swept to Colt.

"I'll take her to her parents' house."

"Good." He turned a stern face to Caitlyn. "And I want to see you again tomorrow. Call me tonight if your head hurts any worse or if you feel nauseous or dizzy. Okay? Also, stay away from video screens or anything that strains your eyes."

Caitlyn gave him a mock salute. "Yes, sir." She hopped off the exam table and grinned up at Colt. "Colt, as Goose's wife says in *Top Gun*, 'Take me to bed or lose me forever!'"

Blake shook his head and pierced Colt with a glare. "And absolutely none of that."

Colt raised his hands in surrender. "I'm dropping her off with her mother and I'm going home by myself."

"You both are *so* boring." Caitlyn teased, knowing she'd be lucky if she could stay awake until she got into Colt's Jeep.

McKenzie almost dropped her champagne flute when the Reeds' front door suddenly swung open, and Colt carried a sleeping Caitlyn into the living room followed by Renegade. Caitlyn stirred and looked around the room in temporary confusion. Colt kissed her temple and said, "We're here."

Dylan moved a long, flat box off the sofa, and Colt set her on the cushion next to John. Colt sat next to her, unwilling to be any farther away.

Caitlyn's dark eyes narrowed. "What the hell is going on here?" She glared first at a white, crystal-encrusted gown draped over one of McKenzie's arms, then panned her gaze to Stella.

Stella rushed to Caitlyn's side. "Honey, are you alright? Blake called to tell me you were on your way. From what he said, you're lucky to be alive." She swept assessing fingers over Caitlyn's face and into her hair, pulling long locks aside so she could see the bandage-covered stitches.

"I'm fine." Caitlyn drew away. "Why is McKenzie holding a wedding gown in her arms? And why are you all drinking champagne? You just can't help yourself, can you, Mom? What—I don't even get to choose my own gown? Because I have to tell you, that dress is as far from something I'd wear as I can imagine." Caitlyn's face flushed with anger.

"Mind your tone with your mother, young lady." John sat up straight and glowered at his daughter.

McKenzie hid her grin behind white folds of tulle and waited for the scene to play itself out.

Stella leaned back and frowned. "You're out of line, Caitlyn, and you'd know that if you ever bothered to return my calls."

"Uh—I've been a little busy trying to catch drug-dealing killers, and I was almost blown up twice for my efforts. It's been one hell of a day. Sorry I didn't call to chat about dresses and napkin colors."

John stood and pressed his hands on his hips. "That is enough, Caitlyn Rose!"

Caitlyn looked up at her father and burst into tears. The stricken look on his face made McKenzie cringe. She laid the dress over the back of a chair and rushed to Caitlyn, taking John's vacated seat. Her friend had burrowed her face in Colt's shoulder, so she rested her hand on Caitlyn's shoulder blade.

Colt looked helplessly at Stella and John. "Catie has a concussion, and she's exhausted." He wrapped his arms around her defensively.

"Caitlyn, this dress is not for you." McKenzie brushed a lock of hair from Caitlyn's face. "Look at me for a second."

Caitlyn peered at her with tired eyes that held a deep sorrow, belying her sharp attitude.

McKenzie took Caitlyn's hand and was thankful she didn't pull away. "Everything is going to be fine, but we need to get you to bed. You have most certainly been to hell and back today." Colt kept a protective arm around Caitlyn, and McKenzie glanced at Stella. "A pot of tea might be just the thing."

Stella nodded and left for the kitchen.

"Catie-girl. I'm sorry, I..." John stammered.

McKenzie reached up and squeezed John's arm. "It's not you, John. Caitlyn has a concussion. She's also simply worn out and needs to get some sleep. We can talk about everything tomorrow."

Caitlyn turned her face to McKenzie. "What do you mean, that dress isn't for me?" She sniffled.

"Well..." Despite her best effort, a huge smile filled McKenzie's face.

Dylan took position behind McKenzie and rested his hands on her shoulders. He grinned at his sister. "McKenzie and I are getting married. Not everything is about you, you know," he teased.

Caitlyn stared at her brother. "What?"

"You heard me." Dylan twined his fingers through McKenzie's hair, and she nodded. It might have been an inappropriate time to share their exciting news, but she couldn't wait either. Maybe a little happiness would help keep the darkness of the day at bay for a while.

"So... That's *your* dress?" Caitlyn's bruised face filled with confusion.

"It might be." McKenzie giggled. "We went to Spearfish today to see what the bridal shop had in the way of wedding gowns and bridesmaids' dresses, and I ended up trying this gown on and I loved it. Later, while Dylan and I were at dinner, your mom bought the dress as a surprise when she was trying on mother-of-the-bride dresses. She must have had an inkling, because later, Dylan proposed!"

"Then what the hell is Dylan looking at your dress for?" Caitlyn shot to her feet but then swayed and Colt pulled her back to the couch. "He shouldn't see the gown before the wedding!"

Caitlyn slumped against Colt, and he said, "You need to go to bed. We can congratulate Dylan and McKenzie in the morning." His tone held a slight chiding note.

"You're right. I'm being a jerk. What I meant to say is, it's about damn time." She grinned and closed her eyes. Dylan chuckled at her and taking McKenzie's hand he pulled her to her feet.

"Come on, you." Colt nudged Caitlyn and gave McKenzie a silent, apologetic grimace. "Your mom can bring your tea up when it's ready." Colt lifted Caitlyn from the couch and carried her to the stairs. Renegade followed them.

Caitlyn opened her eyes and smiled. "I'm sorry, Kenze. Dylan, I hope you know how happy I am for you. For you, both." She wiggled out of Colt's arms, and he set her on her feet. "We'll celebrate tomorrow." She patted Renegade's head. "Come on, boy. You've had a rough day too."

31

Dirk called first thing in the morning to check on Caitlyn, and she assured him she would be fine after a few days' rest. She didn't mention the searing headache she had.

"Glad to hear it. The sheriff down in Mammoth had one of his deputies drive your truck up here to Billings. He thought it would be more convenient for you than driving all the way back there to get it."

"That's much easier. I'll have Colt drive me up."

"Good. Listen, I wondered if you wanted to go with me to see Laurie and Caleb. I need to make sure she's taken care of. See if she needs anything." He was silent for a moment. "I can't believe Sam's gone," he murmured.

"I know. Me either." Caitlyn wiped at a rebel tear. "Absolutely, I want to come with you to see Laurie. Have you heard how Caleb is doing? He worshiped his daddy. Do you know what the plans are for a memorial service?"

"We're working on coordinating everything. It will probably be next week." Dirk didn't answer for a time, and finally he cleared his throat. "I talked with Laurie on the phone. She said Caleb hasn't spoken at all since he heard the news."

"Poor little guy." Caitlyn's heart hurt for the boy. She thought back to the last time she'd seen him. It was the last time Caleb and Sam were together. Caleb had been laughing and playing with Renegade. "When are you going to see them?"

"I'd like to go on Friday. I have a ton of BS paperwork to do, but I'm off on the weekend."

"Sounds good." Caitlyn was relieved to have a few days to recover. "I'll meet you at the Billings field office before noon."

"That'll work. Are you gonna be okay to drive your truck home?" Dirk's concern warmed her.

"I will be by then. Will you let me know if there is anything Laurie needs? I feel so helpless, so sorry..." Caitlyn's voice trailed off. Guilt overwhelmed her. It should have been her—not Sam.

"The Marshal Service will make sure she has everything she needs. There's nothing we can really do besides be there for her."

Caitlyn nodded. "Yeah. I'll see you Friday."

She got out of bed and stretched. Her head hurt, but not bad enough to alert Blake. In fact, a hot cup of coffee would probably fix everything. Renegade jumped from his bed, ready to play. Caitlyn plodded down the stairs to the kitchen followed by her dog. When she walked through the swinging door, she heard barking in the backyard. It wasn't Ren and didn't sound like Larry, so she pulled the curtain aside to look out.

McKenzie sat in the center of a swarm of black and brown puppy fuzz. Thrilled, Caitlyn hurried to the back door and swung it open. "Rottweiler puppies? I thought you were breeding Belgians!" Caitlyn went outside and sat on the bottom porch step, and the gaggle of puppies gamboled over to her. She lifted a fat puppy while another nibbled her bare toe. "Ow! Hey!" She laughed. "I guess I missed out on a lot of things happening around here."

"We'll get you caught up. I *am* going to breed Belgians, but I rescued the mother of these pups, and well… here we are. They all already have owners. All but one." McKenzie grinned. "The one chewing on your foot."

Caitlyn set the plump fella down and lifted the mini chomping machine. "This one? Why doesn't he have a home?"

"He was an extra. The vet must not have seen him when he did his exam. Dylan wants to keep him, but I'll soon be raising and training up half a dozen or more high-energy Belgian puppies."

"Plus, Dylan already has Larry," Caitlyn smirked. "Though he never could resist puppies. Who can?" That's when the idea struck her. "What would you say if I told you I think I have the perfect home for him?"

Dylan, who had come up behind her and was standing in the kitchen doorway, asked, "Where?"

Caitlyn twisted around to look up at him. "Sam's little boy." Her throat thickened, and tears clouded her vision. "I bet a puppy would be just the thing to help him get through the long months of grief he's facing after losing his dad."

Dylan's expression softened. "I think that's a great idea, Caitlyn."

AT THE END of the week, Colt drove Caitlyn, Renegade, and the Rottie pup up to Billings to get her truck. "Sure, you don't want me to wait for you and follow you back home?"

"No. I'm fine. The dogs and I will be home late tonight, though. I'll call you."

"Okay but promise me you'll be careful. Trouble seems to seek you out."

Caitlyn slid her arms around Colt's neck. "I will. And when I get home, we can set a date and plan our ceremony."

"Good. Though the heat is off since your mom is distracted by Dylan and McKenzie's wedding." He chuckled and kissed her goodbye.

Colt left for town, and Caitlyn played with the dogs for a few minutes before she mixed up a milk substitute for the baby and bottle fed him. She lost herself in the comfort of his warm little body snuggling onto her lap. She didn't look forward to facing Laurie and seeing the depth of her loss in her eyes. A loss that should never have happened.

She and Renegade entered the Billings Marshal's office to meet Dirk, carrying her surprise gift for Caleb as they rode up two floors on the elevator. When the doors opened, Dirk was there waiting for them.

"Perfect timing. Ready to go?" He stepped into the compartment.

Caitlyn backed up to give him room. "Ready as I'll ever be. Honestly, I dread facing Laurie."

"Me too, but we need to." He ran a hand over the puppy's head. "Who's this?" Dirk, not one to show emotion of any kind, fought the appearance of a smile—and lost.

Caitlyn grinned at him. "This is my gift to Caleb. If it's okay with Laurie, that is. He's still too little to be away from his mother for too long, so I'll have to take him home for a couple of weeks, but I'm hoping he will cheer Sam's boy up a little."

"Worth a try. Poor kid." Dirk led the way to his all-black SUV.

They rode together to Laurie's house. Dirk turned off the engine, and they sat in the car for several minutes, trying to gather the courage to face Laurie and Caleb. Taking a deep breath, Caitlyn opened the door. "Let's do this."

She left the dogs in the car with the windows down. She hadn't asked Laurie if Caleb could have the puppy, and belatedly worried it would make things worse if the little boy saw the tiny dog. What if Laurie wouldn't let Caleb keep him? *I'm such an idiot!*

With heavy feet, Caitlyn and Dirk walked up the path and knocked on the front door. Laurie opened it to them and gestured for them to come in. "Thank you for coming. Have a seat," she said before lowering herself onto the couch in the darkened living room. She gripped a worn tissue in her fingers and dabbed at her red, puffy eyes.

"Laurie, I'm so sorry." Caitlyn sat next to her. "I—"

Laurie reached for Caitlyn and embraced her, cutting off her words. "Sam thought the world of you, Caitlyn, did you know? He probably never told you." The woman drew back and offered Caitlyn a watery smile that crushed her heart. "He bragged about how you saved him from the bear and could shoot a shotgun one-handed." Laurie's little laugh brought fresh tears.

"The admiration was mutual," Caitlyn murmured, overwhelmed by Laurie's kind words.

Dirk lowered himself into a side chair, and they all sat without speaking for a long while, each lost in their own thoughts and memories. Caitlyn's stomach roiled when Caleb entered the room. The little boy didn't look up at anyone as he made his way to his mother's side. He leaned into her and kept his eyes glued to the floor.

"Hi, Caleb," Caitlyn tried. But he didn't respond. "Laurie, can I see you in the kitchen for a minute?"

Laurie nodded and kissed Caleb on the top of his head. "I'll be right back, sweetie. Stay here with Uncle Dirk."

The women went to the other room, and Caitlyn took Laurie's hand. "I had an idea. You see, my brother's fiancée is a dog trainer, and she currently has a litter of Rottweiler puppies. I brought one up here for Caleb. I thought, if it's alright with you, the puppy might help him get through this horrible time."

Laurie shook her head. "That's very thoughtful of you, Caitlyn. But I don't think I have the strength to care for a puppy right now. I'm sorry. I know you're just trying to help."

Caitlyn's cheeks heated. It had been foolish to bring the puppy all this way. "Of course. I understand. Don't give it another thought. The puppy is too young now, anyway. As it is, I've had to bottle feed him on this trip. I need to take him back to his mother for another month, but if you change your mind, he'll still be there."

"I'm sorry you went to all the trouble of bringing the puppy here. Where is he? In the car?"

"Yes. I left him there with Renegade. If you said yes, I didn't want to only have a picture for Caleb. I thought it might help for him to see the puppy. Then he'd have something to look forward to."

"That's very sweet, Caitlyn. But it's too much right now." Laurie gave Caitlyn a wan smile and squeezed her forearm. "Thank you for thinking of Caleb, though."

"Mom!" Caleb called from the other room. Seconds later, the screen door slammed shut

Laurie's eyes rounded, and her mouth dropped open. She glanced at Caitlyn. "Caleb hasn't spoken a word since Sam's death." She ran to the living room. Caleb had bolted out the front door, and the women rushed after him. Outside, Dirk had taken the puppy from the car and set him in the yard. Caleb was now rolling in the grass with the exuberant black and tan bundle of fur.

"Mom! Look! Unka Dirk has a puppy!"

Laurie's eyes filled with tears, and she gripped Caitlyn's hand. "I think you might have performed a miracle." They went out to the yard and watched the puppy soothe the broken heart of a little boy. "Thank you, Caitlyn." Laurie whispered. "I might not be ready, but I think we'll be raising a puppy after all."

Caitlyn slid an arm around Laurie's shoulders. "I'm so

glad to see Caleb's smile. There's nothing better for a boy than a dog."

Caleb ran to his mother. "Isn't he great, Mom?"

"Yes, he is. What will you name him?" Laurie wiped her son's face with her thumb.

Caleb's eyes—his dad's eyes—widened. "I getta keep him?" He bounced up and down on his toes. "I'ma name him Bear! Like the bear Daddy fought in the woods with Unka Dirk and Caitlyn!"

Caitlyn's gaze flew to Dirk's, and for a long second, they shared a stunned look. Then, at the same time, they shared a soft laugh. Caitlyn wiped tears from her cheeks. "That's the perfect name, Caleb. Bear will always remind us of your daddy."

The little boy looked at her solemnly. "Me too."

A minute later, the puppy nibbled on his shoelace, and Caleb smiled. The unsteady Rottie pup flopped onto his back. Caleb looked up at Caitlyn, "Can Ren come out of the car and play with us, too?"

32

One week later, Caitlyn stood with Laurie and Dirk in front of the church which Laurie had requested for Sam's memorial service. Her exhausted heart ached, and she couldn't fathom how Laurie was coping with the burden of her grief. Caitlyn's US Marshal windbreaker was hot in the sun, but it served as her uniform for the day. That and her five-point Marshal badge that carried a black band of mourning strapped across the front. Laurie positioned herself behind Caleb, who stood tall, wearing a little blue suit and tie. Renegade sat stoically at Caitlyn's feet.

The small group watched the mile-long procession that had started at the Billings Marshal's Office and led to the church. Motorcycle officers, black unmarked USMS Chargers and SUVs, along with first responders from all over Montana and Wyoming comprised the honor parade. The diverse array of emergency vehicles entered the church parking lot under an Arch of Honor created by the Mammoth fire truck ladders. The firefighters had draped their ladders with American flags.

When the lead vehicle carrying Sam's tactical helmet, rifle, and boots pulled to a stop at the steps before them, Caleb saluted the car. Caitlyn stood ramrod straight, swallowing rapidly while a rogue tear escaped and trickled down her cheek. It was hard to breathe past the pressure crushing her chest. The weight of Sam's death sat heavily on her shoulders. This ceremony should have been for *her* death, not his. Now, Sam's little boy stood bravely by as the honor guard carried his daddy's battle gear up the stairs and past them, into the church. The crowd followed them in. Caitlyn and Dirk sat with Laurie and the Dillinger family in the front row.

Because Sam died while he was on duty in her region, Marshal Laila Williams, of the Wyoming District, was the first official to speak After her thoughtful comments, the Marshal of Montana gave the eulogy.

When he finished, Dirk stood to make a few remarks. "First of all, on behalf of Sam's wife, Laurie and their son, Caleb, I want to thank you all for coming to honor Deputy US Marshal Samuel G. Dillinger. Your presence and support are received and deeply appreciated." He nodded at Laurie and Caitlyn took her hand. "Those of you who knew Sam personally know that he was a diligent man. Every one of us welcomed the opportunity to work with him, and I was blessed to be his partner. Sam was the guy who was always cutting a joke." Dirk waited while the mourners laughed at their memories. "He was always positive, always willing to step in. Sam was as tactically sound as any man or woman here. He was the kind of guy you were glad to work with, knowing he always had your six.

"In the end, Sam made the ultimate sacrifice, and his actions saved countless lives. Deputy US Marshal Sam Dillinger lived his life all the way to the end as a true hero."

Laurie's cold fingers tightened their grip on Caitlyn's hand. Silent tears shook the young widow as she fought to be brave. Caitlyn whispered, "I've got you, Laurie. Grip my hand as hard as you need to."

"Now, the DEA is flying an aerial salute in honor of our fallen brother. If you'll all make your way outside, they'll be overhead in ten minutes." Dirk walked toward them and held his hand out to help Laurie to her feet. Together with Sam's parents and sister, they exited the building first. Dirk led them to a small lawn at the front of the church. White chairs stood in a line for the family. Once the Dillingers sat, Dirk and Caitlyn took standing positions behind them. Renegade sat next to Caleb's chair and rested his chin on the little boy's leg. All other mourners filed out into the parking lot.

The distinctive wop wop wop wop of five Black Hawk helicopters permeated the silence. They made their first pass, low and fast in a combat V formation. At the horizon, they circled back for their final pass. Marshal Williams spoke into an amplified megaphone. "Deputy US Marshal Samuel Dillinger." She paused, before calling out his badge number three times, symbolically calling his name and number for his last radio call. Then her strong voice uttered, "Samuel G. Dillinger this is your end of watch. You are gone but not forgotten."

As she spoke the traditional words, the helicopters approached on their final fly-by. When they were directly overhead, a solitary airship representing Sam pulled sharply up, pedal-turned, and flew west. The four remaining Black Hawks flew on in their missing man formation. Caitlyn's heart wrenched, and she was glad for the loud rotors as she resisted the sob in her throat.

A color guard approached the flagpole at the center of the grassy area near the family. The flag bearer's voice rang out. "Color guard, retire the colors." He counted aloud to three and led the guard in a rock-back salute. He then lowered the flag into the hands of the guard as a single bugle played "Taps." He unclipped Old Glory from the hooks: stripes first, then stars. The color guard pulled the flag taut, horizontal to the ground, and folded it into a tight triangle, tucking the end into a fold. The flag bearer then carried the stars and stripes to Laurie and knelt before her. He turned the triangle so that the long end faced her and handed her the flag. "On behalf of the United States Marshals Service and a grateful nation." He stood and saluted the family before marching away with the rest of the guard.

Laurie pressed the flag to her heart, bowed her head, and wept. Her family was quick to circle her, protecting her privacy in her moment of pure grief.

Later, at the reception for family and friends, Caitlyn looked for Colt. He'd been there in the crowd all day, but now she needed him with her. Needed to hide in his arms. Acting brave and stoic during the ceremony had been exhausting. Now, all she wanted to do was find a quiet corner and burst into tears. Sam's death was so unfair.

Laurie was now forced to face a future without the love of her life, and sweet Caleb… Caitlyn sucked in a breath and blinked her eyelids to prevent the tears that were burning for release.

Her knees almost gave way when Colt's arms wrapped around her from behind. She turned in his embrace and pressed her face against his chest as she slid her arms up his back and held on.

He tightened his grip on her. "That was an incredibly honoring ceremony," he said against her ear.

Caitlyn nodded but had no words. What could she say? Nothing she said or did would bring Sam back or ease Laurie's pain. Nothing could make this better except for time. Her first sob shook her body. The noise was lost inside Colt's shirt. He tucked her under his arm and led her outside to a private corner in Laurie's backyard. He pulled her close as soon as they were alone, and Caitlyn released another cry. She was losing it. Thank God, Colt was there.

"Go ahead and cry, Catie. Let it out. Your heart is broken for your partner and friend." He stroked her hair and held her tight. He was exactly what she needed right now. She needed this man like she needed air. Gratitude swirled through her agonizing grief, and she slid her hands around him and held on for the torrent of emotion. He held her while she wept.

When Caitlyn's tears were spent, she stepped back and gazed up at him through wet spikey lashes. "Thank you, Colt. You always know what I need." A slight smile warmed her lips. "And what I always need is you."

33

The following week, Caitlyn stood in front of her full-length mirror and stared at herself in her yellow sundress. She ran her fingers over her few scrapes and bruises. They had mostly faded, and she covered them with a little face powder. She was a different woman than she was last summer when she wore this dress for the first time to her law enforcement academy graduation party. What a year it had been. It seemed she was a hundred years older and at least that much wiser now.

She heard Colt's Jeep pull up out front. Looking forward to a night set aside for Colt, she dabbed some clear lip-gloss on her lips and grabbed her sweater.

Renegade followed her to the front door, and she reached down to pat his head. "Don't wait up." His tail swished happily back and forth. She opened the door just as Colt started to knock.

"Hey, don't you look handsome?" She admired the crisp white button-down he wore under his suit jacket.

"It's been a long time since I've seen you in anything other than your uniform."

Colt's appreciative gaze made her feel self-conscious. "I love you in that dress." He tilted her chin up and kissed her. "You're beautiful."

Colt took her to the golf-course restaurant—the nicest place within an hour's drive. He had reserved a table by the windows with a view of the course and the mountains beyond. They sipped a rich cabernet as they held hands across the table, gazing at each other. Caitlyn's phone buzzed with a text.

Colt smirked. "Go ahead, read the message."

Caitlyn gave him an apologetic smile and turned her phone over to read the screen. Her mouth formed an O.

"What is it?"

"It's from Dirk. Listen to this," Caitlyn read Dirk's text. "Both Elaine Woodrow and Ben Kanoska were found dead in their jail cells when the guards brought their dinner."

"You're kidding!" Colt sat forward. "How did they die?"

"He says Elaine had a bedsheet twisted around her neck and Kanoska was shanked."

"Someone clearly wanted to keep them quiet."

"That's not all." Caitlyn thumbed her screen. "They never found Ray Burroughs's body buried in the rubble after the fire."

Colt released a sigh. "So, the hunt continues?"

"Damn straight. And I think the trail will lead us all the way through Tito Garza and beyond. All the way to the crime syndicate in New York. I am now one hundred percent convinced the capital T in *rockeT* stands for Tito —that self-centered, arrogant son-of-a-bitch!"

"When will you and Sterling head out?"

She scrolled through the rest of Dirk's message. "Not until we find something solid to go on. Dirk's looking for leads." She tucked her phone into her purse. "Either way, tonight belongs to us."

Their waiter approached the table with a bottle of champagne and two glasses.

"What's this?" Caitlyn smiled.

"From the gentleman across the room." Colt and Caitlyn turned to look in the direction the server indicated. Blake and Kayla sat on the other side of the dining room, and they raised their wine glasses in a silent toast. Caitlyn waved and Colt lifted his glass in return.

"They make a good couple," Caitlyn mused.

"As long as he's distracted from his infatuation with you, I don't care who he dates." Colt chuckled.

Caitlyn turned to him. "Speaking of infatuation... I heard Allison Snow is in town."

Colt choked on his sip. "Yeah." He blotted his mouth with his napkin.

"You've seen her?" Caitlyn watched him closely, but his hazel eyes pierced hers.

"She's been around, but she doesn't matter, Catie. You are my life, and you know it."

A soft smile curved Caitlyn's lips. "I do. And you're my life too, Colt. You're my whole heart. How does November eleventh sound for a wedding date?"

"November eleventh? That's the day my dad died, Catie."

"I know." She reached for his hand. "You came to our house that afternoon, remember? You sat with my dad under the old cottonwood tree. The one with the tree swing."

"I remember. You came out. You didn't say anything, you just sat next to me and held my hand."

Caitlyn nodded. "That's when I first knew I loved you."

AFTER DINNER, Colt and Caitlyn drove back to town to get an ice cream cone. They walked arm-in-arm along Main Street licking their desserts. "This is nice. It's been a terrific night. I don't think I've fully relaxed since I got home. Thanks for this." Caitlyn stretched up to kiss Colt's cheek, leaving a smudge of triple-chocolate brownie fudge on his jaw. She giggled and wiped it off.

Colt grinned. "Let me have a taste of that." He bent down and kissed her sticky lips.

Caitlyn laughed, unable to take the kiss seriously. She tried to shove him playfully away, but he pulled her in tight, kissing her deeper. Vaguely aware of some people trying to pass them on the sidewalk, Caitlyn turned her face from his. "Sorry. Excuse us," she said. Laughter danced with her words until she saw the people scootching past them to climb the steps to the café.

She pulled back from Colt and narrowed her eyes at the group—her jovial mood evaporating. "Allison?"

Colt's grip tightened on Caitlyn's waist, but she ignored him and pushed away.

"Hello, Caitlyn." Allison's gaze bobbed to Colt and

back. "Colt." The woman attempted to steer her little family group up the stairs.

Caitlyn continued. "I heard you were in town."

"Yes. Visiting my folks." She nudged the people in front of her to keep going.

When Mrs. Snow got to the top of the steps, she turned back. "It's Caitlyn, isn't it? You're the Reed girl." Allison's mother must have been in her late fifties but was still beautiful, and she had a kind smile.

"Yes, ma'am."

"Come on, Catie." Colt tried to steer her away, but Caitlyn wanted to stake her claim.

She gestured to him. "And this is my fiancé, Sheriff Colt Branson."

"Yes, Sheriff." Mr. Snow reached out to shake Colt's hand. "I believe it was you that Allison sat with here, at the café for a little while, when we came to dinner the night she first got home."

The boy with them turned and peered up at them from under sandy bangs. Caitlyn sucked in a breath and stared. Her mouth jaw dropped. Before her stood an exact replica of Colt at age ten or eleven. She couldn't breathe.

Mr. Snow grinned. "This is my grandson, Jace."

THANK YOU FOR READING JUSTICE.

I hope you enjoyed riding along with Caitlyn and Renegade as they chased fugitives across Wyoming and Montana. Bloodline, the next book in the Tin Star K9

Series continues their story and their fight for Justice, Integrity, and Service with the US Marshals Service.

Order Bloodline Now!

If you enjoyed reading Justice ~ Book 4 in the Tin Star K9 Series, I would be most honored if you would please write a quick review.

Review Justice

Thank you!

***

Next!
Book 5 in the Tin Star K9 Series

BLOODLINE

When her personal life spins out of control, Deputy US Marshal Caitlyn Reed is quick to volunteer for a case hunting a murderous fugitive in another state, far from home. She and Renegade escape the tangle of relational issues and jump into a forthright battle against crime.

Sheriff Colt Branson must grapple with the shock of family turmoil and a run-away fiancée. While dealing with emotional upheaval in his world, Colt continues his search for the murderer of a local father and son that took place in Moose Creek months ago. His investigation uncovers the killer's connection to a New York crime syndicate.

When Caitlyn suddenly falls off the radar, Colt risks everything to find her. He has nothing to go on besides Renegade and Caitlyn's abandoned truck. Colt joins forces with a team of US Marshals led by Caitlyn's mentor, Dirk Sterling. Together, their unit has the combined skill and manpower, but will they get to her in time?

Order your copy today!

~

For free books and to join my reader group,
Please visit my website.
Jodi-Burnett.com

ALSO BY JODI BURNETT

Flint River Series

Run For The Hills

Hidden In The Hills

Danger In The Hills

A Flint River Christmas (Free Epilogue)

A Flint River Cookbook (Free Book)

FBI-K9 Thriller Series

Baxter K9 Hero (Free Prequel)

Avenging Adam

Body Count

Concealed Cargo

Mile High Mayhem

Tin Star K9 Series

RENEGADE

MAVERICK

MARSHAL

JUSTICE

ACKNOWLEDGMENTS

First, and always, I thank God for blessing me with a vivid imagination, work I love, and for the inspiration with which to do it.

I am enormously appreciative for my team. I am beyond grateful to Kae Krueger who is the first to see my words and check my stories. A huge thanks to my team of beta readers who help me see the forest for the trees. You all are integral to my writing process. Thank you, Chris, Emily, Sarah, Jenni, Brooke, Jerry, Sheila, Elle, Barb, and Kay.

I owe a huge debt of gratitude to the Castle Rock Police Department, specifically Officers Matt Fellows, and J.R. Gondeck and their K9 partners Shogun, and Maverick. These officers generously took time out of their day and allowed me to interview them. I learned so much about the day-to-day life of K9 officers and the rigors of working with such high-energy and intelligent dogs. Thanks guys!

I could not do without the support and encouragement of my family. Writing can be such a solo venture. Thanks for pulling me out of my cave and loving me through the rough spots. I cherish the inside jokes, all the sports, and most especially the way we love each other. My cup overflows.

Most of all, I thank my husband Chris, who helps me flesh out my plots, and reads all the words. He listens to my crazy ideas, accompanies on my grand adventures, and loves me through it all. I rely on his strength and encouragement. I love you, Chris, with all my heart.

First, and always, I thank God for blessing me with a vivid imagination, work I love, and for the inspiration with which to do it.

I am enormously appreciative for my team. I am beyond grateful to Kae Krueger who is the first to see my words and check my stories. A huge thanks to my team of beta readers who help me see the forest for the trees. You all are integral to my writing process. Thank you, Chris, Emily, Sarah, Jenni, Brooke, Jerry, Sheila, Elle, Barb, and Kay.

I owe a huge debt of gratitude to the Castle Rock Police Department, specifically Officers Matt Fellows, and J.R. Gondeck and their K9 partners Shogun, and Maverick. These officers generously took time out of their day and allowed me to interview them. I learned so much about the day-to-day life of K9 officers and the rigors of working with such high-energy and intelligent dogs. Thanks guys!

I could not do without the support and encouragement of my family. Writing can be such a solo venture. Thanks for pulling me out of my cave and loving me through the rough spots. I cherish the inside jokes, all the sports, and most especially the way we love each other. My cup overflows.

Most of all, I thank my husband Chris, who helps me flesh out my plots, and reads all the words. He listens to my crazy ideas, accompanies on my grand adventures, and loves me through it all. I rely on his strength and encouragement. I love you, Chris, with all my heart.

ABOUT THE AUTHOR

Jodi Burnett is a Colorado native and a mountain girl at heart. She loves writing Mystery and Suspense Thrillers from her small ranch southeast of Denver, where she lives with her husband and their two big dogs. There she dotes on her horses, complains about her cows, and writes to create a home for her nefarious imaginings. Burnett is a member of Novelists, Inc. and Sisters in Crime. Connect with Jodi at Jodi-Burnett.com, on Facebook @ JodiBurnettAuthor, on Instagram @ JodiBurnettAuthor, or on Twitter @ Jodi_writes. Get free books by Burnett on her website

Made in United States
Orlando, FL
25 July 2022

20134036R00182